A small smile [P9-DNT-207] but his eyes narrowed.

"You're not crazy. You were in a stressful situation. *Are* in one. I'd rather have skipped the nighttime jog through the woods, but I get why you ran. No need to apologize."

"I'm still sorry," she replied.

"Well, then. You're forgiven."

"Thanks."

He stared down at her for several long moments, his face unreadable. What was going through his head? Reggie thought maybe he wanted to add something else. His mouth twitched as though he was holding back. And she had a strange urge to coax whatever it was out of him. To reach up and touch his cheek and tell him he could share whatever he wanted to share, and it would be just fine with her.

* * *

Be sure to check out the next books in this miniseries.

Undercover Justice: Four brothers-in-arms on a mission for justice...

* * *

If you're on Twitter, tell us what you think of Harlequin Romantic Suspense!
#harlequinromsuspense

Dear Reader,

One of the things I was really excited to do in this brand-new series was to create a fantastic contrast between its warm, community-minded setting and its seedy underworld. I loved the idea of creating a bustling town that can't help but have interconnected characters who all know each other's business while also being blissfully unaware that there's a snake among them.

So welcome to Whispering Woods, a fictional town in Oregon. Nestled in the mountains, it was once a thriving forestry community. Now, though, it relies on tourism to keep its year-round residents afloat. Well. Tourism. And (of course) a criminal mastermind.

I hope you enjoy your stay!

(Skiers, hikers and murder, oh my...)

Melinda

CAPTIVATING WITNESS

—

Melinda Di Lorenzo

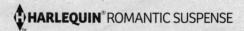HARLEQUIN® ROMANTIC SUSPENSE

Recycling programs
for this product may
not exist in your area.

ISBN-13: 978-1-335-47201-4

Captivating Witness

Printed in U.S.A.

Amazon bestselling author **Melinda Di Lorenzo** writes in her spare time—at soccer practices, when she should be doing laundry and in place of sleep. She lives on the beautiful west coast of British Columbia, Canada, with her handsome husband and her noisy kids. When she's not writing, she can be found curled up with (someone else's) good book.

Books by Melinda Di Lorenzo

Harlequin Romantic Suspense

Undercover Justice

Captivating Witness

Worth the Risk
Last Chance Hero
Silent Rescue

Harlequin Intrigue

Trusting a Stranger

Harlequin Intrigue Noir

Deceptions and Desires
Pinups and Possibilities

For my husband.
I could dedicate a thousand books to you,
and it would still never be enough.

Prologue

The four boys stood in an awkward square, no one quite daring to make the first move, no one quite willing to speak.

Brayden Maxwell, who knew he was already the quietest of the bunch, couldn't force even a single word. He just shifted from foot to foot, wishing he could get out of the monkey suit his mother had forced him to wear, lock himself in his bedroom and pound away on his drums. Problem was, earlier that week, the repo guys had come by and taken the drum kit. The TV and the new kitchen table, too, though the drums were the part that mattered most to Brayden. They'd been a gift from his dad. The last thing given to him before the always-laughing, always-joking, always-in-your-face man had died in the line of duty.

It was crap. Even at fifteen years old, Brayden could feel the unjustness of the situation. Three cops dead. Four kids—him and his little brother included—without fathers. No one to play catch with, no one to wink at and point out the pretty girls with.

No one to pay the damned bills.

He winced, thinking his mom wouldn't appreciate his use of the word *damned*, even in his own head. Those kinds of things were important to her. Swearing, cheating and lying. All high on the mom list of punishable offences. Except right now…dropping a mental *damned* was the least of Brayden's worries.

A year had gone by since the deaths of their fathers, and the man who'd done it all was getting off without a day served in prison.

It was why they'd gathered together today. To hear the announcement as it was made public. To stand by their moms—widows now, which seemed like a weird thing to call a bunch of women in their thirties—and watch as the infamous Freemont City Bomber walked out of the courthouse. It made no difference that his face was shielded from the cameras, his identity undisclosed because of his age. It was obvious what would happen. He'd return to his everyday life, while things for *them* would never be the same.

Brayden looked at each of the boys in the room, feeling the burden of being thrust into his role as their leader.

Anderson Somers was the kindest. The slowest to anger. The one whose intelligence sneaked up on you, every time.

Harley was Brayden's own little brother. Not quite two years younger. Sensitive, prone to doodling and always empathetic.

Rush Stephenson was tall and wide and a year older than Brayden and Anderson. His temper was well-known, and it took little to fuel the fire.

Brayden, though, was the one with the most forethought. The one who reasoned things through and came up with the plans. The one who would gladly step up and take the blame when their shenanigans went awry.

Which is why they needed *him* to bring this plan to the table.

So he finally cleared his throat and said, "This isn't a funeral."

"Feels like it," replied Anderson.

"Feels *worse*." That one came from Harley, who looked down at his feet as he spoke.

It kinda killed Brayden to see that his brother's confidence had been stripped away like that. To recognize that no matter how hard he tried, he couldn't build up the kid the way that their father had.

Failing, he thought, with far more bitterness than any fifteen-year-old should.

He took a breath and said what they were all thinking. "We need to find out his name."

Rush spit on the dusty floor. "Whoever he is, I'd like to wring his neck."

"We all would," Brayden said back. "But since you're probably the only one who could *reach* his neck…"

"It's not funny," Harley told him.

Brayden sighed, lifted his fingernail to his mouth, remembered he'd promised their dad he'd stop chewing, then dropped his hand to his side. "I'm not making a joke. Not really. I want to take the guy out just as bad as Rush does. But Dad—all of our dads—would want us to do it the right way."

"What's the right way?" Rush sounded furious, as usual. "Weren't you paying attention, Bray? The system failed."

"It wasn't the system," Anderson interrupted. "It was a loophole."

"A loophole?" Harley repeated. "What does that mean?"

"It means that murderer isn't rotting in prison the way he should be," Rush all but growled.

Brayden lifted a hand. "A loophole means that his lawyers are smart, and they found a legal way for him to *not* go to jail. For this anyway."

Anderson's eyes whipped to Brayden's face. "You think he's committed more crimes?"

Brayden nodded. "Don't you? Someone living a straight life doesn't just set off a bomb in a police station."

"So what do you want to do?" Rush asked.

"I want to catch him."

"Ourselves?" Harley said. "By the time we're old enough to try, we'll be too old to even do anything about it."

Brayden fought an urge to give his brother a solid kick in the butt. "We'll be in our twenties, not dead."

There was a weird silence then, the word *dead* hanging in the air. Because people *did* die young. Their fathers were proof of that. Anderson's dad, who'd still been a junior in high school when Anderson was born, had been just twenty-nine.

Finally, Rush spoke up again. "What's the plan, Bray?"

Brayden managed a smile. He reached into his back pocket and pulled out the tidy stack of pamphlets. He handed one to his brother and to each of his friends.

Anderson was the first to look up. "You want us to become cops?"

Brayden nodded. "I want us to become cops. And I want us to track him down and catch him."

The room went silent again, and he was sure he could feel what each one of them was thinking. Rush would be bucking against the idea of working within the system. Anderson would be digesting the idea slowly, weighing the pros and cons. Harley would be hating it, thinking it was too far-fetched and too far in the future and too unlikely to succeed.

But it was his brother who spoke up first. "I'm in."

Brayden couldn't mask his surprise. "You are?"

"Yeah. Dad would want this."

"I'm in, too," said Rush at the same moment that Anderson chimed in with "It's a good idea."

Relief swept through Brayden. "All right."

A final silence descended on them, brief this time. Then they all started talking at once. And none of it had to do with the stress and fear and sadness of the last year. It was as though making a plan—even one that extended so far into the future that it seemed like a dream—released all the tension. And for a while, at least, they could go back to being teenage boys.

Chapter 1

Fifteen years later...

Reggie Frost pressed the wash button on the industrial-sized dish sanitizer, then looked up and sighed at the big old-fashioned clock on the wall at the Frost Family Diner. It wasn't even eight at night yet, but she was already exhausted. And an hour behind schedule.

Two of the other servers had come down with the flu, so she'd pulled an open, then worked a crazy busy lunch rush, a sleepily slow dinner hour and was now doing a close, too. She was just thankful that Fridays were notoriously slow before the start of the summer tourist season. Any other day of the week, and she would've been stuck there for the late-night snack crowd, too. And a week or two from now, when Whispering Woods was overflowing with out-of-town guests, she would've been lucky to get off work before midnight.

Small things to be grateful for, Reggie acknowledged.

It helped, also, that tonight was the kickoff for the annual Garibaldi Gala.

Hosted by its namesake, the party started out with fireworks on the Friday before the so-called official opening of tourist season. Everyone who didn't have somewhere else to be was on the other side of town, jostling for free cotton candy and the best view of the soon-to-start light show. But even before she got saddled with the never-ending shift, Reggie hadn't been planning on attending the late-night festivities. She was working on a plan. One she hadn't yet disclosed to anyone. One she *wouldn't* disclose unless it worked out. And in order to make it happen, she needed Jesse Garibaldi's attention. She had to make sure the man knew without a doubt that she was as committed to the community as he was. It was the main reason she'd signed on to help out at family-friendly fair the following morning.

And she wanted to be well rested enough that she could cheerfully paint two hundred sticky-with-cotton-candy faces, work the lunch rush—again—then attend the Saturday night dinner and dance. The last part was key. The party was an exclusive one. Accessible only to those who worked for or with Garibaldi. And the man of the house *always* attended in person. Her hope was to speak to him directly. To present her request and hope that he'd bite.

No point in passing up on free food and drinks, either.

She tapped an aching foot, waiting for the cycle to finish its run. With the exception of the last load of dishes and a final trash bag waiting its turn to be run to the bin outside, the diner was in shutdown mode. Everything was tidy, all the floors sparkling. Reggie was sure even her long-passed grandmother—who had opened the place back when the town was still a forestry one—would be pleased with the way it looked at the moment.

And, she thought, *it'll prove to Dad that I can do it on my own.*

"That'll teach him to call me a slacker," she grumbled.

But it was an affectionate complaint. She'd left the tiny town twice. Once, in pursuit of an education in psychology. Another in pursuit of love. Neither had panned out, and her dad teased her all the time about giving up. But the truth was, the time she'd spent away from Whispering Woods had put her life in perspective. She really did prefer the tight-knit community to all else. She enjoyed being near her father. She even liked the idea of inheriting the management of the diner over the management of potential future clients. Besides which, Reggie was convinced that she could learn far more about the human psyche while waiting on tables than she could from a textbook.

Those things made her more than happy to set up a permanent life in the touristy town.

Dishes and all, she thought with a smile.

As if on cue, the sanitizer buzzed, and she quickly turned her attention to putting away its contents. Plates in their slots, mugs on their racks, cutlery in its case. In minutes, she had it sorted out. With another sigh—this one satisfied—Reggie grabbed the green bag from the ground and marched toward the rear door of the diner.

Five minutes, she said to herself. *Then you'll be on your way home. A half hour, and you'll be in the bath. And tomorrow night, you'll be sitting somewhere else, sipping champagne and eating canapés. And hopefully celebrating a victory.*

But she no sooner had the door cracked open than one of her no-nonsense work shoes got caught in a groove in the cobblestone just outside, sending her flying. As she fell forward, one knee smacked the ground and the bag flew out of her grip. Reggie watched in disappointed frustration as the bottom split open and bits of leftover food and soggy napkins rolled out. All *right* beside the Dumpster that had been her destination in the first place.

"You've got to be kidding me," she muttered.

She started to push herself up, then went still as the sound of feet thumping on concrete reached her ears. A heartbeat later, there was a wordless cry, then a thump as something—some*one*—hit the other side of the big bin. The whole thing rattled. Even the lid shook in protest.

Then a man's voice—laced with obvious fear—carried through the alley.

"I swear," he said. "I swear that I wasn't planning to say anything."

A second man replied immediately, his tone calm and controlled, but somehow full of derision, too. "The thing is, two minutes ago, you told me there *was* nothing to say. Now you're telling me you won't say anything. Which is it?"

There was the sound of a muffled sob. "Both."

"Both?"

"Yes!"

"That answer just doesn't fly, my friend. You should never have come back to town. You were told what would happen if you did, weren't you?"

The Dumpster rattled again, and Reggie cringed backward as a narrow-shouldered man dived out from behind it. He tried to tear across the alley, but the man chasing him was faster. Bigger. And wearing a police uniform.

For a second, Reggie was so startled that she almost forgot to stifle a gasp. She didn't recognize the first man. But she *knew* the man in the uniform. A rookie named Chuck Delta. He'd moved to town very recently, hired on for the upcoming tourist season, and he came into the diner every morning to grab a bagel and a coffee.

Was he there on official business? Was the man he now held by the collar a criminal? Should Reggie make her presence known?

But before she could work through an answer to the last question, the first two were answered.

"You're supposed to *help* people," said the smaller man. "And I haven't done anything wrong."

The big one shook his head. "Maybe not this time around. But I recognized you. And that's enough."

Chuck took a step toward the stranger, his hand stretched out toward the man's mouth. And in a futile attempt to escape, the stranger flailed, then cringed back against the wall.

Something worse is going to happen.

The second the thought popped into Reggie's head, it came to fruition.

A flash of metal.

A muted bang.

A muffled cry.

Reggie stumbled backward fearfully, trying to right herself and instead scraping against both the ground and the discarded garbage scattered over it. A soup can—which had somehow sneaked out of its rightful place in the recycling—rolled across the road. She froze, watching it make its way out into the open, *ping-pinging* along.

Too much noise!

Her eyes lifted fearfully just in time to see as the first man slumped forward, and Chuck started to turn. And the need for self-preservation finally kicked in. Reggie's feet smacked against the cobblestone, her brain urging her along in time with the beat of her flight.

Run-run, run-run, run-run.

She pushed out of the alley and hit the concrete sidewalk.

Quick-quick. Quick-quick. Quick-quick.

She hit the corner, then continued straight onto the pavement.

Go-go. Go-go. Go—

The screech of tires was the only warning she had as she darted out, and her chanting brain didn't have time to catch up. With her feet still moving, she raised her eyes in horror. A slick black car was sliding toward her, kicking up the scent of burning rubber as it skidded over the road at a wild angle.

But Reggie couldn't stop herself.

Biting down on her lip so hard that she tasted blood, she flew straight into the driver's-side headlight. Or maybe it hit her. The sudden, sharp pain all the way up her body made it impossible to say which was true. She crumpled to the ground.

No!

She couldn't afford to stop here. She had to keep going. So she fought to get to her feet, her hands flailing to grab something—anything—to pull herself up. What she found was a warm hand. *Two* warm hands, in fact. One wrapped around her own, and another on her shoulder.

Wide. Tall. Strong.

A man.

And Reggie's first instinct, spurred by the violence she'd just witnessed, was to fight him off. Tooth and nail if she had to.

But he was mouthing something at her. Words she couldn't quite make out. And his eyes—light brown and as warm as his hands—were staring down at her, full of concern. A little familiar. And genuine. She was almost sure. But was it enough?

She swiveled her head in the direction she'd just run from, and the world spun. It would have to be.

"Help me," she said, her voice not much more than a croak.

He replied, and it sounded like "I'm trying."

"Please."

His expression went from concerned to puzzled, to even *more* concerned. But thankfully, he didn't argue. He just bent down, lifted her from the ground and tucked her against his broad chest. She closed her eyes and sank into him gratefully, praying he could keep her safe from the craziness she'd just witnessed.

Detective Brayden Maxwell inhaled as he shifted his hips to accommodate the added weight, and a lightly spiced scent hit him. Pleasant. Just like the feel of the girl—who he recognized from the quaint little restaurant a few blocks over—curled up in his arms.

Reggie, wasn't it?

He glanced down. Yep, her name tag confirmed that he had it right.

Just two minutes earlier, he'd been on the phone with his brother, telling him that things were going smoothly. The plan didn't have a hitch. Finally, after a decade and a half of searching, he was sure, all but 100 percent sure that they'd located their target. The man who'd walked away without a scratch, but left them with deep scars.

Now this.

What had spooked her so badly that she'd run out in front of his car like that? He hadn't seen anything himself. Heck. He'd barely seen *her*. He was just glad he'd had enough time to swerve as much as he had. She'd smacked herself pretty hard against his bumper, but three seconds *less* notice…he shook his head at the thought, then inhaled again, and the sweet smell filled his nose a second time.

Cinnamon, maybe? Pie from the diner?

He studied her for another moment. She was always smiling while she served at the restaurant. One of those big smiles that lit up her whole face. It was almost too big for her very petite form. Perfect for her sparkling eyes, though, which were the greenest he'd ever seen. Which were all but closed now. Fluttering just a little. Her body was shaking a little, too.

Yeah, she was definitely more than shaken up. Maybe not in medical shock, but definitely under a great amount of emotional distress.

Not good.

Brayden frowned and brought his attention to the street. He scanned it carefully. Up. Then down. Then both ways again. He couldn't see a shred of anything suspicious. Or anything much at all, for that matter. The sky was dim, but

the streetlights—few as they were in this small town—
hadn't yet come on. The moment hovered right between
dusk and true darkness, and his eyes hadn't quite adjusted.

He gave himself one moment more to study the surrounding area. Nothing jumped out, but his instincts were
definitely alight.

He decided not to waste any more time looking for—and
thinking about—something that might not even be there.
The girl was scared. Possibly hurt. Both those things necessitated his assistance, even if he didn't factor in her spe-
cific request for help.

"All right," he murmured. "Let's get you somewhere
you can feel safe."

Where that was, he didn't know yet. But his experience
with trauma victims told him that getting her away from
the scene would be a good start.

He stared at his car for a second, then decided it would
be easiest to transport her in the back seat. She could lie
down instead of trying to keep upright. As Brayden tugged
open the door and laid her down, she started to shiver even
more, and her teeth were chattering, too. The evening air
was far too warm for that kind of chill.

Definitely something close to shock.

"Hey," he said, careful to keep his voice low and gentle. "I've got a blanket in the trunk. Sit tight while I grab
it, okay?"

She gave him just the barest hint of a nod. It would have
to do. He strode to the rear of the car, popped open the lid,
then retrieved a thick duvet from the pile of items he'd just
washed at the Laundromat. It still had a hint of warmth,
leftover from the dryer.

Perfect.

He slammed the trunk shut, then moved back to the side
of the car, where he carefully tucked the blanket around
Reggie's tremor-riddled form. He made sure to cover her

completely, shoulders to toes, noting that one of her shoes was missing. A quick glance in the direction she'd sprinted from told him the missing piece of footwear was nowhere close.

"Okay," he said to her. "We'll worry about that later. For now, I just want you to lie still. Can you do that?"

She gave another tiny nod, the duvet bouncing with her agreement.

"Good." He put a hand on her covered shin, glad to see that her shivering had tapered off already. "You're going to be fine. I promise."

Then Brayden closed the door and made his way back to the driver's seat. He turned the key and eased the car onto the empty street. He drove along slowly, mentally assessing what his destination ought to be.

The local doctor? He'd heard there was a man who ran a practice from his home, but it had to be after hours now.

Her place? He hadn't a clue where it was.

The diner where she worked? Fine, unless she'd just run from there. It was only a few blocks over, after all.

Maybe Brayden's own rented cabin? He paused to think about that possibility a little further. His temporary home was out of the way. But at least he knew where it was, and was familiar with its resources. Of course, having guests over wasn't on his list of priorities. He had his mission—his one and only reason for taking up residence in the tiny town—and getting to know the pretty waitress wasn't a part of it.

Because running over her with your car was?

Brayden stifled a sigh. Yeah, that hadn't been on his to-do list, either. But adjusting to accommodate unexpected scenarios was a pretty key element in his work. So he'd just have to do it now.

As he put his foot to the gas, he let himself lift his eyes to the rearview mirror. Reggie had disappeared into the bulky blanket; her waiflike form was but invisible. Only a wisp of her dark hair peeked over one corner. For a second, it actually made him smile.

Then a flash of red and blue caught his eye, and as he adjusted his gaze to find the source, his smile dropped off completely. Straight ahead, a police car was cruising toward them. Flashers on. Sirens off. A solo, uniformed man at the wheel.

Something about the sight of the car deepened his worry. Generally speaking, when working a case that crossed jurisdictions, his boss made sure to alert the local authorities. Brayden knew that wasn't the case here. His captain at the Freemont City PD had authorized the investigation—even if he hadn't provided the time and the resources—and that sanction was enough. But the man they were investigating had entrenched himself in the Whispering Woods community. He had the mayor's ear, and many pieces of the town's property in his pocket, and the local police probably wouldn't take kindly to having one of their favorite citizens investigated. So the case was more covert than most, and Brayden's presence a well-kept secret.

Moments later, the cruiser pulled up behind him. The cop inside pointed sideways, and Brayden's concern spiked. Still, he had no choice but to pull over. He flipped on his signal and slowed the already moving-at-a-crawl vehicle. The cop waved again, and Brayden pulled the car over completely. He rolled down his window and waited with barely contained impatience as the other officer climbed out.

Brayden noted that the man was barely more than a kid. Clean shaven, fresh faced. But with a stiffness to his shoulders. Straight out of the academy, maybe, with something to prove.

Brayden sighed, forced a smile and readied his license and registration. "'Evening, Officer."

"Sir." The younger man gave the paperwork a cursory

once-over, then handed it back. "You're not a local. You just passing through?"

The question made Brayden want to frown, but he held it in. No one just passed through Whispering Woods. There was one road into the town, and nothing but mountains and trees on the other side.

"I've got a business venture in mind," Brayden said. "Got a short-term lease on one of the cabins out by the creek."

"Ah."

"Yep. Was I speeding, Officer?"

The kid shook his head. "Nah. I'm just investigating a report on a disturbance."

Brayden felt his eyebrow twitch. The guy *had* to be inexperienced if he was giving even that bit of information away so freely.

"Anything I should worry about?"

"Nah," the rookie said again. "What about you? You see anything suspicious happening around here in the last few minutes?"

Brayden made himself laugh. "Around *here*? I've been in town for over a week and I don't think I've even seen a misbehaving squirrel."

The kid's face relaxed marginally. "Does tend to be a bit quiet. From Freemont City myself. Used to a faster pace."

Freemont.

The mention of his own hometown made Brayden want to stiffen. He guessed it wasn't entirely improbable that it was a coincidence. Whispering Woods was two hundred miles north of the Oregon city, and even though it was a bit off the beaten path, it was still a decently popular tourist destination. That didn't mean he wasn't going to file away the information for later. He made a mental note, then relaxed his face into another smile.

"Guess that'll do it," Brayden said. "Good to be vigilant, though. Even in a small town."

"You bet." The kid gave his bare face a scratch, then stepped back. "Have a good night."

"You, too."

Brayden put the car back into Drive and flicked on his signal. He didn't make it as far as pulling out, though, before the young cop called out again.

"Sir?"

"Yep."

He braced himself for a question about the human-shaped pile of blankets on the back seat. It didn't come. Instead, the officer held out a business card.

"That's my direct line," the kid said. "If you *do* see anything, feel free to skip the middleman and call me right away."

"You got it."

Stifling a relieved sigh and suppressing a need to hit the gas as hard as he could, Brayden eased the car onto the street. As he pulled out, he glanced in the rearview mirror. What he saw just about made him swerve into a fire hydrant. The kid had turned away and was heading back to his patrol car. And jammed into his belt at the rear of his waistband was a woman's shoe.

Chapter 2

Reggie kept her mouth shut. Partly because she was still terrified. Partly because her head ached. And partly because she wasn't sure exactly what to say to the big man who'd scooped her up like she weighed nothing, then tucked her into the back of his car with a gentleness that was completely at odds with his obvious strength. Especially since he'd—*thank God*—hidden her presence from Chuck, the gun-wielding cop.

Why *had* he done it? Normal people went *to* the police when there was an issue. And having a panicked woman run straight into your car was definitely an issue.

So maybe he's not normal.

She hazarded a tiny peek over the edge of the warm blanket. She didn't have the best view of him, but she could tell that his eyes were fixed on the road ahead. And she could also see that there was a definite edge to the way he held himself. His stubble-covered jaw was stiff. The hand he had on the steering wheel was tight. Tension everywhere. Maybe from lying to the cop. Maybe from something else.

Remembering she'd thought there was something familiar about him, she studied his features surreptitiously, trying to see more. When he cast a quick glance in the sideview mirror, she got a fuller look at his face. He had wide lips and a well-proportioned nose. His eyes were a pale brown that bordered on amber, and thick lashes framed them, making their unusual color stand out all the more. Beyond a doubt, he was one of the best-looking men she'd ever seen. But she couldn't place where exactly she knew him from. The diner, probably, but she was sure he wasn't a regular, and she doubted a tourist would be so eager to mislead the local police.

She closed her eyes for a second, considering whether or not the bump on her head was making her short-term memory fuzzy. A strong possibility. When she lifted her lids again, he'd turned back to the road, and all she could see now was his profile. She had to admit to a weird stab of disappointment that she couldn't stare at him for a bit longer.

Apparently the bump didn't affect your libido, she thought sarcastically.

Reggie fought the need to study him further, knowing full well that she should be worried about what he planned to do with her rather than be distracted by his looks. She had no clue where they were headed or what his intentions were. Something in her gut told her she could trust him, but at the moment, she wasn't sure she should rely on the instinct. If someone had asked her twenty minutes earlier whether or not Chuck was a good guy, she probably would've said yes without even considering another answer.

She fought a shiver as the memory of his furious tone came back to her. The man in the front seat was a far better option than being back there. He had to be.

At least until I'm far away from Chuck. That's all that matters right this second.

Except as quickly as the thought came, it was replaced with the realization that it wasn't quite true. In her panicked run, she'd forgotten all about the man on the other end of the gun.

"Oh, my God!" she gasped.

The man in the front seat tossed a concerned look over his shoulder. "What's the matter?"

"We have to go back!"

"What?"

"The man...the other one..." She tried to push up to a sitting position, but a wave dizziness hit her, overriding the worry and guilt and keeping her in place. "Oh, God."

"Take it easy."

She shook her head, making the dizziness even worse. "I can't."

"Just give yourself a minute. Breathe."

Reggie closed hers eyes and took his advice, her mind reeling. What had happened to the other man? Could he possibly have lived? Should she be calling someone for help? Probably. Yes. Definitely, actually.

But who?

Clearly the police were out of the question.

"We have to go back," she said again, this time in a mumble.

"I get the feeling that would be a bad idea."

"We have to. *I* have to."

"We're over halfway to my cabin."

"Your cabin?"

"Wasn't sure where else to take you."

"Oh."

"You need to tell me something?"

She chewed her lip nervously, trying to decide what to say. "Someone's life might depend on whether or not I go back."

He met her gaze in the rearview mirror, and he didn't look as startled as she thought he should. "And *your* life?"

"What?"

"That cop back there..."

Those four words were enough to make Reggie's heart beat at double time, and her hands tightened on the blanket. "Yes. That's Chuck Delta."

"Well, Officer Delta had your shoe."

Reggie glanced down at her feet, then recalled one of the slip-ons had fallen off during her hasty escape. And it wasn't exactly good news that it was now in Chuck's possession. But even that wasn't the most pressing of her issues right then. She needed to help the victim. If he could still be helped.

"Bad time to play Cinderella," the big man pointed out, then sighed when she didn't respond. "All right. You tell me where you need me to go and I'll circle back."

"The Frost Family Diner."

"Got it. But the second I see anything I think is dangerous, I'm hitting the gas. That includes running into the cop again."

Reggie breathed out, glad he'd conceded, even with his conditions. "Okay."

She closed her eyes, letting the rhythm of the tires under her back lull her. After a few silent moments, though, one of his statements came back to her.

His cabin.

And finally she placed him.

"Tuesday, table five. Two eggs, over easy, dry toast," she said, opening her eyes again.

A smile tipped up both sides of his mouth and showed a row of nice even teeth before his gaze went back to the front windshield. "I usually go by Max. But that works, too."

Reggie felt her face warm. "Sorry."

"Don't be sorry. It's not like customers wear name tags." His teasing gaze found hers in the mirror again. "Actually, I'm kinda flattered you remembered my meal."

"You left one of the girls a twenty-dollar tip when she complained about the price of diapers. She talked about it—*and* you *and* your plans to start a bed-and-breakfast— for an hour after."

"Ah. My wanton display of wealth. Should've known."

"Generosity with no strings," she corrected, then blushed a little more at how emphatic she sounded.

"Always glad to help," he said with another glance at her in the mirror. "Never any strings."

She sensed a question in the words, and she wasn't sure what it was. Which made it even harder to answer. After a moment, she settled on something easy.

"Thank you. For picking me up and for taking me back, too."

He replied just as simply. "You're welcome. And speaking of which...we're here."

She fought the dizziness and propped herself up to look out the window. The street was eerily empty. And even though she knew it was because Jesse Garibaldi owned the whole block and all the owners were probably just getting ready for his party, it still made her shiver. Even the familiar sight of her family's restaurant couldn't help her shake her unease.

"See anything you don't like?" Max asked.

"I don't see anything at all," she admitted. "But I still don't like it. Could you drive around to the alley?"

"Sure."

Very slowly, he guided the car to the end of the road. Reggie didn't have to strain to see that it was as empty as the street.

Unless there's a body behind the Dumpster.

She swallowed nervously and reached for the door handle.

"What are you doing?" Max demanded immediately.

"I need to get out and check."

"Check *what*?"

Ignoring his question—mostly because she wasn't sure she could answer without panicking again—she pushed open the door. From the front seat, the big man muttered something unintelligible, and before Reggie could even get both feet on the ground, he'd flung open his own door and made his way to her side of the car.

He positioned himself in front of her, arms crossed over his wide chest as he repeated, "Check *what*?"

She met his gaze as steadily as she could manage with her head swimming the way it was and made herself say the words. "Check for a body."

Max's eyes widened, then darkened as he shook his head. "We're not checking for a body."

"We have to."

"Body checking is a police job."

"Unless the police *created* the body."

"Chuck?"

Reggie nodded, wincing at the sharp pain the motion caused. "There was a gun and another man and cop or not… I'm sure it wasn't something legal."

"Then you *definitely* shouldn't be checking."

"I have to, Max. What if the other guy is still alive and needs help?"

His mouth twisted like he wanted to argue, but after a second, he just shook his head again. "I'll go."

"No."

"The second you step out of the car, you're going to fall over. What's going to happen if someone *is* back there, and he's not happy to see you?"

Reggie wanted to protest that she wasn't anywhere near falling down, but it would've been a lie. Her head definitely didn't feel right. But she wasn't excited about the idea of him risking himself either. Not for her sake.

She swallowed. "I don't think it's very safe."

"I've got some experience dealing with the shadier side of life," he assured her.

"That's not exactly reassuring."

"It just means I can handle whatever's around the other side of that Dumpster."

"You're sure?"

"A hundred percent."

She took a breath, then nodded. "Okay."

He studied her for a second longer—like he was trying to figure something out—then moved to the passenger-side door on the front of the car. He opened it, then the glove box, too, and pulled out something shiny and metal.

A gun.

Reggie was shaking her head—pain be damned—before he even brought it back and held it out. "I can't take that."

"You're scared. And for a minute or two, you're going to be alone. This'll give you some security," he said.

"I don't even know how to fire it."

"This is an easy one. Flick off the safety, then click, point and shoot." He demonstrated the steps once, then twice, then handed the weapon to her and made her repeat the sequence herself. "Good."

Reggie couldn't think of a worse word to describe the situation. Less than an hour ago, she'd been worrying that she wouldn't have time to do her nails before Garibaldi's party. Now she was sitting in a stranger's car with a gun in her lap. And the stranger was telling her things would be fine and holding out his hand and expecting her to just take it.

"C'mon," he said. "I'll help you into the front."

As she closed her fingers on his, a startling tingle shot up her arm. The sensation was strong enough that it momentarily blocked out the buzz in her head. Surprise made her loosen her hand, and she shot her gaze up, wondering if he felt the shock of sharp heat, too. But Max was focused on tightening his hold and pulling her out gently.

Reggie made herself dismiss the heady sensation as a side effect of her head bump, and let him guide her to the passenger seat. But it was impossible to deny the jolt of loss as he let her go.

"Key's in the ignition," he said. "If I don't come back

around that corner in five minutes, I want you to drive away. Fast and far enough away that you know your 911 call is going to go to a different city."

Reggie opened her mouth to protest, but he was already closing the door. With her heart in her throat, she stared after him as his pressed himself to the edge of the building, then slipped around the corner and disappeared.

With well-practiced stealth, Brayden eased along the exterior brick wall of the Frost Family Diner. He'd already compartmentalized his worries so that he could focus on the moment. From the shoe in the cop's back pocket to whether or not this whole situation related to his own case, to the fact that he found the pretty waitress's green eyes utterly mesmerizing, everything had been tucked into a tidy corner of his mind. Even the ridiculous prick of heat he'd felt when he took her hand had been momentarily put aside. After all, he wouldn't get a chance to experience it again if he couldn't satisfy her need to check up on whatever had happened in the alley.

He moved along a little farther. He didn't feel insecure about leaving behind his weapon; he was more than capable of winning in a hand-to-hand combat scenario. Even if his opponent came armed, Brayden had a few ways of disarming him without breaking much of a sweat. If worst came to worst, he could always rely on the small knife he kept tucked in his boot.

He had a feeling, though, that neither a knife nor his fists were going to be necessary. In spite of the quiet, uneasy air, Brayden's instincts weren't screaming a warning. His gut wasn't wrong often. Eight years a cop—four of them as a detective—saw to that.

He reached the Dumpster in question and pushed out from the wall to avoid rubbing his back along the sour-smelling bin. He inched along until he got to the corner, where he paused, listening. Not a single sound carried out from the other side. Even the dim light above didn't emit a hum.

Feeling confident that he'd find nothing—but cautious nonetheless—he eased out into the open. Silence continued to reign. Brayden relaxed even more. His gaze swept the area in search of anything out of the ordinary. The alley was clean. Almost weirdly so. He slowed his perusal of the space, now looking for something *in* place instead of out of it. There were no scraps of trash on the cobblestone, no signs of refuse of any sort.

He frowned. There should've been something. A half a dozen businesses shared the alley and the Dumpster. How could it possibly be so clean? The answer was one that made his instincts jump.

Because someone cleaned it up.

The trip between the spot where he'd picked up Reggie and the spot where he'd pulled the U-turn to come back had taken a little more than thirty minutes. If someone *had* come in and taken care of the scene—assuming the waitress was right about what happened—they'd done it in a hurry. Which meant they likely missed something.

Brayden made himself do a third visual inventory, this time square foot by square foot, surveying everything from the walls to the ground. He still saw nothing. Convinced he'd been thorough but with his gut still telling him something was off, he turned to head back to the car. Then he spotted it. Wedged under the door opposite the large bin. A dull metal soup can with a highly-recognizable logo.

With a quick glance around, he took a few steps toward the discarded item. Then paused as something far more sinister caught his attention. Just above the can, at chest height on the wall, was a small, rust-colored smear. A few more steps and a closer look confirmed Brayden's initial suspicion. It was blood. He'd seen enough of it in the course of his career to know.

Now he backed up, trying to get a wider view. The light was growing steadily worse, but he was almost positive that the wall showed signs of a hasty wipe down. An unnaturally even arc of dirt swept around the smear. Like someone had wiped it clean, then tried to mask the wipe down. An untrained eye might've missed it. A few days from then, it would probably be utterly unnoticeable.

Habit made Brayden want to call it in. But the integrity of the local police was more than just in question—it was possible that at least one of them was responsible. He didn't even know for sure what the end result of the shooting was. If the man was alive, he stood a chance of being saved. Except he thought the chances of that were slim to none. If he hadn't been dead when the cleanup happened, he wouldn't have made it for much longer. A shooting in an alleyway wasn't a warning—it was a death sentence.

Make a decision, he ordered silently.

He tapped his fingers on his thigh for a second, said a silent prayer for the man who'd very likely met his untimely fate in the alley, then yanked out his cell phone. As much as mourning the loss of life felt right, it was action that would *make* things right. So in quick succession, he took a series of photos, making sure to get the smear from multiple angles. Then he took a panoramic shot of the alley. As soon as he had a good collection of pictures, he dragged them into an album, added a shorthand note and fired them off to a generic email address that he and his team used for communications like this. What were the chances that a town as small as Whispering Woods was home to two criminal masterminds?

Slim to none.

This had to have something to do with the slippery crook who killed their father. And if for some crazy reason it all turned out not to be related to his own case, it was still a good record to have. Especially if a man *had* been shot, as Reggie said.

Reggie. Right.

He needed to get back to her. His five minutes were more than likely up, and he had a strong preference for *not* walking the fifteen miles back to his cabin. Tucking his phone away, he turned up the alley once more. He only got two steps before a bang rocked the air.

For a second, he was frozen, a tumble of bad memories hitting him hard.

The bomb. The echo. The debris.

Video footage of the tragedy jumped to the forefront of his mind. The remembered sound of it filled his thoughts for a minute, blocking out all else. A teenage boy, knowing exactly what it sounded like on the scene where his father was killed.

Then a second explosion echoed through the alley, and instinct kicked in a little belatedly. Brayden threw himself against the wall and ducked low; his head whipped back and forth as he looked for the source of the noise. Everything was still. There wasn't even a whiff of smoke.

So what the—

A third boom sounded, cutting off his thoughts as he realized it had come from up the alley. Near the spot where Reggie waited in the car.

Panic hit, this time even harder than before and directed outward rather than inward.

A rare curse dropped from Brayden's mouth as he bolted up the cobblestone road. In seconds, he'd reached the street, fear for the green-eyed waitress making his feet move fast. He stopped short, though, when he spotted his car in one piece, Reggie in the same spot he'd left her. Even from a few feet away, he could see the concern on her face, but it was no stronger an expression than it had been a few minutes earlier.

Puzzled, he took a step out. A fourth boom, then three more rapid-fire ones rang out. Brayden flinched. Then the sky above exploded in light, and he realized what it really was and his body sagged.

Fireworks. Seriously?

It might've been funny if it weren't so ridiculous. He almost wanted to laugh anyway. He made himself refrain from doing it, afraid it might come out a little manically if he let it.

"Way to stay calm under pressure, Detective Maxwell," he muttered as he picked his way over to the car and opened the driver's-side door.

"Are you okay?" Reggie asked right away.

"Fine."

"You're sure?"

He forced himself to answer lightly. "This from the woman who got run over by my car."

"I guess. But you do look a little green."

For the briefest second, he considered telling her about his overreaction and where it came from. Something in her gaze made him think she might offer a sympathetic ear. That she might even genuinely care. He shook off the urge. They didn't have time for exchanging stories or getting all touchy-feely. What he needed to focus on was getting her away from whatever had happened back there in the alley. Before someone came back to check on their handiwork.

"I'm really okay," he assured her.

"And there wasn't anything in the alley?" She took a visibly shaky breath. "No body?"

"No body. But there *was* something," he admitted. "I just don't think we should hang around and talk about it here. And considering the fact that Chuck-The-Cop had your shoe, I also think it's probably best if we steer clear of your house. At least for the moment. Any objections to sticking with my original idea?"

"Your cabin?"

"It's out of the way. Not easy to sneak up on. If someone is looking for you, it won't be on their radar."

She pursed her lips and drew in her breath. And before her nod of agreement was even finished, Brayden was turning the key.

Chapter 3

The familiar scenery whipped by in a blur of green and brown, muted by the twilight.

Though she'd grown up in Whispering Woods, she'd never had a reason to check out the little cache of rental cabins at the edge of town that bordered the wildest part of the mountain. Not up close anyway.

Unlike the large, well-visited lodge that sat in the middle of everything, their destination had the inconvenience of requiring a short drive. Most tourists didn't want the effort. And any who were seeking something a little out-of-the-way seemed to gravitate toward the mobile home park on the way into town instead. Maybe because the park boasted its own little shop, running water and the convenience of a clubhouse.

The cabins where Max was staying were older and definitely more rustic. They'd once housed the loggers who used to call the town home. But as they approached the woodsy setting, Reggie could see that it was picturesque. Even in the dark, there was no denying the appeal. On one side of the clearing, four small cabins angled toward a fire pit. On the other, two larger wooden homes sat apart, separated from each other by a six-foot-high hedge. Tall evergreens surrounded all of it, providing a gorgeous green canopy overhead.

If *she* were choosing a vacation spot, it would be this over the lodge or the mobile home park any day.

Max pulled past all six houses and guided his car up a dirt path that could barely be called a road, then parked in front of a seventh cabin that Reggie wouldn't even have guessed was there. It was the biggest of the bunch—though still a single floor—and clearly intended as a more permanent residence than the others. A wide porch went from one exterior wall to the other, and a welcome sign hung over the door. Potted plants lined the railing, and several rocking chairs and a wooden swing decorated one end of the porch, while the other held a cast-iron table and matching seats. Through the window, Reggie spotted gingham curtains, and up on the roof, she could see a metal chimney.

"Home sweet home-away-from," the big man announced. "Sit tight and I'll give you a hand getting out and up to the house."

She started to protest that she was fine, but again, he was too fast. In less time than it took for her to reach for her seat belt, he was opening her door and holding out a hand.

Bracing herself for another zap of attraction, she took a breath and put her fingers into his. And there it was. A goose-bumps-inducing heat that radiated up her arm as he helped her out of the vehicle. Maybe it was simply the skin on skin, maybe it was something more, but either way, Reggie couldn't shake off her awareness of his warmth and strength. And as he adjusted their position so that her hand was resting across his waist for support, it increased even more. The sudden physical closeness turned the prickles of attraction into a fierce burn. It made her stumble a bit before they even made it three steps across the ground toward the cabin.

"You okay?" Max asked, pausing while she regained her footing.

She managed a nod. "Yes. Fine."

"Okay." He sounded a bit doubtful, but he didn't argue. "Let's get you inside."

He pulled her even closer to carefully lead her up the path to the steps, and she realized she was thoroughly enjoying the nearness.

She wasn't usually much of a first-meeting-manhandler kinda girl. If anything, she considered herself to be a bit standoffish with men, prone to assessing from afar rather than jumping in haphazardly. Working in the service industry in a tourist town meant plenty of opportunities for brief encounters. And in the peak seasons—summer and winter—there was a smorgasbord of willing guys coming through the town. She'd made that mistake in her past. Just once. But one slip was all Reggie needed to know better. She barely even noticed the line of guys who paraded through town with their skis or overdone dirt bikes anymore. Especially now that she'd rounded the other side of twenty-five. Something short-term and based on fun and fun alone wasn't what she was after.

Although, judging by the way her body was reacting to Max…there were certain parts of her that hadn't gotten the message.

And whether or not *he* was aware, she couldn't tell.

She inhaled, trying to steady the abruptly staccato beat of her heart as they took the first stair. But the deep breath had the opposite effect that it should've. Because along with a hit of cool, woodsy air, she also drew in a breath of tangy, mouthwatering cologne.

She stumbled again. And again Max steadied her. This time, though, his jacket whipped loose and a cell phone clattered from his pocket to land on the wood beneath their feet. For a second, Reggie stared down at it, her heart sliding up from her chest to her throat.

"You said your name was *Max*," she whispered.

"Yeah?"

She pointed down. "The screensaver says 'Brayden's Phone.'"

"Oh. I can—"

She was off before he could even finish his sentence, one bare foot slapping the ground as she ran. A few steps later and her other shoe slipped off, too. But she didn't stop to grab it, or even to look. Somehow, finding out she'd been deceived by the man who'd saved her brought to a head the gravity of her current situation. Something in her snapped.

A man had been shot. Not just in her sleepy little town, but behind her own family's diner. The person who shot the man wasn't some stranger or criminal. He was a police officer. And maybe he hadn't seen her. But maybe he *had*.

And now...

Now she had nowhere to go. She was stuck on the outskirts of town with a man who'd lied about his name. A small, simple thing. The easiest thing to tell the truth about. She'd been too distracted by his eagerness to help. Too naive to think that he might have some ulterior motive.

It was just a name, said a little voice in her head.

She shoved it down.

Just a name, she replied to herself silently. *That's the whole thing. Why lie about such a small thing?*

But the why of it all didn't really matter. Not right then. All that *did* matter was getting away. Putting some physical space between herself and the big man. Even if that meant being unreasonable. Because clearly being near him clouded her judgment.

Reggie pushed past the tidy cabins. Rocks and pine needles and other, unknown bits of debris cut into the tender soles of her feet. She ignored the little stabs and kept going to the bottom of the driveway. There she paused.

The road or the woods?

The road would take her back to town. But Max—no, Brayden—would know that. If he was following her, he'd be expecting her to try to get home. And going home wasn't safe anyway. She swallowed, thinking of her dad in his two-bedroom bungalow. Was *he* safe? Would Chuck come by there, looking for her?

Reggie shoved aside the worry. If the wayward cop did find a reasonable excuse for visiting her childhood home, he'd quickly figure out that Reggie hadn't been there herself. And he wouldn't want to make her dad suspicious. Being crooked didn't make him stupid.

She took a breath and turned toward the forest. At the very least, it would provide a place to hide while she sorted through what to do.

"Reggie!"

The yell—up the driveway and as of yet out of sight—was enough to spur her on. She slammed her feet to the ground once more. In moments, she was pushing her way through the low, thick bits of greenery. She moved as fast as she could with the branches slap-slapping against her ankles and calves. Yard by yard, she put space between herself and the cabins. Brayden's voice faded. Then it disappeared. And she kept going.

The shrubs gave way to bigger and bigger trees, spaced apart, their wide roots popping from the ground in a meandering, patternless dance. She didn't let them slow her down.

At last the ground started to slope up, and Reggie knew it would only get more treacherous from there. Her breaths came hard and fast, and her face was covered in sweat. At last she stopped to gulp in some much-needed air and hazarded a look around. She could see the broken path she'd created, and also the way up the mountain. The rest of the area was made of enormous trees and a few crumbling boulders.

Had Brayden figured out yet that she hadn't headed back into town? She couldn't be sure. But she was almost certain that even if he had—and even if he was following her now—he was far enough behind that she could at last take a thirty-second breather. And she really needed one.

So she perched on the edge of one of the big rocks and rested her elbows on her knees, wincing at the sight of her feet. They were ragged. Covered in dirt and so torn up that she could pretty much count on an infection.

And that was almost as bad as the fact that it was nearly pitch-black.

Reggie lifted her gaze. The canopy above was so dark that it almost couldn't be called green. The bits of sky between the covering branches were starless, and there was no moon to speak of, either.

Wondering if she'd put herself in even more danger by running, she closed her eyes and inhaled. Her breathing had slowed, and when a breeze kicked through the air, the dampness of her forehead made her shiver. But the chill brought on by the sound she heard next was far greater. The snap of twigs breaking under heavy feet.

With her heart thundering again, Reggie jumped up. The pain in her feet was immediate. And crippling. A cry escaped her lips, and she fell forward. The rocky ground loomed beneath her face and her eyes closed and her body tensed in anticipation of smacking into it. But before she could land, a strong hand closed on her elbow. It pulled her back, then she slid down to her knees. A second hand joined the first, moving over her shoulders, then under them. Together, they scooped her from the ground. Away from the pain. She knew without checking that it was Brayden. She recognized his touch. His scent, too. And in spite of the way her mind screamed at her that she was running from him, her body wanted to sink into him. Like she had before.

She fought the urge and instead yelled, "Put me down!"

"So you can run off and hurt yourself even more?"

For the first time, he sounded a little impatient. "I don't think so."

"So you're just going to do what? Carry me all the way back to the cabin?"

"Pretty obvious that you can't walk there on your own."

"You can't hold me against my will."

"I don't *want* to hold you against your will. And if you wanted to leave the cabin, you could've just asked. I would've even driven you wherever you thought you needed to go."

"You lied about your name."

"It wasn't quite a lie, and I would've explained it if you'd given me a minute."

"Right."

His chest heaved with a heavy breath. "Listen. My real name is Brayden *Maxwell*. *Max* is a nickname."

Reggie wished her gut didn't want so strongly to believe him. It was hard to argue with the instinct to trust. Especially when her nose was filled with his musky scent and his warm body was holding off the increasing chill in the air. It was a heck of a lot easier to justify running away like a crazy person when he wasn't so close.

"Do you have ID?" she made herself ask.

"I do. Sitting in the center console of my car. Which is back at the house."

"Not good enough."

"What do you want me to do here, Reggie?"

"I don't know," she said honestly.

He went silent for a minute. "Reach into my pocket and take my keys."

"What?"

"My keys. You can use them like a weapon. Stab my eye out if I move the wrong way. Or you can use them to take my car. Either way, they might make you feel a little more secure."

Reggie considered his suggestion. She knew he was probably just placating her. The fact that she was cradled in his arms kind of gave away the fact that he was the more physically powerful of the two of them. And realistically, he probably outweighed her hundred-fifteen-pound frame by a good hundred pounds of his own. He seemed almost oblivious to the added weight. But the idea that he was willing to add some vulnerability to his own side of things just to make her feel better...that was something. Or so she hoped.

"Which pocket?" she asked.

"Inside left."

She lifted her hand and slid it along his chest. All on their own, her heartbeat sped up and her fingers slowed down. Her palm moved across his thick, more-than-obvious muscles, unintentionally exploring a little more than was necessary. No wonder he didn't seem bothered by her extra weight. He was built like a truck. Reggie told herself to ignore it and will her hands to just grab the keys. But as she fumbled to find the pocket, it was impossible not to note the sharp breaths he drew in at each bit of contact.

So. Maybe he isn't as oblivious to your presence as you thought.

The realization warmed her face, and she was glad it was dark enough that he couldn't see her unexpected blush.

Her hand closed on the key ring then, and she yanked out the little stack of metal. Before she could get them all the way out, though, Brayden sat down on one of the big boulders and settled her in his lap. He adjusted, and then his thick fingers landed on top of hers. He spread apart her knuckles and dragged a key between each one.

"Like this," he said. "Makeshift brass knuckles."

Reggie stared down at the homemade weapon in her hand, and she wasn't sure if she wanted to laugh or cry. The latter was definitely winning.

"I'm sorry," she said softly.

"For what?"

Brayden sounded genuinely puzzled, and when Reggie lifted her eyes, she saw that his expression matched his tone. Those caramel irises of his were fixed on her and narrowed a little in a confused squint. And a laugh won out. A little giggle—maybe a touch hysterical—escaped her lips.

"Are you serious?" she wondered out loud.

"Yes?"

The unsure reply made her laugh a second time. "You saved me from Chuck. You took me back to the diner when I asked you to. And when I realized your name wasn't Max, I assumed you were lying to me and I ran off like a crazy person. But you're asking what I'm sorry for?"

A small smile tipped up his lips, but his eyes tightened. "You're not crazy. You were in a stressful situation. *Are* in one. I'd rather have skipped the nighttime jog through the woods, but I get why you ran. No need to apologize."

"I'm still sorry," she replied.

"Well, then. You're forgiven."

"Thanks."

He stared down at her for several long moments, his face unreadable. What was going through his head? Reggie thought maybe he wanted to add something else. His mouth twitched as though he was holding back. And she had a strange urge to coax whatever it was out of him. To reach up and touch his cheek and tell him he could share whatever he wanted to share, and it would be just fine with her.

Seconds later, she was startled to find her hand *had* lifted. Her fingers brushed the edge of his jaw, tingling as they followed its strong line. It wasn't quite smooth, but it wasn't quite rough, either. Reggie wondered if he'd shaved that morning. Very abruptly, a vision of that filled her head. Brayden in front of the mirror with a straight razor in his hands. Lathered up in shaving cream, and wrapped in a towel.

With an embarrassed gasp, she dropped her fingers. But his palm came out to stop them from falling away completely. He cupped the back of her hand with his own and brought it up to his lips. He placed a swift kiss right in the center.

Heat—searing and nearly shocking—slammed into the skin there. It didn't bloom out the way his other, inadvertent touches had. Instead, it clung to that one spot. Like a tattoo. Or maybe a brand. She closed her fingers around the feeling, savoring it, even though she couldn't quite say why she felt the need.

Then Reggie dragged her eyes up to meet Brayden's. He looked as surprised as she felt. But he didn't say a word. He just shifted on the boulder, cradled her to his body once more, then stood up and started to walk.

Chapter 4

Brayden cursed himself for giving in to a rare moment of spontaneous emotion. Though *giving in* implied he'd done it consciously. The move had been pure instinct. The impulsive seizure of a moment. Not something he'd consider doing under normal circumstances.

And for your moment, you chose a kiss on her hand? Really, Maxwell? When her mouth was just as close?

But he couldn't deny the impact of the small gesture. He could still taste her salty, dust-covered palm. Still feel the coolness of it on his lips. It was a sharp contrast to the warmth everywhere else their bodies had touched. Continued to touch. It dulled some—if not all—of his irritation at her sudden flight and brought him back to his typically patient self.

"M—er, Brayden?"

"Mmph," he mumbled back.

"Aren't we going the wrong way?"

"Nope."

"I came in from the other direction."

"Yeah. And you kind of ran in a circle."

"I did?"

"That's how I managed to catch up with you," he said, grateful for the distracting conversation. "Took me about ninety seconds to figure out you were too smart to head right back into town. Went back to the house to get a flashlight so I could search for you, and I heard you crashing around *above* the cabins."

"Crap."

"Yep."

"I guess I'm not very experienced at running and hiding."

"That's a good thing. Most of the time anyway."

Brayden pushed through the last thick patch of trees. The far-range, motion-detection light came on immediately, illuminating the rear of his rented cabin.

"See?" he said. "Here we are."

Reggie blinked at the light. "Wow. I'm not just bad at running away. I'm terrible."

Brayden couldn't help but laugh. "I'd tell you it takes some practice, but that probably wouldn't be very reassuring."

"Definitely not."

He moved quickly from the back of the cabin to the front, where he paused at the bottom on the stairs and asked teasingly, "You ready to be carried over the threshold?"

Even in the dim light, he could see the color bloom in her cheeks. "I could *try* walking."

He glanced down at her dirty, battered-looking feet. "Might be better not to. Unless you want to add splinter removal to my list of first aid duties. And call me crazy, but I think checking you over for a concussion and tending to those cuts is probably enough of a first aid order for one night, don't you?"

She wrinkled her nose. "Ugh."

"What?"

"Now I can't insist on being independent without making it seem like I'm trying to create more work for you."

"I'd apologize, but I'm not really sorry."

"Fine. Carry away."

Grinning to himself, he took the steps quickly, then

paused at the door and adjusted so he could drag out his key. He held her tightly all the way into the house, not releasing her until he'd flicked on the lights in the rustic cabin and made his way through the country-style kitchen into the living room. There, he settled her onto the love seat and took a step back.

"How's your head?" he asked.

"Not too bad."

"Still dizzy?"

"Just a bit," she admitted. "Mostly when I move quickly."

"Like when you run through the woods barefoot?"

"Funny."

"I thought so. Any nausea?"

"No."

"All right. Close your eyes, count to thirty, then open them and look up at the light."

"Okay."

She dropped her lids, but when Brayden moved closer and positioned himself over her, her eyes flew open again immediately.

"I don't think you counted to ten, let alone thirty," he said.

Reggie blinked. "Uh. No."

"Makes it a little harder to check your reactivity to light."

"Oh."

"Wanna try again?"

"Yes."

She closed her eyes a second time, and Brayden counted the seconds off in his head. One for every rise and fall of her chest. He was hyperconscious of their physical closeness. Every breath brought in that light cinnamon scent of hers. By the time he finished ticking off the moments, she bumped her leg against his. Twice. And she didn't open her eyes at the end, either. She just continued to sit there, one lip sucked under the other, cheeks slightly flushed, and her long, dark lashes resting lightly on her skin.

Can't beat this view, Brayden thought, drinking in the sight of her for a few seconds longer before speaking. "I think you're good now. I'm at a count of fifty-three."

"Right."

As she opened her eyes, he brought his finger to her chin and tipped her face toward the light overhead. He held her still as he examined her, and when he did let her go, he had to admit it was with genuine reluctance. At least it was until her green eyes found his gaze and held it. He'd be happy to lose himself in that stare for a ridiculous amount of time.

"So?" she prompted softly.

"So?"

"Do I pass?"

"I wouldn't recommend running into any more cars tonight, if you can avoid it," he said, offering her a small smile. "But I don't think you're concussed."

"That's good news."

"Sure is." He eased up off the couch. "I'm going to grab the first aid kit. You want something to drink?"

"Just a glass of water, maybe?"

"On it."

He pushed up off the couch and moved toward the kitchen. Digging through the cupboards gave him a moment of reprieve from the unusual onslaught of emotion gripping him. There was no denying the effect Reggie Frost had on him. Though he couldn't pinpoint why, she definitely stirred every protective feeling he had.

And a few not-so-protective ones, he though as he paused in the doorway to admire her profile.

She was leaned over a little on the couch—not slumped, just resting—and she'd tugged her hair free so that her thick tresses covered her face completely.

Real shame to hide that, he thought absently as he stepped into the room and offered her the glass.

"Your water?"

"Thanks."

Their fingers brushed as he handed it over, and unsurprisingly, another wave of desire swept through him. She met his eyes, and he could swear he saw the same want reflected in her eyes before her gaze dropped and she took a deep sip of the liquid in the cup.

He had to really work to focus on the more pressing needs of the current situation. He unzipped the first aid bag and dug through it for some antiseptic and some gauze.

"This is going to hurt, isn't it?" she asked.

"Might sting," he agreed. "Why don't you distract yourself by walking me through what you saw back there in the alley?"

She shivered. "I already told you about the guys and the gun."

"Walk me through again anyway, starting at the beginning. I want a full picture."

As Brayden dabbed the first of the cuts, she drew in a sharp breath and launched into the story.

He listened intently as the pretty waitress told him what she'd seen. About recognizing Chuck and about his threats. About the frightened man on the other end of the weapon and their brief exchange. She was just as scared herself. It was clear in the way she kept worrying at her bottom lip, and the slight quiver in her voice as she spoke. He couldn't blame her for the fear, and it made him itch to reach out and comfort her. To bend down and touch her face and tell her it was all right. Maybe sweep back the stray strand of dark hair that kept slipping down to her cheek.

It was a strange urge for him, and it felt almost as odd to fight it as it did to have it in the first place. He might even have given in to it if his hands hadn't been busy.

Back home, Brayden had a reputation for being cold and calculating. Though he'd never confirmed its validity, he'd even once heard a rumor that everyone in his department called him Ice when he was out of earshot. It didn't bother him. Being calculating made him better at his job. Being cold meant he could stay detached. It was part of what made him such an effective cop. It was also the reason he'd been nominated to come to Whispering Woods first. He'd watch. Listen. Gain some insight into what exactly Garibaldi was up to in the tourist town.

So why is that coolness so hard to come by right now?

He studied Reggie for a second, watching her kissable mouth work as she talked.

He had no problem admitting that he found her physically attractive. He'd touched her less than a handful of times—albeit a few *extended* times—but each had been a bit like being hit by a lightning bolt. It'd taken a sincere amount of effort to not stop and assess it each time it happened.

Actually acting on the feeling was a whole other story. In that, he had a choice. Brayden picked whom he let into his space very carefully, and he could count on one hand the number of women he'd let get close in all his thirty years.

Not like you've got much choice here, he reminded himself.

It was true. This situation wasn't intentional. But it was also true that holding the waitress up while she leaned on him for support was nowhere near unpleasant. It felt good, actually, to be so thoroughly needed. So much so that he almost didn't notice she'd stopped talking until she cleared her throat.

"Brayden?"

"Yeah, sweetheart?"

"What do you think happened to him?" she asked softly. "The man who got shot?"

"Yes."

Brayden hesitated. His instinct was to keep as many details under wraps as he could. The detective in him didn't like the idea of oversharing. Especially with a civilian. He sensed, though, that not disclosing things would put up a wall, and he was sure he was going to need this woman's trust. He sat down on the edge of his coffee table and met her eyes.

"I don't know," he admitted. "The alley was clean. Except for one small thing."

"Which was?"

"A half-inch-long, rust-colored smear on the wall."

"Blood."

"Likely."

"So it wasn't just clean. It was cleaned *up*."

She was as intuitive as she was pretty, he had to give her that.

"That was my first thought," he agreed.

She closed her eyes for a quick second, then opened them to meet his gaze. "Chuck's a *cop*, Brayden. What does that mean about the rest of Whispering Woods PD?"

Brayden didn't even have to consider his answer. "They could be involved, too."

"But someone needs to be told what happened. State police, maybe?"

"We don't know what there is to tell," he reminded her. "Definitely not enough to bring them all the way out here fast enough. And to be honest, they might just go ahead and alert the locals anyway."

"So what do I do?"

This time, he took a moment to think about how to answer. It would be easy enough to tell her the truth—that he was a cop himself and would do his best to find out what was going on. It wasn't technically a true undercover assignment. Just a covert one. An exploratory mission that was a lot easier to do when no one knew who he was.

So you don't need to leap in and give yourself away to a virtual stranger. Especially when you haven't even finished what you came here to do.

He decided to see if he could get away with not disclosing his identity—yet anyway—and instead asked, "What were you *going* to do, before all of this?"

"Go home. Sip wine. Prepare for tomorrow."

"Tomorrow?"

"I'm signed up to run the face-painting station for a few hours in the morning. I've got the lunch rush at work. Then I'm supposed to get into a really uncomfortable pair of shoes and get ready for the dinner."

"The lunch rush is the only part of that I understood."

"The Garibaldi Gala is tomorrow."

"Right."

The exclusive party had slipped his mind in the height of all the excitement. He'd spent the week hearing about it. Even inquired about somehow getting a ticket only to be told it was absolutely invite only. An event catered to stroke the egos of local businessmen. Every one of whom would be in attendance.

Except Reggie, if she stays here.

"No one will miss you at the fireworks tonight?" he asked, careful to keep his voice neutral.

She shook her head. "I was skipping them in favor of resting. Is that bad?"

"It's fine. Just don't want to draw any more attention to yourself than necessary. Chuck'll already be on high alert. He doesn't know for sure that you witnessed what happened. You said yourself you don't think he saw you. And even though it's not proof, he does have that shoe of yours. If I were him, I'd be trying to find out exactly what you knew."

Her face pinched with worry. "So you think he'll be looking for me?"

"I think you should find a way to let him know *not* to be looking for you."

"How?"

"Got a friend you can call? One who'll be at the fireworks and be willing to lie for you with no questions asked?"

"I think so. Why?"

"I want you to fake an illness. Nothing too serious. Just a good excuse for keeping out of sight unless you *have* to be seen."

"Okay. I think I'll call—" Her face fell as she reached for the pocket on her uniform. "I left my phone in my locker at the diner."

"You can use mine." He went for his own pocket before remembering. "Which you dropped outside."

She smiled ruefully. "Sorry. Again."

"Forgiven. Again. I'm almost done with your feet, and as soon as I am, I'll go grab it." He lifted a fresh wipe from the first aid kit, then said, "So. Your invitation to the Gala. Does that mean your family works for Garibaldi?"

"No. We don't work for him. But we do lease the diner from him," she replied. "You don't know Garibaldi's story?"

"Not really."

It wasn't quite a lie; Brayden knew the man's history, not his current story. It had taken him and the other guys nearly two years just to track him to Whispering Woods. So when he'd asked around a bit, he'd done his best to be subtle. All he got in response was a lot of people singing Garibaldi's praises. Like he was the town's personal savior. Something in Reggie's tone as she explained made Brayden think she didn't necessarily share the sentiment.

"Well," she said, "when the forestry industry bottomed out fourteen years ago, a lot of people foreclosed. Or just walked away. The minimal tourism wasn't enough to maintain their homes and businesses. Then Garibaldi showed up. He assumed a few dozen mortgages. Then a few more. He invested a lot of money in the town and built the lodge."

Brayden finished with the antiseptic and moved on to the bandages. "You don't sound all that impressed."

"I don't want to seem like I'm not grateful," she replied. "Without his help, we would've had to leave town, too, I'm sure."

"But?"

"I don't know. I was just barely a teenager when Garibaldi showed up, but the whole thing gave me a weird feeling."

"No one questioned his interest in the town?"

"Honestly?"

"Yes."

"There *were* a couple of business owners who weren't all that happy. They got kind of vocal."

"People you knew well?"

"You could say." She offered him a ghost of a smile. "All three were local businessmen. One of them happens to be the man who plays Santa Claus every year in the little parade we have."

Brayden fastened the last of the bandage on one foot, then moved on to the next. "No one listened to them?"

"They left town."

"What?"

"Two of them moved away. Only Santa Claus stayed."

"Well. Santa Claus *does* have a certain amount of obligation." He patted her foot and smiled. "All done."

She sighed and leaned back. "So what next?"

"After tonight, you mean?"

"Yes."

"If you're feeling up to it tomorrow, you do exactly what

you were planning on doing. Go to work. Then go to the Garibaldi Gala."

"Really?"

"It's the least suspicious thing *to* do."

"I don't know if I *can* do it. I'm scared."

"Rightly so. But the alternative will draw more attention than you want. You can probably get away with lying low tonight, but after that…anything out of the ordinary is going to seem like you're hiding."

"Because I *want* to be hiding."

"You could leave town."

"But my dad…"

"So the Gala it is."

Reggie was quiet for a long moment before sitting up abruptly, a hopeful look on her pretty face. "You could come with me."

Brayden frowned. "I don't think I'm on the guest list."

"The invite was for a plus-one."

He started to protest, then realized that the idea actually had appeal. On multiple levels. He could stick close to Reggie. He might even get a chance to speak to Garibaldi directly—something he'd been trying to do for a week without success.

He nodded. "All right."

Relief filled her face. "Do you have a suit?"

"I do. And I'm even willing to put it on. But first. The phone call to your friend. I'll go grab my cell from outside."

He gave her shoulder a quick squeeze as he pushed to his feet, and before he could stop himself, he bent down to tuck her hair behind her ear. For a second, she looked startled. Then she smiled up at him. A small, appreciative look that carried up to her eyes, and warmed him from the inside.

"Thank you, Brayden," she said. "Again."

"No problem."

He slipped out of the cabin, his mind working to process

what she'd told him about Garibaldi and the men who opposed his takeover of Whispering Woods. If all three had left town under the described circumstances, it would've raised a lot of questions for him. As it stood now, the circumstances were still suspicious enough that he wanted to talk to the one who'd stayed behind.

Santa Claus.

At least the idea of interviewing Saint Nick provided some comic relief. All he had to do was ask the pretty waitress for an in.

Brayden snagged his phone from the ground, then made his way back inside, the request on his lips. "Reggie, do you think you could—"

He stopped immediately when he spotted her. She'd tucked her legs up onto the couch and pulled her arms in to her body. Her eyes were closed, and her breathing was slow and steady.

"Reggie?" he called softly.

She didn't stir.

For a second, he contemplated waking her. Even though he was sure she didn't have a concussion, there was no such thing as being too careful, and there was the phone call he'd asked her to make. He moved toward her. Then stilled again as she let out a little sigh. She was far too peaceful to disturb, and the call could wait and be altered to suit their needs. No one would be looking for her here.

The couch, though, was a cringeworthy place for a solid rest.

Brayden crossed the room, then bent to carefully scoop her up. She mumbled something incoherent, pressed her head against his chest, then settled in like she belonged there.

With his own sigh and a strange tightness in his chest, he carried her from the living room to the bedroom, where he tucked her soundly sleeping form into his own bed.

When he was satisfied that she was comfortable, he moved to leave the room. He found that he couldn't quite do it. So—chalking it up to a need to ensure Reggie's safety—Brayden settled into the overstuffed chair in the corner of the room and closed his own eyes.

Chapter 5

Reggie woke with a start, her heart hammering hard against her rib cage. It was utterly dark, and she was in a strange bed. Pushing up in a panic, she whipped her gaze around the room. Nothing was familiar. But when her gaze landed on the hulking form lying next to her, her memory finally did its job and reminded her of the night's frightening ordeal.

Brayden.

The gunshot.

Chuck.

The run through the forest.

More Brayden. And—

Wait.

What was the big man doing in the bed beside her?

She took a steadying breath and reached out a hand to touch his shoulder lightly. Too lightly. He didn't move.

"Brayden?"

She waited. Still nothing. She tried a combo instead. Squeezing his elbow and speaking a little louder.

"Brayden."

And that got a response. Sort of. He rolled to his side, flung an arm over her legs, then slid it up to her hips and dragged her into a backward embrace. Reggie was so startled by the abruptly intimate contact that she let herself be pulled into place without protest. And just like that, she was spooning with a man she barely knew.

But it felt good. Comfortable. His large form was warm and safe, and without meaning to, she wriggled a tiny bit closer, inhaling the woodsy scent that emanated from his body. Her rear end fit snugly against his upper thighs.

More than snugly, really. Perfectly.

It was kind of a strange realization, and it made her heart skitter nervously. With a sigh that had more than a hint of regret, Reggie slipped her hand over top of his and slid it out of its resting place just to the side of her stomach. Very gently, she eased it off and inched away. But when she pushed back into a sitting position again, Brayden's eyes opened, too, and he blinked at her a little sleepily. He looked rumpled and confused and far sexier than was fair.

"Hey." His gaze cleared a little as it landed on her. "You better?"

"Better?" she repeated.

He stretched and put one hand behind his head. "Think you were having a bad dream. Sat down beside you to try to wake you up. Kinda grabbed my sweater and held on. You've got a heck of a death grip. I must've dozed off, too."

Warmth crept up Reggie's cheeks. "Sorry."

"Minor inconvenience," he teased.

"I actually don't even remember falling asleep. Wait. What time is it? You wanted me to phone my friend."

"Decided it could wait." Brayden rolled over and pulled his phone from the nightstand. "It's a little after seven in the morning."

Reggie's chest squeezed nervously. "Seven? But it's pitch-black."

"Room-darkening blinds." He reached over to the window and flicked open the fabric just enough that a soft light filled the room.

"We slept the whole night?"

"Looks like it."

"Why aren't you more worried?"

"We're safe here at the cabin. Doors are locked, alarm is set and I'm not on anyone's radar. You can still call your friend and give your excuse retroactively."

She exhaled, then slid back onto the bed—closer to him, but not quite touching—and held out her hand for the phone. "I'll send a text."

Brayden handed over the slim device. "I'll make some coffee."

She waited until he'd left the room before keying in the number for her best friend—whose family leased another shop from Garibaldi—and typing, Hi, Jaz. It's Reggie. U up?

She knew before even asking that her friend *would* be awake. With a newborn in the house, sleep was an elusive thing for the other woman. The reply came through a few seconds later, confirming it.

Ugh. Baby's been awake since five. Whose phone is this?

Reggie winced. She hadn't thought of an explanation for that. She decided to ignore the question for a moment.

I had such a headache last night, she wrote, feeling a little guilty at the fabrication. Crashed before the fireworks even started.

Hope ur not getting that flu that your staff has had.

I think it's just a migraine. But I'm gonna rest for a while longer, just to be sure.

U still coming to the fair?

As long as it turns out to be just a headache. Can u let the right people know that I'll still be there? Don't want anyone to think I'm not coming.

Yeah. Sure. What about work?

I'll get one of the girls to cover my lunch rush.

Good plan. Do u need me to bring u anything right now?

Reggie's guilt slipped away at the thought that her friend might insist.

She punched in a quick reply. Thanks, but no. If I do turn out to be sick, I don't want to share.

Good point. But u sure u don't want soup or something?

Yep. Thanks.

Reggie breathed out, relieved the deception had gone smoothly. But she didn't get off quite so easily. The phone pinged again. She looked down with a groan.

One more thing, though… Jaz had written.

What?

WHOSE PHONE IS THIS?

Reggie sighed. Left mine at work. Borrowed one.

There was pause. At seven in the morning? Another pause. Omg. A third pause. U MET A MAN!

She debated lying. She hadn't met a man in the sense that Jaz meant. At least…not really.

Her gaze lifted from the phone in her hands to the

slightly ajar door. On the other side, she could vaguely hear the sound of dishes clattering, and what she thought was the soft hum of music. And a vision of Brayden making breakfast while he sang along to some oldie pop song filled her head. It made her smile before the buzz of the cell phone jerked her back to the moment.

How did u meet him? her friend wanted to know.

The question wiped the smile from her face immediately. In spite of how attractive Brayden was, the circumstances were just the opposite. But she couldn't very well explain any of that to Jaz.

I didn't meet a man. I borrowed a phone.

From who?

Customer at the diner. Close enough to the truth.

Is the customer a man?

Yes.

Aha! And aren't u working at lunch?

Did I say I was working at the diner right this second?

...

I've gotta go lie back down.

Reggie. Seriously.

What?

U okay?

Fine. Really.

Not kidnapped by aliens and forced to send these vague messages that I'm sure are half-truths?

Reggie smiled. Hardly.

It was easy to picture the resigned look on Jaz's face as the next message came through. K. My parents r manning the bouncy castle today. I'll make sure they tell people ur alive and well.

THX.

Luv u.

Likewise.

Reggie let the phone rest on her knee, guilt tickling at her again. She wasn't in the habit of lying to anyone, let alone to her best friend. She hated that this situation necessitated it. And she had a feeling it would get worse before it got better.

And what about Dad? You'll have to talk to him soon, too.

She cringed at the thought of trying to fool him. He was sixty-five, but he was as sharp as ever. Maybe sharper even, with his age. Reggie had never been able to sneak something by him—not as a kid, not as a teenager and definitely not now as an adult.

She inhaled and straightened her shoulders. The simplest way to avoid having to deceive him would be to figure out what was going on *before* she had to talk to him. Maybe she could even enlist Brayden's assistance. He seemed eager enough to help her. And he already knew what was going on and was aware of the danger but didn't seem too concerned about it. Working together might be the perfect solution.

"That's an awfully determined look on your face." The amusement-laced statement made her jerk her head up.

She found Brayden standing in the doorway, a tray of food in his hands and an apron tied around his waist. For a second, she forgot what she'd just resolved to ask him. The domestic look somehow suited him and was out of place at the same time, and the result was...good. Better than good. But more complicated words failed Reggie right then.

Was there anything more seductive than a man who brought her breakfast in bed?

"Toast?" he offered, then stepped closer.

As he set the tray on the bed, his scent mingled with the coffee aroma, and the combination made Reggie's body warm. And it made her stomach growl.

Brayden laughed. "I'll take that as a yes."

"I haven't eaten since yesterday at about lunchtime," Reggie admitted.

He tipped one of the mug handles her way and lifted a plate. "Don't be shy."

"Thanks."

She devoured the first piece of toast quickly, offered Brayden an unapologetic shrug, then helped herself to another slice before adding a splash of cream to her coffee and taking a hearty slurp.

"Good?" Brayden asked.

"Perfect."

"So."

"So?"

"You going to tell me why you were making that gotta-get-it face when I walked in?"

She swallowed another bite of toast before answering. Was there a tactful way—without coming across as totally lascivious, either—to say that *he* was the "it" at the other end of her determined expression? Probably not. So she decided not to bother trying to find one.

"I want your help," she stated. "Or I guess I should say *more* of your help."

He took a thoughtful sip of his coffee. "Hmm."

Her heart dropped a little. "That's not an encouraging sound."

"Just wondering what more you need. I've already run you over with my car, carried you through the woods and agreed to be your date to the prom. Er, Gala."

Reggie relaxed a little. "Hilarious."

He dropped a wink. "What do you need help with?"

"Figuring out who was on the bad end of Chuck Delta's gun."

Brayden's face immediately stiffened. "That's a job for the police."

"I know. But you said yourself that there's no way to know if the rest of the local cops are in on…whatever this is. What's wrong with a little amateur sleuthing?"

"Aside from the danger to your life?"

"Aside from that…yes. What's the problem?"

He set down his mug and met her eyes. "I need to tell you a secret."

Reggie's heart did a nervous jig as she waited for him to confess something terrible.

Brayden resisted an urge to get up and pace around the room. Guilt tickled at his mind, and he sighed and ran a hand over his hair, trying to convince himself that it wouldn't do any harm for her to know why he was really there. In fact, with the danger she was already in, she'd probably *want* to know. Especially if she thought she ought to be digging into what happened. The idea that she might wind up on Garibaldi's bad side made him grind his teeth together with worry.

She needs to know, he thought. *But she also needs to agree not to share the info with anyone else.*

"Can you say something?" she asked, her voice a little shaky. "You're just sitting there. Brooding."

"Sorry. I just don't want this to come out the wrong way."

"Oh, God."

"What?"

"You're married," she stated.

He stared at her for a second and said again, "What?"

"You're married. And we just slept together." He cheeks went pink. "I mean. Not like that. But still."

He couldn't fight a laugh. "No, Reggie. I'm not married. I'm very *un*married."

"Well…what then?"

"I need your word that you'll keep this between us."

"How can I agree to that when I don't even know what it is you're going to tell me?"

"I wouldn't ask you if I didn't think you'd be willing. I'm trusting you with a secret. It's not a bad one. I just want you to respect my need for confidentiality."

Brayden saw her suck in her bottom lip, considering it. Finally, she sighed.

"So long as it's nothing illegal."

He fought another laugh. "Hardly something illegal."

"Okay. Then you have my word. I won't tell anyone your secret. Whatever it is."

"I'm a cop."

She flinched, and he knew she had to be thinking about Chuck.

"I'm a *good* cop," he clarified. "A Freemont City detective. I can dig up some proof, if you want to see it."

She shook her head. "I believe you."

"That easy?"

"It wouldn't make sense for you to lie after what I saw a cop do last night." She swallowed nervously before adding, "Besides. You seem far more policemanish than businessmanish."

He lifted an eyebrow. "You saying my cover's no good?"

Reggie shrugged. "I tend to notice things."

"Like?"

"The wrong name on your phone. The fact that you weren't wearing a suit the day you came into the diner and that you weren't wearing one tonight. Not until I asked you about putting one on anyway."

"So all businessmen wear suits?"

"All the ones who're trying to convince someone to sell them something."

"Hmm. Think I got made by everyone else in Whispering Woods?"

Her mouth tipped up. "Made?"

Brayden smiled back. "TV-cop talk isn't good?"

"About as good as your real estate developer story. But don't worry. We're all TV-small-town-naive around here," she said teasingly.

"Except you."

"Well. I would've fallen for your clever ruse, too, if it hadn't been for everything that's happened tonight."

"Maybe *you* should've been a detective."

She laughed, the sound filling the room pleasantly. "Thanks. But I think I'll stick to running the diner. Pay might not be as good, but the uniform suits me far better than a badge and a gun."

Brayden found himself grinning. "I dunno. I can kinda picture you in Kevlar."

"I can't tell whether or not that's a compliment."

"Definitely is. Looking good in body armor isn't a feat just anyone can pull off."

"I'll keep that in mind next time I'm in the market for a new outfit."

"Please do."

She went quiet for a second, then said, "Can I ask you something?"

Brayden willed himself not to tense up. "Sure."

"You're here conducting an investigation?"

"Yes."

"And I guess you probably can't tell me what it's about."

"Not really," he admitted. "And it also means I'm not going to let you chase down leads on Chuck Delta or put yourself in any kind of danger."

"Can you at least tell me if it has anything to do with what I saw in the alley?"

He hesitated. Sharing too many details could compromise a case. And with this particular one…there was the far more personal aspect to consider. That alone was enough to make him hold back. In the end, though, he opted for some more honesty. If nothing else, it would make her cautious enough to keep relying on him to protect her.

"I'm not sure," he said. "The guy I'm after… I've been chasing him for a long time, and he's capable of some pretty bad stuff. It would genuinely surprise me if the two things weren't connected. So I'm going to treat it as if they are."

"And that's why you're helping me."

"It's in my job description to help people. And it's in my nature, too." He smiled. "I guess you could say that I habitually go out on a limb."

"Oh."

Did she sound a little disappointed? He thought she did. For a several moments, he was puzzled. Aside from her impulsive and ill-timed run through the forest, she hadn't fought his assistance. Didn't she want to be helped?

A strand of dark hair stuck to her cheek, and his hands itched to pull it away and tuck it behind her ear.

So glad it was her who came flying out in front of my car.

The thought—a little absent, a little ridiculous—made him pause as he clued in to a possible explanation for her let-down tone. Maybe *she* was glad *he'd* been on the saving side of things, too.

He reached across the bed and squeezed her hand, and another jolt of electric attraction passed from her fingers to his. "Hey. Can't say I'm not *enjoying* helping you. If I had to pick who to rescue in Whispering Woods, you'd be at the top of the list."

Her eyes lit up. "Maybe you just haven't seen enough of what Whispering Woods has to offer. Have you met Wanda from the health food store?"

"Don't think I have. Don't think I need to."

"What about Sarah at the grocery store?"

"Nope." He slid his palm from her hand to her forearm, liking the tiny shiver the action produced.

"Olivia at the gas station?" Her question came out a little breathless.

"Uh-uh." He dragged his fingers up to her elbow, then past it, and inched closer.

"Ummmmm." She dragged out the sound like she'd forgotten what she was going to say next.

"Um?"

"Helen. Down at the bike rental place?"

"Didn't catch my eye."

"Oh."

Brayden stared down Reggie, admiring her upturned mouth. Her green eyes danced with amusement, and they flicked from his gaze to his lips—where they hung for a moment—then back again. Then the amusement was gone. In its place was something warm. Something interested. Something interesting.

Undisguised desire.

Brayden placed the look two seconds before she lifted

her hand to touch his cheek and pushed forward, tipping her face to his. Automatically, he bent down to close the gap between them. Her eyes dropped shut, and he covered her lips with his in a kiss. It was meant to be gentle. Exploratory. A question, maybe.

Is this what you want?

The second his mouth touched hers, though, his silent query flew away. His ability to hold back went with it.

Her lips were soft and sweet. Still a little bit salty with sweat from her crazy run the night before. Far warmer than the air around them. Brayden devoured them. He sucked the top one, then the bottom. When she let out a little gasp, he took advantage and swiped his tongue between them, and the inside of her mouth was hotter still.

The tray of discarded dishes slid sideways and clattered to the ground as her fingers came up to the back of his neck. She rubbed the short edges of his hair, and Brayden met the attention eagerly. He pressed his palms to the small of her back and held her there, marveling at how right it felt. How natural. Like she wasn't a woman he'd met just a half a day ago. So much so that it took most of his willpower just to break away.

"We should get going," he said against her mouth.

She tipped her face up, her lids still low, her expression noticeably disappointed. "Okay."

"Not because I wouldn't rather be doing *this*. But because we need to stick to the plan and keep to your schedule."

"And we don't want to arouse any suspicion."

"Right."

"So we should probably let each other go."

"Probably."

"All right."

Except he couldn't quite make himself do it. Instead, he kissed her again. A little more slowly this time, but no less thoroughly. Her grip on him tightened, and she dragged him with her as she eased backward onto the mattress. He was almost—but not quite—on top of her now, one knee resting between her thighs as he held himself up with one elbow. He deepened the kiss even further, his body molding to hers. Her petite frame fit perfectly against his large one. There should've been a contrast. An imperfection. Instead, it was the opposite. Like they were built to complement one another.

She let out a little gasp, and he pulled his mouth from hers and dropped it to her jawline instead. He traced the line of it with his lips. The pleasant taste of her exploded in his mouth and made him want more. So he indulged. He nipped at her ear, then ran his tongue down her throat to her clavicle. He tugged on the sensitive skin there while his free hand roamed over her body.

He'd somehow managed to forget she was wearing the short uniform. When his finger clasped her bare thigh, though, and her knee came up to hug his hip, he could think about nothing else.

The space between them was nearly nonexistent. Only as thick as the layers of clothes they wore. The scant half inch was still too much of a barrier. He wanted to tear it away. Skin to skin. He craved the contact. Which made him sure they should stop.

He drew on every ounce of willpower he had, sucked in a ragged breath and pushed up to stare down at her flushed face and wide pupils.

"Hi," she breathed.

"Hey," he said back. "I mentioned that I'm glad I saved you, right?"

She nodded. "Yes."

"Good." He gave another, far more chaste kiss, then pulled himself to a sitting position. "Just double-checking."

She sat up, too, her brows knitting together in worry. "Brayden?"

"Yeah, sweetheart?"

"Everything's going to be fine, right?"

"Yep. I'm here to make sure it is."

As soon as the words were out of his mouth, he knew it was a promise he intended to keep.

Chapter 6

Reggie stole a surreptitious glance of Brayden's profile as he guided the car along the road toward town. They were almost there now, and he'd barely spoken throughout the entire drive. His jaw was tense, his eyes forward. But even though Reggie knew it was more about worry than irritation, she still wasn't backing down.

"You can't drive me to the fair," she said for the tenth time. "People will notice, and it'll be all I hear about for the entire day. It'll be all *anyone* hears about for the entire day."

"I'm coming with you to the party tonight," he pointed out, also for the tenth time. "People will talk anyway."

"Bringing a guest to a party isn't as suspicious as bringing a strange man to my volunteer shift. And besides that, our plan only works if we pretend to meet there. It'll be completely ruined if you start out standing beside me, glowering as I paint cat faces on little kids."

"I don't glower."

"You're glowering right now."

"You do remember that *I'm* the cop, right?"

"And you remember that *I'm* a resident of Whispering Woods?"

"My point is that I'm pretty good at being subtle when the need arises."

"All the subtlety in the world can't shut down rumors in a town like this one."

"Reggie…"

"You said you could use the time to look into Chuck and work on your own case."

"I'm feeling a change of heart coming on. And I don't think you should be alone."

"There are going to be literally hundreds of people at the town square. I won't be alone."

"You'll be alone for the five minutes it will take you to walk from where you want to be dropped off."

"Which is why you gave me the bear spray." She patted her pocket and stifled a sigh at the stubborn set of his mouth. "You said I needed to stick to my routine, and that Chuck wouldn't cause a public scene. Was all that a lie?"

"Of course not."

"We could go back to my first idea."

"I don't remember you offering another option."

"Sure you do. The one where I try to figure out what Chuck's up to, and you help me."

"That's *not* an option."

"So we stick with this, then." She pointed out the windshield. "It's a left up there. Then two more blocks and you'll have to stop so we can move aside the barricade. After that, you can drive up about fifty feet, you'll see an empty lot and a clothing donation bin. You can stop right in front."

He flicked on his turn signal a little more heartily than necessary and pressed his lips together. Reggie fought an urge to give in. She was worried, too. Actually, closer to scared. No way did she want to run into Chuck Delta while she was alone. But she also trusted the things Brayden had said about how to stay safe. She could handle weaving through the few streets she needed to in order to get to the fair. She thought she could anyway.

They reached the line of orange delineators, and Brayden grimaced as he eyed the row of squat houses just behind the blockade. "Doesn't look like a very nice neighborhood."

"It's abandoned. The entire street is waiting to be torn down," Reggie replied. "That's the whole point, remember? No one's here to see us."

"That doesn't mean I have to like it."

"C'mon. The faster we do this, the less likely we are to get caught."

Together, they climbed out and cleared aside the road closed sign and the rest of the barriers. In silence, they brought the car through, then put everything back in place.

Brayden continued to mutter his disapproval as they made their way to the spot Reggie had described, and when he brought the car to a halt, he turned another frown her way. "Why here?"

"You thought it was best if we didn't stop by my place yet. But I still need something to wear."

"And you're going to remedy that…how?"

She ignored the request for clarification in favor of swinging open the door and stepping onto the sidewalk. Her feet ached the tiniest bit, but they were patched enough that it wasn't too bad as she moved quickly to the donation bin. And by the time she reached it, Brayden had caught up.

He eyed the bin, skepticism clear in his single, raised eyebrow. "You're going to steal from the poor?"

"It's not stealing. It's borrowing back my own things," Reggie replied. "They only pick up once a month, and I just dropped stuff off the other day."

She lifted the lid, pushed up to her tiptoes and peered inside. Sure enough, the silver plastic bag she'd filled sat on top. Just out of reach.

"Do you mind reaching that for me?"

"You're kidding, right?"

"No."

"It's basically like reaching into a trash can."

"It is *not*."

"Maybe if I don't reach in, you'll be forced to accept a ride to the fair."

"No. I'll be forced to walk there with bare feet and my work clothes. Which is guaranteed to draw attention," she put her hands on her hips and spun to shoot him a glare as she said it, but when she got turned around far enough to face him, he grabbed her by the elbows and dragged her close, making her forget why she'd been annoyed.

He dropped a swift kiss on her lips, then pulled away to run a finger over her cheek. "I'm allowed to be worried. In my job, I see a lot of terrible things. They make me overly cautious on a day-to-day basis. And with you…"

She tipped her face up, a pleasant tingle in her chest as she asked, "With me what?"

He shrugged with what looked like forced casualness. "I feel the need to be even more careful."

The tingle expanded. "If you *really* think it's going to be unsafe, I'll stay with you. But I can only hide for so long. Sooner or later, Chuck Delta is going to find a way to talk to me. If we do things this way, at least it's under our terms, right?"

He smiled and swept a lock of hair away from her face. "You're sure you aren't a cop, too? Or maybe a lawyer?"

"A hundred percent. Pie trumps the law."

He studied her for a second, then shook his head and raised his hands in defeat. "A five-minute walk, right?"

"Yes."

"And you've got the bear spray, and know how to use it?"

"Yes again."

"And I gave you my credit card to call me from that antique pay phone that you say exists near the fairgrounds."

"It's really there! It's beside the post office, and it's perfectly modern."

"Uh-huh. It's a *pay phone*. How modern can it be?"

"Don't mock it. It's serving a purpose."

"All right. Are we forgetting anything?"

"The clothes?"

"Right." He moved to the donation bin, scooped out the plastic bag and handed it over.

Reggie pulled out a pair of jeans and plain blue T-shirt, glad she'd been purging things that fit rather than things that didn't. She tucked the clothes under her arm, then stuck her hand all the way to the bottom and yanked out a pair of flip-flops.

"See?" she said triumphantly. "Not trash. Turn around while I get changed."

He eyed her up and down. "You're going to get changed on a public street, but you want me to turn around?"

"It's the principle."

"Guess your idea of what constitutes a principle is different from mine."

"Just do it."

"I've got a better idea. How about we sneak into one of these houses, and you can dress there?"

"Detective Maxwell, are you suggesting we commit a B and E?"

"In the name of not exposing yourself to the whole town…yes."

She looked around the empty street pointedly. "The whole town?"

"You know what I mean. C'mon." He held out his hand. "Please?"

"It's so not fair for you to use that big-eyed puppy dog look on me."

"It's so not fair for you be willing to take off your clothes in public but not let *me* look at you."

She narrowed her eyes, but slid her fingers into his anyway. "Puppy dog eyes *and* shameless flirting? You play dirty."

"Gotta have something to break up the monotony of catching bad guys," he said as he led her up the street.

"Ah."

"Ah, what?"

"This is a habit for you." Her tone was light, but she felt a twinge of genuine jealousy at the thought of him regularly running around throwing himself at the women he rescued.

But his next statement reassured her. "Actually. This incredible display of unprofessionalism *is* a first. At least for me. But I'm definitely putting you on my list of perks, and if you had to witness what you did… I'm going to call it a silver lining."

Reggie's face warmed. She hadn't considered that aspect of the situation. But she had to admit that if there was one good thing to come out of it all, it would be meeting Brayden. She opened her mouth to say as much, but he stiffened, suddenly on alert. He put his finger to his lips, then blocked her body with his. And she couldn't help but note that as he did it, his hand went to his side. Straight to the spot a gun would've been if he'd been wearing it. His fingers twitched for a second, then rubbed nervously over his jeans as his eyes fixed on the house in front of them.

"What's wrong?" Reggie whispered.

"Change of plans," he announced, low and grim, as he nodded up the street. "We head straight for that shed over there on the edge of the yard on our left. Got it?"

"Yes."

"Good."

With her heart in her throat—and without knowing what it was that spooked Brayden badly enough that he was squeezing her hand almost hard enough to hurt—Reggie let him pull her quickly to their new destination.

Brayden itched for his weapon. Even though he could fight with his hands if need be, there was something reassuring about the feeling of steel on his hip. Something about the surety. He eyed the car up the road, then did a mental head shake. He'd stowed the gun in the glove compartment, but he didn't dare stop. Not until he was sure Reggie was safely out of sight.

He brought his eyes forward again. The wooden structure he'd spotted was only a few dozen feet away now. He moved faster. They reached it in seconds, and he immediately yanked open the door and gestured for Reggie to get inside. In she went, and he followed, exhaling as he closed the door soundly behind them.

"You okay?" he asked immediately.

She blinked at him, the green of her irises iridescent in the dark. "Is that a joke? I'm scared out of my mind. What happened back there?"

He just barely had enough room to reach up and run a hand over her slightly wild hair. "Sorry. I saw a flash of movement by the shrubs near that brown-and-white house across the street and I just reacted."

"A flash? Could it have been a raccoon or something?"

"Unless raccoons are a lot taller than I recall and have suddenly taken to wearing hooded sweatshirts, it's not a raccoon."

"You saw all that in a *flash*?"

"Nope. Saw that right before we ducked in here. The flash became a person who stopped, looked around, then started walking in our direction."

"They saw us?"

"Hope not. I think our spot beside the donation bin was sheltered enough. Couple more steps and we would've been in his sight lines for sure." Brayden eased sideways and met her eyes, careful to keep his expression a little neutral. "Even if they did... Might not be targeted."

She studied him for a second, then shook her head. "But you don't believe that."

"Do you?" he asked. "You know the demographics of the town. What're the odds that it's a coincidence, and whoever that was, they were just a squatter?"

"Not as likely as I'd like to think," she admitted. "Whispering Woods has a pretty low vagrancy rate. These houses aren't being torn down for another two weeks, and Garibaldi didn't even feel the need to hire security."

"Garibaldi?"

"He's the one who bought up the houses along the block."

Brayden blinked at the revelation. *Garibaldi.* He had to clamp his jaw shut to keep from saying the man's name aloud again, this time like a curse. He'd known there had to be a concrete reason behind his uneasy feeling about leaving Reggie alone for a scant five minutes. Now he had it.

If he'd been aware that the man owned the street they were on—owned the house where the shadowy figure had just disappeared—he would've avoided the area altogether. Insisted on finding another way. As it was, it just served to make him even surer that there was a connection between Chuck Delta and Garibaldi. If the pretty waitress hadn't been at his side, he would've investigated further. Maybe gone into the house in question. Part of him still wanted to. Leaving Reggie alone, though, was out of the question. He had to make sure she was safe before they even made a move.

He focused on Reggie. "We're going to wait a couple of minutes, then I want you to get changed while I make sure we're in the clear."

"How're you going to do that?"

"I'm going to search this side of the perimeter for exposure."

Her face pinched with worry. "Brayden..."

He touched her cheek. "I'm not going far. I won't let the shed out of my sight."

"I'm not worried about *me*, I'm worried about *you*. That

being-allowed-to thing goes both ways. Just because I'm not a cop doesn't mean I'm not aware that bad things happen."

In spite of their situation, Brayden felt his mouth tip up, pleased that she was worried about his safety. "I'll be careful."

She shot him an exasperated look. "All the care in the world isn't going to make you bulletproof."

"What would you rather do? Wait for your friend Jaz to decide you really *have* been kidnapped by aliens?"

"Hey! How did you—" She groaned. "You read the texts."

He patted the pocket that held the object in question. "It's *my* phone. Did you think I wouldn't?"

"I didn't think about it at all. And I honestly don't know how you had time."

"I make time for the things I'm interested in."

"My texts interest you?"

"All of you interests me. But I have to admit…I'm a little disappointed."

"By what?"

"The fact that you don't see me as a man."

Even in the dark, he could see the sudden bloom of color in her cheeks. "That's not what I meant."

"No?"

"No. Of course you're a man."

"But not one you met."

"That's not what I meant."

"So you keep saying."

She made a frustrated noise, and Brayden laughed. "Come here."

"There's literally only two feet between us. How can I possibly—"

He shot his hands out to her waist, then dragged her so she was flush against him. "Like this."

Her face tipped up, her green eyes locking with his. "Oh."

He chuckled. "Tell me what I can do that'll turn me into a man you met instead of just a man…who you met."

Reggie's forehead crinkled up. "What's the difference?"

"Being able to do this." He dropped his mouth to hers in a light kiss.

"You can do that," she breathed as he let her go.

"So then. You *have* met a man?"

"I think my friend was implying something a little more…" She trailed off and lifted her shoulders helplessly.

"A little more what?"

"I dunno."

"Maybe a little more this?" He brought his mouth down for a second kiss, this one followed by a light trace of her lips with his tongue.

"Didn't you say you had something to do?"

"Didn't you say you didn't *want* me to go?"

She shot him a playful look and traced her hands over his chest. "Is staying actually an option?"

"Yep. But only if you want to spend the duration of my investigation locked in a shed."

"Alone?"

"I *do* have a job to do," he teased.

Now her playful look turned serious. "I know. How long do you think that'll be?"

"The investigation?"

"Yes."

"Are you asking because the idea of staying in here appeals to you, or because you really want to know?"

"Is it too soon to admit that it just became the latter?"

"Never too soon for honesty."

"Then honestly… I really wasn't thinking about it before. I guess my brain's been too busy trying to wrap itself around everything else. But now that it's come up, I *am* wondering what you'll do when your case is closed. Leave? Stay? I know Freemont City isn't all that far away, but it's still a few hours' drive. I assume you have a life there just like I've got one here." She paused, looked down and took a breath, then lifted her gaze to his face again. "I'm not much of a casual dater. Or a casual…whatever you call it when you're kissing a man you just met while running for your life."

Brayden couldn't help but laugh at the last bit. "I don't think there *is* a word for that."

"And if there was?"

"It wouldn't apply to me, either."

"So where does that leave this…leave us?"

He didn't hesitate. "I've been chasing this case for fifteen years, Reggie. There've been a hundred leads that haven't panned out. I've never once thought about walking away. Never thought it wasn't worth my time. I'm committed. When I go after something, I give it everything I've got. If you're not interested in taking a chance that I'll be the same way with you, now's a good time to tell me."

"I'm not *not* interested," she said.

"But?"

She shook her head. "Do you really want to hear all about my relationship baggage while we're hiding in a shed?"

"Is there a better place to hear about baggage?"

"Just about anywhere, I think."

"If you don't want to tell me, sweetheart, you don't have to."

"No. It's not that. I just—" She sighed. "How about I'll make you a deal? You go out and do your perimeter search. You come back in one piece, get us through this day and I'll tell you all my horrible secrets."

He kissed her lightly. "Sounds like a bargain."

He pulled away and placed a hand on the door. He only got it open an inch before Reggie's voice stopped him.

"Brayden?"

"Yeah?"

"Seriously. Be safe."

"I will."

Then he slipped out, pushing aside his personal feelings in favor of his professional detachment, and moved silently through the yard.

Chapter 7

Reggie clutched her clothes to her chest, trying to cling to something concrete to steady the rapid beat of her heart and the matching jump of her thoughts. But her mind didn't want to settle. It wanted to bounce around with worry and curiosity. It wanted her to chase after Brayden to make sure he was being as cautious as he said he'd be. And to ask him a hundred questions about the little bit of information he'd just divulged.

Fifteen years.

It was a long time to be following a single case. Or she thought so anyway. Long enough to go cold, for sure. So why was Brayden still following it?

She undid her dress, puzzling it over. And as she slipped on the retrieved jeans, an explanation struck her.

Something personal.

She paused, midzip. Yes, that had to be it. And it seemed obvious now that it occurred to her. What else could make a man chase the same crime for a decade and a half? She didn't yet know Brayden well enough to hazard a guess as to exactly what it was, but she was confident that he was the kind of person who would see something through, no matter how hard it became. And hadn't he said as much? Told her just how committed he was?

She dragged the T-shirt over her head, then ran her fingers through her hair, still considering the various angles of her theory.

The personal aspect fit. But she couldn't picture Brayden going after straight-up revenge. He was too calm. Too logical. He was definitely the kind of man who thought things through. But he was far from cold. Which meant she also couldn't picture him sitting on a personal case for this many years if his only objective was to make the people on the other end of the crime pay. On top of all of that, he was a police detective, sworn to uphold the law. And the thing she could picture *least* was him abusing that role in order to get back at someone.

She slid her feet into her shoes, convinced that she was right about his motivation, but unsure what his end goal was. She'd have to ask him. A trade of information—her somewhat-embarrassing romantic history in exchange for his disclosure.

Except you already promised to share, provided he comes back safely.

And yes, that was definitely more valuable than hearing what prompted him to chase an old case to Whispering Woods.

"Already taking too long," she grumbled at the closed door.

She wanted to push it open an inch or two so she could see him. Just enough to reassure herself that he was fine. But before she could truly consider doing it, a wordless holler—Brayden's voice, she was sure—from outside made her jump back. Then came a crash, which made her shiver with fear, and the thump of receding footsteps, which made her freeze. Finally, a pain-filled groan carried through the wood walls, spurring her to move.

She shoved open the door and almost tripped over Brayden's wide form, which lay sprawled out at her feet. Drawing a startled breath, she managed to stumble past him instead of onto him. But she immediately dropped to her knees anyway, placing a hand on his face as he blinked up at her groggily. Her heart slowed only marginally when he spoke.

"Reggie?"

"Yes. Right here."

"You're all right?"

"I'm pretty sure that's my line."

He pushed up to a sitting position. "Got clocked pretty good in the back of the head. Hurts a bit. Otherwise I'm fine."

"You don't look fine."

"Just startled."

"Startled? That's what you call getting hit in the head?"

"Speaking of which…" He trailed off, sat up a little straighter and swept the space with a heavy-lidded stare.

"I think whoever it was, they're gone," Reggie said. "I heard someone running away."

His shoulders dropped. "Scared 'em off with my incredible collapsing-man act."

"It's not funny."

"I know." He smiled anyway, then immediately winced and put a hand on the back of his head. "Give me a hand up?"

"Do you think you should be standing?"

"I think we should get out of sight."

"That didn't work out so well last time," she pointed out.

"Now who's funny?" he replied, holding out his hand. "Pull."

She closed her fingers around his, feeling immediate relief at how solid and warm and safe they were. She gave a little tug, and he came up easily. Thankfully, he didn't sway or show any other signs of dizziness as he stood. But he did tuck an arm firmly over her shoulders and pull her close.

"C'mon," he said.

"Where to?"

He nodded across the yard. "The guy that hit me came from inside that house right there."

Reggie followed the nod. "The one missing half its roof?"

"Yep."

"And you want to go inside? Putting aside the fact that it's falling apart and probably not even close to safe…what if there's someone else there?"

"They would've come out by now. Taken advantage of me while I was down. Besides that. If he left someone behind, he'd have taken the time to close the door."

"Okay. I'm trusting your expertise. But if we get jumped, don't be surprised when I use you as a human shield."

Brayden pulled her a little tighter and started up the grass toward the house. "Trust me. I wouldn't have it any other way."

He sounded serious enough that her next breath burned. She didn't *want* him to be a human shield for her. Not really. But there was something overwhelmingly romantic about knowing he'd be willing to do it. And something scary, too.

She started to take back her comment, but stopped as they reached the door and she spotted what was inside. The living room, which was adjacent to the entryway, had been converted into a studio apartment amid the mold-stained floor and chunks of broken drywall. A tarp hung on an angle over the spot exposed by the roof. A mattress had been pushed against one wall, while a hot plate and a set of dishes sat against another. A bowl of food—stale looking, but not yet rotten—sat atop a TV tray. The floor on the other side of the room, which presumably led to where the bedrooms once were, was a dilapidated mess.

Reggie swallowed. "Someone's living here?"

Brayden's reply was grim. "So much for the lack of vagrancy."

"I don't even want to look around. It's…" She trailed off, unable to find a suitable word for the squalor in front of her.

Brayden filled in a few descriptors for her as he slid his arm free. "Dirty, dangerous and depressing."

"Yes. That."

"Hang tight here for a second, then," he said.

"You're really going all the way in?"

"Halfway there already. Might as well see if there's anything worth checking out."

"Okay. Just be careful. Again."

"I will."

He gave her a quick kiss, then stepped farther into the room. Fighting a need to drag him back, Reggie watched as he made quick work of examining the room. He lifted the mattress and checked underneath. He examined the accessible corners, checked under the scant few pieces of furniture and dumped out a small bag of rumpled clothes. When he was done, he turned back her way with a disappointed look on his face.

"Nothing?" she said.

"Just the impression that for a little guy, my head basher likes big T-shirts."

"Which doesn't help, I guess?"

"Nope. No other hint of who's staying here. Or why."

But as he crossed the floor, he paused. He stopped and took a step back. Then bounced in place. And smiled.

Reggie leaned forward, curiosity outweighing her nerves as she tried to see what he was up to. "What is it?"

He rocked a heel. "A loose floorboard."

"Aren't they all loose? The place is falling apart."

"Not like this." He bent down, lifted the wood in question and shot her a triumphant look right before digging in to the space. "Definitely something hidden here. Feels like paper. Aha. Yep. Newspaper clippings and some photos."

He held them up, scanning them as he did. Then he frowned, and his face went whiter than she'd seen it.

Reggie felt her own heart skip a beat in response to his expression. "What's wrong?"

He breathed out heavily. "Do you know the name Tyler Strange?"

"Yes. Everyone does. He was the tourist who was accused of lighting a pipe bomb on Main Street quite a few years ago. I don't remember much about it, to be honest. But I do know that the bomb started a fire that destroyed a coffee shop and shut down the whole strip for almost a month. Why?"

"Have a look at this."

He held out the little stack of paperwork, and she flipped through them. The newspaper articles were local. Old and faded and all related to the fire and investigation. The one on the bottom featured a photo of Tyler himself, standing outside the police station. Reggie squinted down at the picture. The man was big and brawny, his clothes disheveled and his hair wild. He looked like the kind of person that would make someone cross the street in order to avoid contact with him.

With a little shiver, she handed the articles back to Brayden. "He was never charged, though. Something went wrong at the last second. Some technicality, maybe?"

"Not a technicality. Lack of evidence," Brayden corrected. "C'mon. Let's get out of here. If we wait much longer, your alien-paranoid friend will call in the cavalry. I'll walk you all the way there."

"I don't under—wait. You're walking me to the fair?"

He nodded. "Don't know why it didn't occur to me before that I could do it. Five minutes, you said?"

"Yes, but—"

"No buts. I'll take you to the edge and make sure no one

sees me, then I'll come back on my own and we'll carry on with the rest of the plan."

"What about Tyler Strange?"

"To start with… I think this might be *his* hideout." He met her eyes. "And that little explosion of his? It's the reason we found Whispering Woods in the first place. I'll explain once we're moving."

Brayden ran his free hand over his hair and squeezed Reggie's palm with the other. He wasn't certain if the latter move was for her comfort or for his. The fact that the person who'd hit him had run off made him think the guy wasn't after a confrontation, but it wasn't a guarantee. Either way, it felt good to keep their fingers locked together. It was somehow even more reassuring than the fact that he had his weapon tucked back in place at his side.

But neither the close contact nor the gun helped him shake his nerves completely. He remained on high alert, scanning the path in front of them, then around and behind them every few seconds as he delivered the explanation he promised.

"This thing with the pipe bombs goes back a lot further than Tyler Strange and Main Street," he said. "In fact, my team and I have been tracking similar bombings for as long as we've been with the force. Looking for one that fit. Do you remember the Freemont City bombing, fifteen years ago?"

"At the police station?"

"That's the one."

"Yes. Vaguely. I mean, I was a kid, but it was still pretty big news. Some people actually died, didn't they?"

Some people.

Even though she'd said it in an appropriately respectful tone, it still sounded far too generic. Far too casual. It made Brayden have to forcibly push past as stab of grief that threatened to derail his ability to speak impartially.

"Yes," he made himself say. "Three officers. They were all working in the evidence room at the time, which is where the explosion occurred. They'd been on a case together and had some kind of breakthrough, but everything they'd gathered was destroyed in the subsequent fire."

Reggie frowned. "And you think Tyler Strange had something to do with it? He would've been a kid at the time, too. I think he's only a year or so older than I am."

He shook his head. "No. I know for a fact that he didn't bomb the station, and I'm reasonably sure he didn't bomb Main Street here in Whispering Woods, either. But that's exactly what we've been looking for. An MO that matches the Freemont incident but that doesn't fit with the suspect."

"And those are the leads you've been chasing? You think the original bomber is somewhere in Whispering Woods."

"Yep. Until now, none of the clues have ever turned out to be anything related to our case. But Tyler…even though he was never formally charged, he did spend an awfully long time in police custody. But after they released him, he disappeared. The official story is that there wasn't enough evidence to put him away. I don't think that's true."

"So you think he'd come back now?"

"I don't know." He paused, hesitant to tell her what their working theory had been.

She figured it out on her own anyway, before he could come up with a way to put it gently.

"You thought he was dead," she said.

He squeezed her hand. "There *was* a best-case scenario, where Tyler was wrongfully accused, was let go, then took off because it was in his own best interest. But the worst-case scenario just seemed more likely."

"And that worst case was that Tyler witnessed the Main

Street explosion, and whoever was actually behind it made sure he didn't tell anyone else."

"Exactly."

"But if he *wasn't* killed, and he came back to Whispering Woods now…"

"Then I need to figure out why, in order for us to move on with our case," he said. "It has to be connected."

She drew in a breath, then went quiet for a few moments before speaking again, and when she did, it was slightly off-topic. "You keep talking about your team and saying *we* and *our*. Where are they?"

"Back home in Freemont," he told her.

"They made you come in alone?"

"I guess you could say I'm the scout. Far less obvious to send in a lone wolf than a whole team. And even if that weren't true, some of the guys are a bit more temperamental than I am. I nominated myself as their slow-and-steady man."

"I guess that makes sense." She sighed. "Can I ask you something else? Something personal?"

"Sure."

"Is *this* personal?"

Out of habit, he went for a deflection. He paused in their walk, tugged her to face him and smiled down at her.

"Doesn't it feel personal?" he teased.

She blushed prettily, but she didn't let it go. "The case, I mean."

Brayden cleared his suddenly itchy throat and powered through the truth. "Yeah, sweetheart, it's personal."

"Revenge?"

"Justice," he corrected.

"What's the difference?"

"It's a fine line. But revenge is about anger. About emotion."

"And you aren't angry or emotional?"

"I am," he admitted. "But more at the way the system worked—or didn't work, I guess—and how it let a crime go unpunished. And obviously I'm not trying to take revenge on the system, either. If I were, I wouldn't have joined law enforcement. I became a cop because I saw a gap in the way justice was carried out. I wanted to make sure it didn't happen again. Someone got away with murder, and I don't think there's much more injustice out there than that. But I'm not trying to dole out punishment on my own. I'm just trying to see things put right. Which is what should've happened in the first place."

"You mean the Freemont bombing?"

"Yes." He closed his eyes for a second before continuing. "I was a kid, too, when that bomb went off at the station. And my dad was one of the cops in that evidence room."

Reggie's eyes filled with sadness, and that was the only warning he had before she pushed to her tiptoes and threw her arms around him in a tight hug. For a long second, he stayed rigid. He wasn't accustomed to letting anyone get behind this particular, carefully crafted shield. But somehow, he'd already revealed more to Reggie Frost about his personal and professional life than he had to anyone in years. Possibly ever, if he wasn't counting those who were directly affected by the bombing.

And you've known her for all of five minutes.

But the time frame seemed irrelevant as his shoulders dropped and he lifted his arms to return her warm show of understanding.

"I'm sorry you had to go through that, Brayden," she said.

He could tell her words were more than just an empty expression of sympathy, and he swallowed against the lump in his throat. "Me, too."

"I know what it's like to lose a parent," she admitted softly. "My mom died almost ten years ago, too. Cancer."

He felt a thread of mutual loss form between them, cementing into an unseen bond. "Sorry to hear that, sweetheart."

"Thanks." She exhaled a shaky breath.

"Life's not fair sometimes," he replied gruffly. "Losing my dad was the hardest thing I've ever gone through."

"Another good reason to make sure nothing like this happens again."

"Exactly."

With a sigh, Brayden pressed his chin to the top of Reggie's head, and mentally tested out the waters of the unusual instability in his emotions. His care and caution were still there under the surface. But rising above that, he had to admit to a stronger, wilder pull—an urge to plunge headlong into…something. He wasn't sure what it was going to be. He just knew it was risky and unlike him.

So why do I want to say even more?

The only thing that stopped him from actually doing it was a sudden chime of his cell phone in his pocket.

"Should you get that?" Reggie asked into his chest.

"Probably."

"Okay." She squeezed him once more, then backed up.

When he pulled the phone out, though, the text message wasn't for him at all. Not directly anyway.

I can see u, u giant liar, it read.

Stifling a laugh, Brayden held the phone out to Reggie. "Here, I think this is for you."

"What?" Her puzzlement turned to a groan as she scanned the message. "Seriously, Jaz?"

He followed her gaze as she lifted her eyes to the seemingly empty horizon. They'd left behind the abandoned street and made their way through a series of overgrown paths that led to a thick row of trimmed hedges that blocked out whatever was on the other side. He couldn't see Reggie's friend, or even a hint of where she might be.

"Where *is* she?" he muttered.

"Probably in one of those bushes with her binoculars," Reggie replied.

Unable to decide if he should smile or frown, Brayden asked, "Your best friend is some kind of spy?"

She made a face. "Actually, there's a park on the other side of the hedge. If we take fifty more steps, you'll be able to hear the kids playing. The town square is one street over."

The phone chimed again.

"What's she saying now?"

Reggie glanced back down. "She says that you're *definitely* a man, that my pants are practically on fire and that we should get a room."

The smile won out. "I can't say I disagree. Well. Except for the fiery-pants part."

"Yeah, you two should get along great," she grumbled. "Shouldn't you be worrying about our cover being blown instead of laughing about it?"

"It was *your* idea to keep our meeting a secret," he reminded her.

"Because we don't want Chuck to know."

"It only matters if Chuck thinks we've got something to hide. My cover's still good. And this'll give you and your friend something to gossip about while you're painting all those little faces."

"Is that what you think we like to do? Gossip about questionable manhood?"

"Questionable?"

He grabbed her by her elbows and tipped his mouth to hers. He started out slow, tugging on her bottom lip with his teeth, then sucking it until a gasp escaped Reggie's mouth. Next, he moved to the top lip, this time tracing it with his tongue. He slipped his arms around her waist and pressed his palms to the small of her back, dragging her flush against his own body.

In her hands, his cell phone went crazy, chiming on re-peat. He still didn't let her go. Instead, he kissed her even harder. Even more thoroughly. He could feel the sharp thud of her heart and the quick, unsteady inhales and exhales that drove her chest into his.

His cell phone dropped to the ground with a clatter.

He *still* didn't stop. He dragged one of his hands up again, pushing it along the length of her spine. With the other, her clasped her hip and squeezed possessively. He kissed her once more, then pulled away slowly and raised an eyebrow down at her flushed face.

"How about now?"

"Okay," she breathed. "Not questionable."

"That's what I thought."

He slid his hands down her arms, then bent to grab the phone from the ground. He eyed the screen and smiled.

"Your friend says—and I quote—'O. M. G.' About ten times."

"Of course she does."

"C'mon. You can introduce us."

"Great." Her one-word reply was heavy on the sarcasm.

"It'll be fine." Chuckling at the dubious look on her face, he threaded their fingers together. "You'll see."

"And then what?" she wanted to know. "What are *you* going to do while we 'gossip'?"

Brayden's amusement slipped away, but he kept his tone light. "I'm going to eat cotton candy."

"If you get hurt while I'm painting faces…"

"I won't," he promised. "I still need to hear that sob story of yours, remember?"

One corner of her mouth tipped up. "Right. Something to look forward to."

"So far…every second I've spent with you has been something to look forward to," he said, then pulled her to-ward the row of hedges.

Chapter 8

Reggie breathed out, holding open the tent flap and watching as Brayden stepped into the already-thickening crowd. She had to admit that she already wished he wasn't gone. His presence was soothing. Safe. Without him standing beside her, she felt like something was missing. *And* like she needed to keep looking over her shoulder. She stifled an urge to do it. Even though she had his instructions down pat—smile, be polite, act like nothing was wrong—she was still worried that if Chuck approached, she'd panic and do something rash. The last twelve hours had proved that when the option was fight or flight, she'd take the latter. Her still slightly achy feet were more than happy to attest to it.

She almost couldn't see him anymore. In spite of his height and width, she only caught the occasional flash. Then none at all.

"You were staring at his butt, weren't you?" Jaz's question cut through the tent-muted air, startling her so bad she just about jumped.

"What?"

"His butt."

Her face warmed as she stepped inside and moved to join her friend at the table. "No."

"Liar."

"Shut up."

"I don't blame you. It's a nice butt."

"I did say shut up, right?"

"Fine. I'll keep quiet if you start talking instead. I wanna hear every steamy detail. Before the kids start coming."

"I don't kiss and tell."

"Because you don't normally kiss."

"How would you know?" Reggie said lightly. "Since I don't tell."

"Ha ha. I've been stuck in my house with the baby for a week straight. Spill it."

"Um."

"Um? That's the best you can do?"

"Um. And... Where's that army of kids when I need it?"

On cue, the first little face appeared at the tent opening.

Reggie laughed and picked up a paintbrush from the table. "Perfect."

Jaz stuck out her tongue, then smiled at the kid and said, "Ask for a complicated butterfly. And make sure she does it right."

"I *do* like butterflies," replied the little girl solemnly, which made Jaz snort a laugh.

Reggie lifted her hand to make a face. But really, she was just thankful that the other woman had chosen to be the gushing best friend—raising an impressed eyebrow and mouthing "He's hot!" the second Brayden walked up—rather than coming down on her for going home with some random stranger. Even if the extent of her and Brayden's encounter was exaggerated, it was true enough that it felt good to divulge the fact that her interest had been genuinely piqued. The tidbits of information she doled out between their miniature customers were genuine. She *did* like him. She *was* excited about seeing him again. Soon, she hoped.

And truthfully, she couldn't blame her friend for being a little enthused. To say her last encounter ended badly was like calling a tornado a little windstorm. It didn't even begin to cover the fallout.

"Now you're thinking about *him*, aren't you?" Jaz asked, dragging a final, smooth stroke across a little boy's face to create a spiderweb.

The kid grinned at his reflection in the handheld mirror, then leaped up and ran from the tent, leaving them momentarily alone.

"Not him," Reggie corrected. "Just *it*."

"Aha. But the fact that you *are* thinking about it means this is significant. Have you told Brayden anything?"

"Not yet."

"Not yet," her friend repeated pointedly.

And Reggie realized that she was right. Those two words alone were enough to prove that her mind had already decided on something serious.

"But I've only known him for half a day." She said it more to herself than to Jaz, but her friend's hand found her arm and squeezed anyway.

"Quality not quantity."

Reggie stifled a snort of amusement. If the other woman had any clue what had prompted so-called quality, she'd be dragging her away from Brayden as fast as she could.

"Are you laughing at my superior wisdom and experience?" her friend asked.

"I wouldn't dare."

"I think you *are*. And I don't want to have to remind you that I'm always right about these things. I did try to warn you about you-know-who."

"You can say his name."

"I know." Jaz made a face. "I just *really* prefer not to."

This time, Reggie couldn't hold in the laugh. It bubbled out and filled the small space. But as quickly as her amusement came, it died. Because just a moment after she gave in to the giggle fit, the tent flap lifted and Chuck Delta stepped into view.

* * *

Brayden dropped his phone into his pocket and lifted his eyes. The outdoor party was in full swing now, with parents and kids waiting in line at bouncy castles, a guy with a guitar strumming out family-friendly tunes and the scent of fried food everywhere. It was a welcome, happy sight. Especially when he contrasted it with the past forty-five minutes of frustration. Alternating between having his team look up related details in the police database, and using the tiny screen on his phone to comb through relevant newspaper articles, he'd come up with nothing more than he already knew.

Nine years earlier, Tyler Strange had come to Whispering Woods for an unknown reason—possibly a seasonal tourist, possibly not. He'd been in town less than a week when the explosion occurred. For ten days after, he'd remained in police custody. The main pieces of evidence had come down to two things. First, his proximity to the fire. Second, the fact that he'd been unable to provide a valid excuse for being there. With no fixed address and a history of petty crime—vandalism, public intoxication, theft—he'd been the perfect suspect. Except then he wasn't.

The Whispering Woods PD cut him loose with almost no explanation. The explosion became secondary to the repair of the damaged area. Garibaldi had swooped in and taken over, covering costs that the insurance wouldn't, promising that the new buildings would be even greater than the old ones and even staging a grand reopening of the block.

Ingratiating himself to the locals yet again, Brayden thought with a grimace.

But the sequence of events that followed made him sure Garibaldi's tactics were a deliberate distraction.

Tyler Strange disappeared.

The senior officer at the station retired.

The new one didn't pursue the case at all.

The entire crime became a side note.

Brayden just wasn't sure how the pieces fit together. What was Garibaldi distracting the residents *from*? How were the shady man and Tyler Strange connected? And maybe most important, how did all of it relate back to what Reggie had seen?

With a sigh, Brayden lifted his eyes over the crowd again. He immediately zeroed in on the face-painting tent, and his frustration took a temporary back seat. He smiled. Even though they'd only been apart for less than an hour, he felt the separation with a surprising acuteness. There was little he wanted more than to get back to Reggie, steal another kiss or two and get to know her a little better.

He took a step forward, then paused. A group of people ahead had separated, giving him a better view. A man stood in the tent flap, blocking access. It only took Brayden a second to place the figure. Dark blue shirt, fringed with gold. Shaggy blond hair. Wide stance, set on intimidation.

Chuck Delta.

His teeth ground together, fueled by worry, and he strode ahead. If he could've gotten away with running, he would've. He had to settle for a hurried pace that wouldn't attract attention. The minute-long trip from one end of the town square to the other seemed to take an hour, and each step heightened Brayden's concern. His mind swirled.

Shouldn't have left her.

Should've expected him.

You did *expect him. You told her what to do.*

Still shouldn't have left her.

When he at last reached the tent, it took a large chunk of his willpower to keep from simply grabbing the corrupt cop and flinging him aside.

He forced himself to clear his throat instead. "Officer. I wouldn't have pegged you for the face-painting type."

The other man spun, puzzlement turning to recognition

as he eyed Brayden up and down. Before Chuck could say anything back, though, Reggie let out a little laugh that drew the cop's attention—and Brayden's—back to the tent.

The pretty waitress's face was a little pale, her smile a little shaky, but otherwise she looked fine.

Thank God.

"Hey!" she said cheerfully. "We were just talking about you."

Brayden kept his reply neutral. "Were you?"

Reggie nodded. "Officer Delta was telling me there was some kind of disturbance near the diner last night, and I was saying how that made me glad I closed up early and went home to get ready for our date."

Chuck tapped his fingers against his thigh. "Didn't realize *you* were the date in question."

"Do you two know each other?" Jaz interjected.

"Met briefly last night," Brayden confirmed. "Right when I was on my way to grab Reggie, actually. Does this mean you didn't figure out what the disturbance was? Should we be concerned?"

The other man shook his head. "Nothing to be concerned about. Starting to think the report was a hoax, actually. No one nearby heard a thing."

"Good to know. Feel a lot safer with you on the job, Officer Delta."

The cop's face relaxed into a self-assured smile that didn't quite touch his eyes. "Just doing my job. Enjoy the rest of the fair."

"Sure will."

Brayden stepped aside to let Chuck pass, then immediately dropped the flap and moved to Reggie's side. He crouched down and pressed his forehead to hers.

"You okay?"

She nodded, her eyes flicking toward her friend. "Yeah.

Just shaken up a bit at the thought of something going on near the diner."

"Sounds like everything's all right, though. Officer seems convinced anyway." He leaned back and gave her a look meant to convey the fact that he thought the officer was anything but convinced.

Her face paled and she breathed out, seeming to understand. "I guess he's pretty good at his job."

Brayden cupped her cheek. "Seems like it."

She leaned into the touch. "Good news."

Jaz groaned. "Would you two please just get a room?"

Reggie pulled away, her cheeks pink. "We're not that bad."

"You really are," her friend argued. "Seriously. Skip out on the next hour of volunteerism and go be sappy in private."

"I'm not abandoning you."

"You'd be doing me a favor."

"You say that now, but I'll hear about it for the next twenty years."

Brayden cut in, shaking his head. "How about I just agree to sit quietly in the corner and keep my hands to myself while you ladies finish up?"

"Think you can actually follow through on that?" Jaz wanted to know.

"I can try."

"Don't be surprised if we ask you to pick up a paintbrush and help out."

"That'll only last until you see how bad my art skills are," he teased.

"Don't worry," Jaz told him. "My expectations are low."

"I'll be counting on it."

"Charming, aren't you?"

"Gotta get by somehow."

"All right," Jaz agreed, then waggled a finger at him. "But no ogling, googly eyes or kissing."

He put up his hands in a surrendering gesture. "Got it."

The tent burst open then, and a group of excited kids clambered inside, stalling any further conversation.

Reggie was impressed at how wholeheartedly Brayden jumped into the role of face painter extraordinaire. In spite of his claim of a poor ability to draw, he was able to whip up some pretty decent cat and dog faces, managed to craft a few flowers and even turned a kid into a turtle. When their shift finished, he almost seemed disappointed to be done. And once they'd walked Jaz to her husband and baby, exchanged pleasantries there and moved into the fair crowd at large, he didn't seem to be in a hurry to rush off, either. Not even when every third person stopped and asked for an introduction. He seemed happy to repeat his businessman-on-a-mission story ad nauseam.

"Everything okay?" Reggie asked, when they finally got a moment alone.

"Yep."

"Really? Because I feel a little like this is the calm before the storm."

"Maybe more like the eye in the middle of it." Brayden grabbed her hand and smiled. "But also about as close to perfect as things can be under the circumstances. You want to get some lunch?"

She frowned. "Um. Sure?"

He nudged her shoulder, then pulled her toward one of the food truck lines. "C'mon. Things are going our way, at least a little."

"How do you figure?"

"Well. Your friend liked me. We've legitimized our one-day dating life and gone public. There's still the Tyler Strange angle to think about, but we're waiting on a call-back from my guys, so we've got time to enjoy a bit of the day. Act like normal people."

Reggie couldn't help but laugh. "Is that a rarity for you?"

He shrugged. "Mostly. Work eats up a huge chunk of my time. And when I'm not focused on day-to-day stuff, I'm concentrating on things related to the Freemont City bombing."

"What about friends? Family?"

"All cops, too." He smiled when he said it. "Well, not my mom. But she was a cop's wife and her sons are both cops, so she's almost worse. We make delightful party guests, by the way."

"I bet."

"Try not to sound so disbelieving. We do have our moments." Then his face sobered. "But to be completely honest, this case has made us all put our lives on hold a bit."

"Is it personal for the whole team?"

"All sons of the cops who were slain in the bomb."

Reggie's stomach turned. "Sorry. We don't have to talk about it."

"No. Feels good to get it out, actually. Said more to you in a day than I ever said to my grief counselor as a kid." He shook his head ruefully. "Hard to say if the guy was right all those years ago, or if it's just you."

Warmth spread out in her chest. "Both, maybe?"

"I'll give you most of the credit."

They reached the front of the line then, and paused to order their hot dogs and drinks before heading to an empty park bench on the periphery of the fair. For a few minutes, they ate in companionable silence, and it was Reggie who finally broke the illusion of normalcy.

"You really don't think there's a chance that Chuck believed us?" she asked.

Brayden took a slurp through his straw and shook his head. "I've got a decent track record for reading people.

Officer Delta might've *wanted* to believe that you weren't there at the diner. Easier for him all around. But he seems like the kind of guy who needs solid proof. Who'll keep digging until he's covered all his angles and filled in all his blanks. Too bad he's corrupt, or he might actually be a good cop. He'll probably be looking for another opportunity to question you."

"That's not exactly reassuring."

"Well. If it makes you feel any better, it means I'll need to stick even closer to you to keep you safe."

She swallowed. "I'm not sure you can *get* close enough to make me feel better."

He tossed their trash into the can, then slung an arm over the back of the bench and pulled her in. "I can try."

She rested her head on his solid chest and breathed in his tangy, unique scent. "We still don't know who he shot. Or why."

"No. But we have time to breathe while I try to figure it out, and while I confirm that it connects back to my own case."

"While *you* try to?"

"I'm not going to keep you inside an active investigation if I don't have to."

Reggie's heart dropped, and even though she knew she should be relieved, she felt disappointed instead. She had a hard time keeping her reply light. "So that means what? That you just drop me off at my apartment and go around getting yourself into trouble without me?"

"I won't leave you somewhere unsecured, but I've got to do what's safest for you, sweetheart. Even if I didn't feel the need to protect you personally, I'd feel obligated professionally."

"I don't know if I should feel offended or flattered."

"Neither." His hand came down to her shoulder and he rubbed his thumb soothingly over its curve. "It's just the truth. Your life matters to me. *And* I'm good at my job. The fact that I can use the latter to ensure the former works in both our favors."

She wriggled a little closer. "Is that how you're seeing this?"

"Yep. Definitely." He adjusted his body, too, using his other hand to push aside her hair so he could nibble at her neck.

Reggie's pulse jumped. "Maybe instead of just dropping me off at home, you could come in."

His mouth pressed against the not-so-gentle throb of her neck. "I might be able to be convinced."

"Might?"

"Mmm." His lips found her jawline. "You owe me a story."

"I do?" she breathed.

"Uh-huh. Something about a torrid relationship that ruined you for good."

"Oh. *That* story. For some reason, I can't focus."

"Should I stop?"

"I really want to say no. But I think there's a kid over there whispering to his mother about us."

Brayden jerked up so fast that Reggie just about slid halfway off the bench. "Where?"

She laughed. "I was kidding. But I thought you were *happy* about going public."

He grabbed her by the arm and pulled her sideways into his lap. "I am. But I don't want to be the cause of some birds 'n' bees conversation."

"Birds 'n' bees? Really? That's what you're going with?"

"If some imaginary kid can see us, he can probably hear us, too."

"Then I guess I shouldn't tell you all about my horrible past here," she teased.

He lifted an eyebrow. "That bad?"

She sighed. "No. Well. Maybe. I guess it depends on your definition of bad."

"Try me."

Swallowing, Reggie straightened her shoulders a little, then slid down to the spot beside him, nervous about disclosing the details of her past. It wasn't that it was long or even truly lurid. It wasn't that she felt awkward being honest, either. If she were truly embarrassed, she would never have come back to Whispering Woods at all when it all ended.

But a little tickle of self-doubt hung on. It grew worse when she looked down and saw how their hands were woven together. His strength was undeniable, even in that small pose. Rock solid. She liked it. A lot. But what would it mean for her when he heard about how flighty she'd been? How would he—the self-proclaimed commitment king— feel when he learned she was just the opposite?

She tried to think of a subtle way to explain. To make herself seem like less of a child than she'd been.

But you were a kid, she reminded herself. *Or not much more than one anyway.*

So after a long moment of thought, she decided not to sugarcoat it. "Five years ago, I was going to college with the intention of becoming a psychologist. I was three years into my degree when I came home from school for summer vacation. I worked at the diner for my dad, and I met a guy there. Avid outdoorsman. Too many tattoos to count. He convinced me to leave my education behind. And my family. We got married—spiritually, not legally, just in case you were wondering—in some naturalist commune, where he expected me to live."

Brayden's voice stayed neutral as he replied, "How long did it last?"

Reggie breathed out. "Three months."

"And then?"

"And then I came to my senses. I realized I'd married a man who had a strong preference for living in a yurt. Year-round. And let's just say I'm not as much of a fan of the great outdoors as he was."

She hazarded a look his way and saw that he'd cracked a small smile.

"Running-water-and-a-soft-bed kinda girl?" he joked.

"Not ashamed to admit it." Then she shook her head. "But I *was* ashamed to come back. Especially considering how vehemently my dad objected to me leaving in the first place. No twenty-one-year-old wants to hear such a resounding 'I told you so.' In fact, I would've come home sooner if I hadn't been dreading that part of it. And trust me. I spent the entire next year listening to variations of that phrase on repeat."

"But you didn't go back to school when it ended?"

"No. If I'm being totally honest, I have to acknowledge that it was the one good thing that came out of the whole experience. I realized that I had no interest in *actually* becoming a psychologist. Or of doing any more schooling." She shrugged. "My favorite times as a kid were when my grandma let me help her in the kitchen. And those few years I spent away at college, I looked more forward to coming home than I did getting back to school. So I decided to stay."

"Impressive."

"Uh. What?"

"You were stubborn enough to live in a yurt for three months to prove a point. That takes a special kind of fortitude."

The pressure in Reggie's chest eased. "I think that's the first time I've ever had *that* reaction."

"What were you expecting?" he replied. "For me to shove you aside and go running for the hills?"

"More or less."

He smiled. "I'm not that easy to scare off. And besides that, I think I can one-up your story."

In spite of herself, Reggie smiled back. "You think you can one-up a fake marriage, a *really* long walk of shame that led straight back to my dad's house, where I lived for a whole year with my face covered in a paper bag, while being the biggest source of town gossip for nearly half a decade?"

"Okay. Maybe not *quite* enough to one-up that. But mine's still pretty good."

"All right then. Spill it."

"I will," he said. "But not until—"

He stopped speaking abruptly, his grip tightening and his body stiffening. Automatically, Reggie lifted her eyes to examine his face. And his expression startled her. It was hard. Angry. Utterly focused. He almost looked like a different man than the one she'd spent the last few hours with. She studied the lines of his face. She couldn't help but be curious about what it was that made the otherwise methodical man crack his calm exterior. There was no doubt about the anger hidden under the surface.

What changed?

She moved her gaze away, straining instead to catch sight of what he was looking at, and as she tilted her head up, she spotted the part in the crowd. And the man in the middle of it.

Jesse Garibaldi.

Anxiety spiked her pulse, and she tugged on Brayden's hand. There was no doubt now in her mind that the property mogul was her date's target. Garibaldi—who really was a fixture in the town—was at the heart of the case the big, protective cop had been running down for fifteen years.

His face said it all. And anyone who looked their way would know it, too.

Chapter 9

Brayden wished the sight of the man didn't send a wave of futility through him. He wished it didn't propel him back fifteen years to a time when he was helpless to do anything about what had happened. To the one other moment he'd glimpsed Jesse Garibaldi's face in person, before he had a name to attach to the gruesome crime.

Weak, he thought now, unable to shake the rumbling fury and accompanying loss.

The laughing, smiling man, who was slapping someone on the shoulder in a friendly gesture was the one responsible for his father's death. Yet there he stood. Wealthy. In control. No one in Whispering Woods the wiser.

That fact dug into Brayden, and without even realizing it, he started to push to his feet. A tug on his hand stopped him. He glanced down, feeling strangely surprised to meet with resistance. Reggie sat on the bench, her green eyes full of concern.

"Hey." Her voice was low and laced with understanding.

She knows, he realized.

Even if no one else in the town had figured it out, *she* had. And somehow, that was enough. Brayden sagged back against the bench.

"Sorry."

"Don't be."

He ran a hand over his hair, trying to think of something to say. Reggie beat him to him.

"It's him, isn't it? Jesse Garibaldi is the man you said you've been chasing. The one who bombed the Freemont Station."

He managed a nod and a thick, one-word reply. "Yes."

Her gaze flicked toward the other man, then back to Brayden. "We don't have to stay here."

"I'm fine."

"You look a bit like you're going to charge across the square to throttle our host."

"I like to think I have a *bit* more self-control than that." The statement sounded a little forced, and he exhaled a thick breath before admitting, "It's been a long time since I've seen him up close. I wasn't expecting it to hit me quite so hard."

Reggie's hand tightened in his. "We can go somewhere else, Brayden. We can talk about it. Or not talk about it, if that's what you'd prefer. Either way, we really don't have to be here."

He looked down, preparing to choose the *not* talking about it option. Instead, he found himself wanting to say it all, just as he had a few minutes earlier.

And that means something.

"Is that offer to hang out at your apartment still open?" he asked.

"Definitely."

"Then let's go."

As he guided her away from the fair to the street where he'd parked his car, he couldn't stop himself from letting the words overflow.

"I was fourteen when it happened," he said. "Just barely. My brother Harley was twelve. Things were tense in our house because my dad was on some big, secretive case. He'd been spending more time away from home than at it, and it was hard on all of us. My mom was fed up with Harley and me, tired from working herself and they had a big fight just before he left the house the last time. He told my mom that the job was almost over, and when it *was*, his career would be made. She asked if that was just going to mean more cases like this one, and she told him she couldn't handle it if that happened. I remember the whole thing like it was yesterday."

"That sounds hard, Brayden," Reggie replied.

He nodded tightly. "I chased after him when he left that day, and I said a lot of things I regret." They reached the sedan, and he paused in his story for a second to let her in, but started up again as soon as she'd given him the address and they were on the move. "I was so mad. Self-righteously so. And fully on my mom's side. But when I finished ranting at him—in the middle of our quiet neighborhood, no less—he didn't yell back. He just told me really calmly that he needed to see justice served. That he had to take this guy off the street because too many lives were at stake to do things any other way. He said that his family was what motivated him to do it, and that one day I'd understand. I swore I never would."

"But that changed."

He nodded again, recalling the look on his mother's face as he burst into the house a few minutes after the confrontation. "When I turned around and headed home, I was still pretty ticked off. Came home, kicking furniture and swearing. Not my usual MO, and my mom didn't appreciate the sudden change in my demeanor. We fought, too. Then Harley got involved, and it was a real, you-know-what show. Once we all calmed down, though, my mom explained that she was taking out a bad day on my dad. Reminded us that his job was one of the most important ones in the world. Then she called my dad. She made my brother and me listen while she apologized for losing her patience. I think it was her words and attitude that brought me around so quickly. If she'd still been angry when the bomb when off…"

"Then you would've blamed the job," Reggie filled in softly.

"Exactly. Instead, I saw things from my dad's perspective. He was trying to make the world a better place for *us*. He died as a result, but the only thing he would've regretted about it—aside from the family loss, of course—is the fact that he never got a chance to finish his case."

"And that's part of what you're hoping to do. Justice *for* your dad…and on his behalf."

"My gut tells me they'll turn out to be one and the same. There's no doubt in my mind that Jesse Garibaldi is behind the Freemont City bombing. And he'd only have gone after the evidence in that room if it covered up something worse."

"Something worse than murder." Her voice shook noticeably before she cleared her throat and added, "Does your team have a theory?"

Brayden tapped his fingers on the steering wheel. "Not a firm one. Something worth a lot of money, for sure. But it was impossible to know for certain. Every shred of whatever my dad and his partners were working on was destroyed. And the man responsible was never held accountable. And to make matters worse, his identity was a mystery."

"A mystery? What do you mean?"

"The bomber was a minor. He turned eighteen four days after he committed the crime. Our lawyer told us that when my mom wanted to sue privately."

"So he was tried as a minor."

"Yep. Name hidden from the public. And since it took a whole year for the trial to process, he got away with time served. Then…an expunged record."

"But you tracked him down."

"We used the few details we had to keep the search alive. The birth date. The crime signature. We kept things flagged in newspapers and online. Eventually applied all of that to our police resources. And I knew what he looked like. I'd played kid detective and went to court one day. Sneaked into the closed session, and actually lasted all of five minutes before I got caught and kicked out." He paused, recalling how he'd stared and stared, memorizing the details of his father's killer's visage, vowing never to let them go. "It was a good enough look to embed his face in my mind for good. So I'd know it was him even if everything else didn't line up."

"And now that you've found him?"

"My brother does some work in records. Since we have a name, he's digging through to uncover anything and everything about Garibaldi's past. I'm slotted to stay here and uncover anything current."

"And I guess you found something."

"Guess I did."

He might have added something else, but they'd reached her street, and he was on automatic alert, looking for signs that anything might be wrong. A suspicious car or an out-of-place person. But the road was empty, the short row of apartments still. Extra quiet because of how many people were at the fair rather than at home. Satisfied that they weren't under any obvious surveillance, Brayden flicked on his signal and pulled the car into the parking lot at the side of her squat-looking apartment building.

As he brought the vehicle to a halt, he threw Reggie a quick glance. Her gaze was fixed on her building, and that plump bottom lip of hers had been pulled between her teeth once more. She made no move to exit quickly. A strand of dark hair stuck to her cheek, and this time he didn't hesitate to pull it away and tuck it behind her ear.

She tipped a little smile his way, but it faded away as quickly as it'd come.

"What?" he said.

"I was just thinking about the dress I'd planned on wearing to the dinner tonight."

"And?"

"And it crossed my mind that it wouldn't look very good over a bulletproof vest. I should be worrying about whether my purse matches my shoes well enough, and instead *that* goes through my head."

"You can think about the shoes and purse," he assured her, reaching over to close his fingers on hers. "I'll take care of the insane part."

"You've got a lot of experience with bulletproof vests under dresses?"

"None. But I've got a fair amount of experience keeping people safe."

After a final squeeze, he released her hand, then let himself out and moved around the car. By the time he reached her side of the vehicle, her attention was focused on the apartment building once more.

"Something wrong?" Brayden asked.

"I'm not sure."

"Not sure?"

"The third window from the left…that's my living room with the yellow light shining through. But I'm almost positive that two seconds ago, that light was off."

Brayden turned his attention to the window, his gut already churning.

There it was. A dim yellow glow in an otherwise-dark, shade-drawn building.

He studied it for a long moment. In a normal situation, he'd call for backup, then go after the invader himself. This situation, though, was far from normal. He couldn't very well leave Reggie in the car on her own. No way did he want to bring her along, either.

What other choice is there? Drive away? Find somewhere to hide? Maybe head back to the fair and pretend we never saw the light?

He shook his head to himself, his mind working through it quickly. Whispering Woods wasn't exactly a mecca of secret spots. Without tourist season in full swing, anonymity was an impossible dream. Fewer people meant no crowds to blend into. On top of that, if someone *was* in Reggie's apartment, he wanted to know who and why.

Could it be Chuck?

He really thought not, though he supposed nothing was 100 percent certain.

Maybe the guy who clocked you over the head back near Tyler Strange's hideout? Or Tyler Strange himself?

He glanced up again. There was nothing to say that whoever was up there wasn't simply lying in wait. One of the only things they had going for them was the possible element of surprise. If he could use that, he would.

"Reggie…" he said, looking down at her in the passenger seat. "Can you see the courtyard and parking lot from up there?"

Her inhale was audible. "As in, if someone was inside, could they see *us*?"

There was no point in denying the intent behind his question. "Yes. Exactly."

She shook her head. "I don't think so. If I'm standing right at the edge of the living room window, I can only see as far as that big shrub right there."

Brayden followed the incline of her head, relaxing a little as he spied what she meant. The bush had a ballooned-out top that bowed out below the second story. A perfect, natural shield.

"And what about if we walk across the lot?" he asked.

"If we move along the edge there—" She paused to indicate a low wall between the concrete stalls and a grassy area. "Then I think we'll be fine. If someone happened to be looking out the window at the exact moment we crossed to the patio by the door, they *might* see us. But not well."

"Is there somewhere out of sight in the lobby?"

"Somewhere out of sight?"

"A place to hide."

She groaned. "Again? Seriously?"

"Let me know when you've got your firearms license, a black belt and eight years of field experience, and we'll talk about *not* hiding you."

She sighed. "There's a supply closet for the maintenance guy."

"Good enough."

He climbed out, then moved to her side to open her door, too. He wiggled his palm, and she sighed again, then took it and let him pull her out. Spontaneously, Brayden brought the back of her hand to his lips. He lingered for a second before releasing her, then bent to grab his weapon from the glove box. He snagged his clipable belt holster, too, and with habitual ease, fastened it to his side and secured the gun inside.

"Ready?" Brayden asked.

"Never been more prepared to hide in a closet in my life."

With a dark chuckle, he reached for her hand again so they could move together—closely—to the hip-high wall. They reached the door quickly, and Reggie freed her hand and shot him a rueful smile as she pulled out a small ring of keys—which had been fastened to the hem of her uniform using a safety pin—and held it up.

"Learned that trick was I was kid," she told him as she shoved one into the lock and twisted it. "Lost a lot of keys when I was about twelve."

Brayden smiled back, then reached out to grab the door. As his hand closed on the metal handle and yanked it open, the muted thump of boots on linoleum carried to the lobby from above.

His smile fell away—the noise could belong to someone who *should* be there, but it could also belong someone who shouldn't.

"Normally I'd insist on ladies first," he said. "But right this second I'm going to suggest coming in behind me."

"I won't argue."

"Good. Put your hand just below my shoulder so I can feel where you are."

She complied, and Brayden stepped forward, his fingers finding his gun. He moved quickly but cautiously, taking in every detail of their surroundings as they entered. Four couches, pushed together at their corners, formed a centerpiece for the lobby. In the middle of those was an obviously fake tree. The rest of the space was open. One wall held a row of mailboxes, another a community board. A third wall served as the entrance to the first-floor apartments. The final wall was home to both the marked stairway and the closet Reggie had mentioned. Brayden studied the latter for a second. Its door had angled slats on the top and a solid bottom. Not lockable, but it would do.

"No elevator?" Brayden asked, his voice automatically dropped low enough for her ears only.

"No," she whispered back. "Only three floors. No real need."

He didn't like the idea that there was only one way up and one way down. It made it that much more likely that he'd run into someone.

And how will you know if it's a friendly neighbor, or a gun-toting thug?

Thinking quickly again, he led Reggie toward the closet. "Do you know everyone in the building?"

"Not well. But to look at, yes."

"Give me the fastest rundown in the world. No names, just descriptions."

She closed her eyes and reeled off a list, "First floor. Asian couple in one, guy in a wheelchair in two. Three is vacant, and four is a brunette with a Yorkie. Second floor. Five and six are one unit, guy's an artist and he looks like one—beard and ponytail, always covered in paint. Seven is an older man with an anchor tattoo on his left hand, eight is me. Third floor. Spinster sisters in nine—they never leave the apartment. Ten is our local dental hygienist, red hair down to her butt. Eleven is the hygienist's boyfriend, buzz cut and an eyebrow piercing. Twelve is a single mom, baby's about six months old." She opened her eyes. "Good?"

"Perfect."

He pulled open the closet door and was relieved to see that it was spacious and not filthy. At least while she was hiding, she wouldn't be suffering. He stepped back to make room for her and found her staring at him, worry evident in her green eyes.

"Everything all right?" he asked.

"Aren't you going to repeat it?"

"What?"

"The list."

"Worried I might coldcock one of your neighbors?"

"It's not funny."

He exhaled. "I know."

"So?" she prodded.

"Asian couple, wheelchair, Yorkie, beard, anchor tattoo, spinsters, redhead and pierced boyfriend, mom with baby." Brayden paused to draw in a breath, then winked. "And prettiest brunette in Whispering Woods."

Reggie's cheeks colored. "Thank you. And that was pretty impressive."

Brayden tapped his temple. "Virtual notebook."

She stepped backward into the closet. "Make another note in there, okay? This damsel in distress would like it a lot if you didn't get hurt."

"That makes two of us. I'll be back in five minutes. Seven, tops."

"I'll be counting."

He started to close the door, but her voice stopped him three-quarters of the way there.

"Brayden. Wait."

"What?"

"My apartment key."

He turned back, and found her holding out the item in question. When he reached for it, though, she grabbed his shirt collar. She pressed a swift, firm kiss against his lips, then released him with a breathy exhale.

"For luck," she said, dropping the key into his palm.

"And good motivation to come back," Brayden teased.

"That, too," she agreed.

He pulled her in again, kissed her forehead, then her mouth once more before letting her go. He was smiling as he closed the closet door. His cheer faded, though, as he made his way across the lobby. He could think of a dozen worst-case scenarios. Mistaking a resident for an intruder. Or the reverse. Or getting mistaken for an invader himself.

Stop, he ordered silently.

Thinking through every possibility was neither productive nor cathartic. He shoved the what-ifs to the back of his mind and entered the stairwell cautiously. Slow through the door. Relaxed in appearance. Hand ready to go for his weapon if the need arose.

The concrete interior was empty, and silent except for the buzz of the industrial lights that hung from the wall.

Good.

Brayden quickened his pace. The faster he got to the second floor, the less chance someone had to intercept him. He took the steps two at a time until he reached the landing. There, he paused. No sound carried through the door. Vigilant in spite of the quiet, he eased open the door. Then stepped into the hall.

A crash and a muffled curse lifted from behind one of the walls and put him on alert, and Brayden's thumb automatically flicked open the holster while his palm closed on the gun.

Steady, he cautioned.

The self-directed warning was unnecessary, really. Over the course of his career, he'd only fired his weapon twice in the line of duty. It was a last resort both times, and even though it wasn't something he was afraid to use again, it was still an option taken only when words wouldn't work.

At the moment, though, it just felt right to remind himself of that fact. There was a lot at stake. His and Reggie's lives. Putting away a man he'd been after for a decade and a half. He didn't need to blow any of it by having an out-of-control moment.

He stood still, waiting. No further disturbances came to life, and after a few seconds, the familiar sound of a popular game show carried through the door labeled seven.

Anchor tattoo, Brayden thought. *Getting his quiz skills sharpened.*

Letting out the breath he'd been unconsciously holding, he chalked up the previous clatter to some domestic mishap. With his hand back off his weapon, he slid past and moved toward Reggie's unit. Careful to be as quiet as possible, he tried the knob. Left, then right. It didn't budge either way. He turned it a second time, just to be sure it was locked. It definitely was. It just didn't quite feel like good news. Not yet anyway.

Brayden dug Reggie's key from his pocket and eased it into the hole. The mechanism inside clicked loud enough to make him wince. He waited for a reaction. There was none—just reigning silence. So he turned the handle again, this time all the way, and pushed the door open. As it swung inward, he turned sideways and flattened himself against the wall. Still nothing.

A quick glance into the apartment entryway yielded total darkness.

So what about that light?

He'd seen it himself from the parking lot. Wondering about it made him draw out and ready his gun. It also made him move slowly. In past the little rack of shoes. Along the overstuffed coat closet. To a hasty halt at an open archway.

With extra caution on his mind, he tipped his head around the wall, half expecting to be either jumped or shot at as he did. All that happened was that he caught a glimpse of Reggie's kitchen. Stainless steel appliances and a few dishes on the counter. A cutout over the sink that led to the living room. Everything looked normal.

Brayden breathed out slowly, then crouched down a little and moved on. The living room was equally still. The overhead light was out, and a fish tank glowed an eerie blue in one corner.

He scanned it all quickly but thoroughly before slinking along the wall to the short, adjoining hall. At the end of it, the bathroom door sat open, and in the mirror, he could see that it was empty. The clear shower stall and pedestal sink left nowhere to hide.

Next was the bedroom, and Brayden was torn about entering it.

On the one hand, he was genuinely curious about where the pretty waitress slept. Bedrooms were intimate. They provided clues into people's preferences. Silk sheets or flan-

nel, a tidy space or one cluttered with mementos. In his police work, he often found unexpected but invaluable clues
inside the private spaces.

Though in this case, of course, it was a personal curiosity. His attraction to Reggie made him interested in her
habits.

*Does she leave the bed a mess in the morning, or is she
more fastidious than that*? he wondered.

That question alone was enough to give him pause. He
would've preferred to be *invited* into her room, not forced
in by circumstance. He stared for a long moment at the
white door, wishing the circumstances were different. He
made himself go in anyway.

A long window, covered in a nearly sheer brown curtain let in enough light that he could see just fine without
turning on a light. The bedroom was spacious, especially
for an apartment. There was more than enough room for
the king-size bed—which immediately brought to mind a
tumble of dark hair on white sheets—and still space leftover for a lumpy reading chair, a tall armoire and an old-
fashioned dressing table. Her closet was open, revealing
an obvious love of all shades of green.

Probably to go with her eyes, Brayden thought absently.

His own gaze swept the room, making sure it was clear,
but also noting the details. Hints of Reggie's life were
everywhere. A ribbon name tag from the Frost Family
Diner hung from a mirror. A framed picture of an older
couple decorated the solitary nightstand.

Half-made, Brayden observed as he bent to check under
the bed, amused by how one side was smooth and the other
was shoved back to reveal a well-loved pillow.

He let himself stare for one more moment before deciding the room was as empty as the rest of them, then pivoted
on his heel and started to walk out. A flash of out-of-place
color caught his eye and made him stop. Tucked just under

the corner of the curtain was a familiar shoe. One he'd last seen sticking out of Chuck's waistband.

Brayden's heart rate jumped, and he grabbed the shoe and took off from the apartment at a run.

Chapter 10

Reggie held her breath, watching through the skinny slats in the storage closet door for Brayden to reappear. But truthfully, her mind was more interested in thinking about him than it was in waiting for him.

The past fifteen years couldn't possibly have been easy on him. Losing his dad, searching for the killer... And yet he'd managed to carve out a successful life, as far as she could tell. He was obviously good at his job, and took it seriously. Which meant that he was capable of putting aside his own issues in favor of the greater good. That required a lot of strength.

Reggie wondered if she'd have been able to do anything close, if it had been her. She'd had time—a year of chemo and year of remission and another four months of illness— to prepare, but losing her mother had still nearly broken her. Recovering from that loss... Well, it ended in a failed fake marriage, an ended education and a feeling that she constantly needed to prove herself.

Until now anyway.

Brayden somehow changed that. For one, he seemed to take her history in stride. And he was easy to talk to. Easy to relate to. In a single day, she'd become more comfortable sharing herself with him than she had with anyone since before her mom died. She felt more secure—more grounded—than she had in literal years. Which was especially crazy considering the fact that she'd been more or less running for her life since about two seconds before they met.

Amazing what the heart can do. The thought jerked her out of her wistful reverie. *The heart?*

Attributing her insta-comfort to her heart was almost as crazy as everything else. But that didn't make it something untrue. Carefully, she probed the warm corners that Brayden seemed to occupy. Yes, there was something there. More than a passing physical attraction. She could feel it threading through her. Settling in. Wanting to grow.

Too bad she was now being forced to hide, when she was sure she could be helping him right that second.

With a sigh, she opened her eyes, which she hadn't even realized she'd closed in the first place, and just about screamed. Directly in her narrow line of sight, a hooded figure dropped down—seemingly out of the sky—and landed on the cement patio outside the glass front of her building.

Reggie clamped her mouth shut and flailed to keep upright as she jumped back in fear.

What the hell?

She breathed in through her nose and out through her mouth for second, reminding herself that there was no way whoever it was could see through to where she hid. She pushed forward again, squinting. The figure's head swung back and forth as if in search of something.

Or someone.

The thought made Reggie shiver, and she had to force herself to keep from backing away from the door a second time. She inhaled and made herself keep watching. The figure drew a phone from the sweatshirt, and for a moment the dark shadow of a beard made an appearance.

At least I know it's a man.

It wasn't much consolation at all. Where had he come from? And what was he doing there?

She continued to stare as he continued to speak into the cell, one hand gesturing emphatically as the conversation carried on. Suddenly, he seemed to pause. He pointed straight up, as if the person on the other end could see. And that clued Reggie in.

He climbed down the building.

Her gaze flicked up nervously. She couldn't see anything past the glass doors and the hooded man. But she was pretty sure of what was up there. Her own apartment. Now her gaze shifted from the man to the door that led to the stairwell. Had Brayden run into the man? The building seemed quiet. If there'd been a fight, someone would've heard it, wouldn't they? There'd be a commotion. The nature of living so close together in such a small building was that no one had any privacy. Reggie once had a bird fly through her open kitchen window. Less than five minutes later, two neighbors had been at her door, offering to help her. So if they'd heard anything, they would've reacted.

She swallowed as another idea occurred to her.

What if the attacker sneaked up on Brayden? What if he hurt him? Or worse?

She shook her head. She wouldn't even consider the last thing as a possibility. But her feet itched to move out of the closet.

What if he needs my help?

She shifted back to looking outside, wondering if she could somehow sneak by unnoticed. But when her eyes found the spot where the man had been standing a couple of moments earlier...it was empty.

Dammit.

She scanned the patio as best she could, standing up on her to toes to try to see better. But her view was still far too limited. She could swear she could see even less than she could before.

Somewhere close, tires screeched a little noisily, and she had a feeling she knew who the impatient driver was.

Dropping back down to her heels, Reggie exhaled in frustration. She had to get out. To check on Brayden. She put a hand on the handle and started to push. And she froze. The door to the stairwell squeaked, then flew open so hard that it smacked backward and hit the wall behind it.

Brayden.

The big man stumbled through the door, his gun in his hand. His gaze whipped around the empty lobby before he strode purposefully toward the closet door. Gasping with relief, Reggie threw herself out and dived into his arms. His hands came down to her waist, and his tight squeeze was reassuring. She felt safer just being able to touch him. And he didn't seem to find her enthusiastic—almost desperate— greeting over-the-top, either. He just pulled away enough to smooth back her hair, then touch her cheek.

"You're okay?" he asked.

"Me? I'm fine. What about you? I saw—" She cut herself off as movement outside the building caught her eye.

Without thinking about it, she grabbed his hand and tugged him toward the closet.

"What're you doing?"

"Shh." She dragged him inside, then slid her arm around him to pull the door shut, then dropped her voice to the barest whisper. "Sorry."

"What's going on?" he whispered back.

"I saw someone before. And maybe again just now."

"Who?"

"A man I didn't recognize. Black hood and—" She stopped abruptly again as the lobby door shuddered open noisily.

Brayden's palm came to her waist again, and he angled them sideways so they could both look out. Reggie sagged with relief almost immediately. A familiar brown fur ball was jumping up and down at his owner's feet as the woman opened her mailbox.

"Yorkie." Brayden spoke very softly, his mouth so close to her ear that she could feel his warm breath against the sensitive skin there.

"Yes," she whispered, suddenly acutely aware of just how small the space was.

His hand slid a little lower, his palm resting on her hip. She couldn't help but lean into the touch. Brayden's body was solid against her and just a few degrees hotter than her own. Distracted by the pleasant sensation of being chest to chest, Reggie pulled her eyes away from her neighbor and looked up at the big detective instead. He was staring down at her, too. His gaze was heated. Full of desire that even the dim light couldn't hide.

"Hey," he murmured.

"Hey," she breathed back.

Her hands crept up to his shoulders, then snaked around his neck to toy with the short bristles of his hairline. He groaned a little at the attention, and it made Reggie smile.

Her heart.

It ached with need.

She pushed up to her tiptoes and dragged her lips over his. Sharp heat spread like fire. From her mouth to her jaw to her throat. And down. Into her chest and ballooning outward so that her limbs tingled. She deepened the kiss, darting her tongue out to taste him. Brayden's palms came around to press into the small of her back, pulling her impossibly closer. And this time, it was Reggie who groaned. He felt so good. Better than good. Amazing. Incredible. Too good to let go.

But a sudden yip from the Yorkie outside the closet door forced her back to reality. Pulling away and regretfully, Reggie turned her eyes to the lobby. The little dog was straining against his leash like crazy, trying to get closer.

"What's going *on*, Bruiser?" his owner murmured, yanking him back gently. "Got a problem with brooms all of a sudden?"

A laugh threatened to burst out of Reggie's lips, and she buried her face in Brayden's shirt to keep from being heard. His shoulders were shaking a bit, and she was sure he was battling the same amusement. The dog continued his persistent attention all the way to the entrance that led up to the first-floor hall. And even once they'd disappeared from view, his little barks still carried through. Fighting her giggles, Reggie didn't bring her head up again until the sound of a door slamming cut off the yaps. And when she did meet Brayden's eyes again, his immediate question sobered her once more.

"I take it that wasn't your hooded man?" he asked.

She shook her head. "No. Although my guy was about as hairy as the dog."

"It wasn't someone you recognized?"

"No. This guy was small. Older, I think. And he had a beard. I didn't see much else. He was on the phone and kind of worked up. Then he took off."

"Took off?"

"I heard a car drive away pretty fast," she explained. "But, Brayden...I think he came down from the balcony in my apartment."

His inhale was sharp enough that she could feel it as well as she could hear it. "The balcony?"

"It's off the bedroom. Did you go in?"

"Yeah. But I didn't notice a balcony." He sounded annoyed at himself.

Reggie felt a need to soothe the irritation away. "It's small. Barely big enough to fit two people."

"Where in the bedroom?"

"Behind the brown curtain. It probably looked like a window, and—what's wrong?"

"He was in there when I was."

"You're sure?"

He reached into the inside pocket of his suit jacket and pulled out one of her practical, good-for-waitressing shoes. Then the other.

"I grabbed one of these when I was chasing after you," he told her. "I grabbed the other from the floor in your bedroom just now. You know where I saw this last?"

Ice cut through Reggie's stomach, and the fear kind of took her breath away. She could barely manage a nod. It was one thing to worry that someone had violated her space. It was a whole other to know it. The tight space in the closet no longer seemed intimate. Instead it was cloying. Suffocating.

Reggie swayed on her feet. She put up a hand to steady herself. But she failed. Her fingers landed on a metal shelf, and the shelf wobbled, then collapsed. Startled, she glanced up just in time to see a metal bucket headed straight for her. Before she could raise her arms to protect herself, the thing cracked her right between the eyes. Her vision blurred. The world spun. And the only thing that kept her from toppling sideways as blank grayness overtook her senses was the fact that Brayden's hands shot out to grab ahold of her.

Brayden twisted awkwardly inside the closet, careful to keep Reggie from falling over.

"Sorry, sweetheart," he said. "Should've held off on the shoe revelation, I guess. I wasn't thinking about—" He cut himself off as she slumped in his arm, and he realized she wasn't just leaning on him for support. "Reggie?"

When she didn't respond, and her eyes didn't lift right away, he had to suppress both a growl and a lick of worry. He stared down at her for a second, watching her eyelids flutter. If he'd been a man who cursed, he would've dropped a dozen really unpleasant ones right then.

"Sweetheart?" He cupped her cheek.

Still nothing. And even in the dark, he could see the welt forming in between her eyebrows. A dozen more curses came to mind.

Balancing the petite waitress on the crook of one of his arms, he reached the other backward to grab the door handle. He paused, though, before opening it. His mind went to the shoe-dropping, hoodie-wearing intruder. Reggie had said she'd heard him leave in a car. But was that a sure thing? There wasn't really a way to know. Not unless he left Reggie behind so he could do a perimeter search. He looked down at her again. He just wasn't willing to do that.

"Just have to trust that you were right," he said to her still form.

He finished the turn on the handle and pushed the door open with his hip. Praying that no one would see them and jump to the worst conclusion, he bent down and lifted her up. His arms ached a little with the effort this time. It almost made him smile. Knowing a woman for a day, but being sore from carrying her around already. Except it wasn't really amusing at all. If he was going to ache from sweeping Reggie off her feet, he'd prefer it to not be because she kept getting hurt.

Frowning instead of smiling, Brayden eased into the lobby. He didn't pause to glance around—there was no sense in wasting the time it would take. A quick deliberation in his head sent him back up the stairs rather than out to the car. At least he could secure the apartment, and at least he knew that someone had already searched it. And that the someone in question chose fleeing the scene over confrontation.

He thought about it as he tucked Reggie closer and moved carefully up the stairs. It was the same choice that the person who'd clocked him over the head had made. Between that and Reggie's description—dark hoodie, small form—he figured they were very likely the same person. Possibly Tyler Strange, though the size factor didn't line up, and he still hadn't confirmed the man's presence as a certainty.

And there's the shoe to consider, as well.

Did its presence mean that the hooded man was working with Chuck Delta? Had the corrupt cop handed it out to some lackey of his the way someone might hand a clue to a bloodhound?

Brayden had a hard time picturing Garibaldi allowing such a reckless move to happen under his watch. The man had flown under the radar for a decade and a half, and it seemed unlikely that he'd risk drawing negative attention to himself. Not if he wanted to protect his reputation in Whispering Woods. To keep what he'd built intact.

So if the shoe hadn't come down *that* line, where had it come from?

A gut-churning answer came to mind.

The shoe dropped in the apartment wasn't the one from Chuck's pocket. It was the one from Brayden's house. Which meant that whoever had sneaked into the apartment—Tyler Strange or not—was an entirely separate threat.

Now Brayden did curse. Low and muttered, but a curse nonetheless. Another source of external pressure was the last thing he needed. Garibaldi and Chuck Delta were more than enough on their own.

Reggie stirred in his arms then, and he brought his attention back to the needs of the moment. He'd reached the top of the stairs, and the hallway was thankfully empty.

"Don't worry, sweetheart," he murmured. "I'm putting you first right now."

He shouldered his way through the partially open door to her unit, then made a beeline for the bedroom. There, he settled her into the rumpled side of the bed and drew up the blankets. When he was satisfied that she was breathing evenly and as comfortable as she could be, he bent down and touched her face lightly with his knuckles—one part caress, one part assessment. Her cheek was cool, her forehead smooth. In the light, the welt didn't look quite so bad. He thought it would probably fade quickly and leave her scar-free. He ran his forefinger around the edges of it. Her skin was soft. Kissable.

Without thinking about it, Brayden bent a bit farther, this time to press his lips to spots he'd just touched with his fingers. When he pulled back, those green eyes of hers fluttered again, then opened slowly.

"Waking me with a kiss? Are you Prince Charming now, too?" she said.

"Hardly." He kissed her again anyway, lightly.

"Did I, uh, get hit in the head with a bucket?"

"You did. Sorry."

"Sorry?" she repeated.

"I guess my hero skills don't extend much past the initial rescue job." He meant it to sound rueful, but it just came out a little bitter instead.

"It's not *your* fault I got hit with a bucket," Reggie told him.

He leaned back. "I should've checked the closet for hazards."

"Are you serious? You saved my life yesterday, remember? Chuck might've—" She paused to draw in a visibly shaky breath. "He *would* have killed me. But you're concerned about a bucket?"

Brayden ran a hand over his hair, worry and guilt competing for supremacy in his gut. "I should call my guys. Have them arrange somewhere safe for you to stay."

She pushed to a sitting position. "In Freemont City?"

"If need be."

"I'm not leaving Whispering Woods."

"Reggie…"

Her face set into a stubborn look. "I live here."

"And you'll stay here even if it's not safe?"

"That's up to me to decide."

Brayden sighed. "Stubborn, aren't you?"

She smiled. "You should see me when I'm not afraid for my life. My dad always—oh, God."

The sudden pallor of her skin filled him with concern. "What?"

"My dad. If someone came here looking for something and they didn't find what they were after, they might go to his house next. I can't believe I didn't think of it before, Brayden. What if Chuck had gone there?"

He reached out to keep her from throwing the blankets back. The expression on her face told him she'd gladly tackle him and steal his keys to get to her father. That kind of passion for family was something he could not only relate to, but also appreciated. It didn't mean he wanted her to hurt herself in an attempt to act on it.

"Listen," he said calmly. "When *you* talked to Chuck, did he seem unreasonable? Would anything he said to you have made you suspicious if you didn't already know something was off?"

"No." She breathed out. "But whoever was *here*…"

"Deliberately avoided being seen."

"I need to make sure my dad's okay."

"So why don't you just give him a call?"

"A call? You think that's enough?"

"I do."

Remembering that she still hadn't picked hers up from the diner, he dug his own phone out of his pocket and offered it to her. She took it gratefully, and as she punched a number into the keypad, Brayden moved away to give her a little privacy. He wouldn't leave her alone completely, but he could at least tune out the conversation. His eyes sought the balcony he hadn't noticed before, and his feet brought him closer. A flick of the curtain revealed that the narrow sliding door was closed, but unlatched.

He wanted to open it. To see what the intruder had seen. He resisted the urge. They could be watching the apartment. Waiting for a wrong move.

Another wrong move, you mean? he chastised himself, unable to suppress a stab of self-directed anger.

He'd left himself vulnerable. Which meant he'd left Reggie vulnerable. As thorough as he'd been in his examination of her apartment, he'd missed a key detail.

Distracted by the fact that it was her *bedroom.*

He ran a frustrated hand over his head. Could he be truly effective at keeping her safe if it was going to be like this? Could he even complete what he'd come to Whispering Woods to do? He'd known Reggie Frost for a day, and he could feel a conflict slipping in already. It was unexpected. Uncharacteristic. But undeniable, too.

Fighting his irritation, he glanced at her over his shoulder. The sight of her got him distracted all over again. She'd worked her hair free from its ponytail and had a strand wrapped around one finger. She let it go, and its length bounced softly against her collarbone, which had become exposed because her T-shirt had slipped down low. She lifted her eyes to meet his, then smiled, pointed at the phone and rolled her eyes.

"Yes, Dad," she was saying, her tone affectionately exasperated. "I realize I didn't tell you before that I had a date to the party, but I just met him. No. For crying out—I'm closer to thirty than I am to twenty."

Brayden smiled, amused at the interaction. But his entertainment was short-lived.

Reggie's eyes widened, and she started to shake her head. "No. Seriously? C'mon, Dad. No."

Brayden mouthed, "What's wrong?"

"He wants to talk to you," she whispered.

"What?"

She gave him a helpless shrug, then held out the phone. "Sorry in advance."

Brayden cleared his throat and offered a cautious greeting into the phone, "Hello?"

A chuckle answered him. "I love giving her a hard time. Don't let on that I think this is funny."

He immediately dropped his face into a neutral expression. "Yes, sir."

"You really her date tonight for the Garibaldi Gala?"

Even though he wasn't sold on the idea that—after her injury—Reggie was feeling well enough for the party, he answered in the affirmative. "Yes, sir."

"Interesting."

"Sir?"

"You met outside the diner yesterday?"

"That's right."

"And you asked her out, and she said yes, just like that." It was a doubtful statement rather than a question, and it made Brayden want to smile.

"*She* asked *me*, actually," he corrected.

"Even more interesting."

"I'm not sure I'm following."

"It's her life, not mine. But as a rule, my daughter doesn't date," the man on the other end said. "And if she did, she wouldn't call and tell me about it. Makes me wonder what she's up to."

At least I know where she gets her powers of deduction from, Brayden thought, turning away so that Reggie wouldn't see his face as he replied. "No good, I'm sure."

"Is she in trouble?"

"Trying to make sure she's not."

There was a long pause before her dad responded. "That's an honest answer, I'm guessing. So I'm trusting that you'll keep an eye on her then."

"I'll do my best."

"Do *my* best," the other man said. "And that's a damned steep order because she's my only daughter."

"You have my word, sir." Maybe it was too earnest, but it was honest, too. "Would you like to speak to her again?"

"Think I'm good. Looking forward to meeting you, son."

"Likewise."

Still mildly amused, Brayden clicked the phone off and turned to face Reggie. She was no longer in the bed. He spun again. She wasn't in the room at all. An unreasonable panic settled in, driving away his amusement.

He dropped the phone and stepped into the hall. "Reggie?"

The bathroom door hung open, just enough to give him a perfect view. She stood at the edge of the sink, an emerald green towel wrapped around her body, a tantalizing amount of creamy skin on display.

And any and all thoughts of her father went out of Brayden's head.

Chapter 11

Reggie felt Brayden's eyes on her even before she lifted her own gaze to meet his in the mirror. The usual warmth in his stare had turned hot. It held her rooted to the spot, and it sent a slow burn from the top of her head to the tips of her toes.

"Hi," she breathed.

He swallowed, his Adam's apple moving up and down heavily in his reflection. "Sorry. I hung up and you were gone, so…"

"Don't be sorry. I was just trying to sneak away so I could change into something *not* retrieved from a donation bin."

"Okay." She watched his Adam's apple rise and fall again before he added, "I'll just let you be then."

But as he turned to leave, Reggie had a sharp need to have him stay.

"Wait," she called.

He paused and swung back, his eyes lifting to her in the reflection again. "What?"

"Can you… I think…" She sucked in a breath and pushed on awkwardly. "I kind of want a quick shower. But I feel a little exposed. Would you mind waiting there for, like, five minutes while I wash my hair? Maybe just talk to me with the door open a bit?"

If he thought the request was strange, he didn't let on. "Sure."

"Thank you."

She waited until he'd closed the door all but a crack, then reached into the tub to turn on the faucet.

"I'm a bit afraid to ask, but what did my dad say?" she called over the running water.

"That you don't date."

Reggie just about fell as she stepped over the side of the tub. "What?"

"That you don't date," Brayden repeated. "I think he was suspicious of our little arrangement."

She couldn't suppress a groan. "Of course he was. I should've given him a more plausible story."

"Like the kidnapped-by-aliens scenario?"

"Exactly." She tipped her head back and let the shower soak through her hair. "I can't believe he'd even say that. What a rat."

"Was he telling the truth?"

"Sort of."

"Sort of?"

"I'm *not* not dating."

"So you *are* dating?"

She smiled at the hint of jealousy in his voice. "Didn't I already tell you my sob story?"

"You did," he agreed. "But you also said you'd been back in town for a few years. A few years is long enough to date again."

"I also mentioned that it's a *small* town, right?" she hedged.

He clearly didn't buy it. "A small town with a big influx of tourists twice a year."

"And look how well that turned out for me the first time."

"Sounds like you're making an excuse," he said teasingly.

Reggie took a second to lather up some shampoo before replying. "For the record, I don't really need an excuse not to date. If I don't want to, that's my prerogative. There's nothing wrong with being a single, almost twenty-six-year-old woman. But I *do* have my reasons. And before you tell me they're the same thing, I'd like to remind you about that fine line between revenge and justice that you so kindly illustrated for me earlier."

He chuckled. "All right. I'm listening."

"Well. I went to school because my parents always said I should. Then I got married—at least partially—to prove that I didn't have to do what they said. And after that, I probably did deliberately avoid dating for a while. I didn't want a rebound or a fling. I *really* didn't want people talking about me more than they already were. But then things settled down, and I clued in to the fact that I never really gave myself a chance to think about what *I* wanted. Everything I'd done up until that point had been either for someone else's expectations, or against them." She leaned back and let the last of the bubbles run down her head as she rinsed the shampoo, then squeezed out the excess water. "So I didn't want to *not* date. Or *to* date. I just wanted to do things because they helped me be…*me*."

"What about now?"

"Now?"

"Are you *you* enough to want to date?"

She turned off the tap, grabbed her towel and wound it around her body again. "That's my whole point. I don't *need* to want to date. But if I met someone…"

"Then you might invite him to the Garibaldi Gala with you?"

"I might."

"Even if he hadn't rescued you from a corrupt cop,

chased you through the woods, charmed your best friend, then let you be assaulted with a bucket?"

Reggie stepped out of the tub and pulled open the door to shoot him a look. "Are you still obsessing about the bucket?"

He offered her a lopsided smile. "Maybe. Or maybe I just wanted to see you in that towel again."

"If that's the case…you could've just asked."

"Is that right?"

Feeling emboldened by the obvious appreciation in his eyes, she crooked a finger. "Come here."

He took an obedient step into the steamy bathroom. "Yes?"

"Closer."

He took another step.

"Closer."

And another.

"Even closer."

A final step brought him near enough that her towel brushed the front of his shirt.

"Close enough?" he murmured.

Reggie tipped her face up to look at him. "Almost." She lifted her arms up and draped them over his shoulders, then threaded her fingers together on the back of his neck. "I like you, Brayden. A lot."

"I like you, too, Reggie." The flicker in his eyes wavered between amused and heated. "Does this mean we can date?"

"I could be convinced."

"Aha. That's a trick, isn't it?"

"How do you figure?"

"Because you just gave me the speech about doing what *you* want. If I have to convince you…" He trailed off and raised an eyebrow.

"So maybe *I* should be convincing *you*."

"How're you gonna go about doing that?"

In response, Reggie pushed to her tiptoes and dragged her tongue over Brayden's bottom lip. Then she sucked that same lip between her teeth and bit down lightly. He let out a groan and put a hand on her terry-cloth-covered hip.

"Reggie…" Her name rumbled from his mouth.

"Brayden," she breathed back.

The hand on her hip tightened, and she let him pull her flush against him, the already-minuscule space between them diminishing to nothing at all. Although the residual dampness from the shower had been keeping her skin cool, there wasn't an icy enough bath in the world to dampen the sudden rise in temperature between them. Reggie dug her fingers into Brayden's hair and pulled him down for a fullmouthed kiss. When she broke for air, she could barely gasp in enough before going back for more. Her heart thundered noisily in her chest, and her lungs actually ached. But she didn't stop. Or maybe she couldn't. It was hard to say. And even if she did have a choice…no way did she want to slow down.

Still holding her—now by both hips instead of just one—Brayden pulled her from the bathroom and into the hall. Reggie eagerly let him tug her along, bumping the wall, then her bedroom door. And by the time his knees hit the bed, she was the one leading. She pushed her hands to the front of his shoulders, and he landed heavily on her mess of sheets. His eyes danced hungrily over her body, taking in every inch and making her burn even more.

The towel had come free somewhere along the way. The bathroom floor? Caught on the door? Reggie didn't know. But she *was* sure that the playing field was uneven. Brayden was fully clothed. She was naked.

"Gotta fix that," she murmured.

"Gotta fix what?"

"This."

She reached for the top button on his shirt, and before he could say a word, she had it—plus the next three—undone. It was still too slow. She gave up any pretense of decorum and grabbed the bottom of the shirt so she could tug it off completely. Immediately, her breath caught. His chest was wide. Lightly muscled. Marked with half a dozen jagged scars. Inch after inch of masculine perfection.

"The rest." The request escaped her lips as a gasping plea, and she didn't care.

Locking his eyes with hers, he slid his hands to his belt. The sound of it unfastening—and the unzip of his pants that followed—echoed through the bedroom. Reggie's knees were already weak with anticipation. And when he dragged his pants and boxers off in a smooth motion, then clasped her wrists to drag her onto the bed beside him, she was desperately thankful not to have to hold herself up anymore.

For a long second, they lay facing each other, their breathing shallow, their skin touching and their gazes unmoving. The quiet, nearly still moment was exquisite.

Then Brayden touched her face, adding to the spell rather than breaking it. "You've convinced me. Just, please…tell me we can date."

Reggie couldn't help but let out a low laugh. "We can date."

"Exclusively."

"Exclusively," she confirmed.

"Should we work out logistics?"

"Um. How about later?"

"You're a tough negotiator," he teased. "But you've convinced me again."

Then Brayden's hands were on her. Touching and teasing and exploring. He kissed and nipped and showered her with more sensual attention than she'd ever experienced. She wanted to reciprocate, but her brain couldn't keep up. So it ceased to try. She let her body take over, falling into his rhythm, riding the waves of warmth that came with each touch. When she got to a point that she didn't feel she could take any more, when she was literally shaking with need, he finally eased away—with one hand still on her unsteady thigh—and looked her in the eye once more, his face a mask of want that matched her own.

"Sweetheart?" The question was clear.

"Yes," she said, her voice far firmer than she expected it to be.

He cleared his throat, a hint of awkwardness brushing his next words. "Do you have a…uh, something for protection?"

With her face as warm at the rest of her body, she nodded. "In the nightstand. Jaz gave them to me for an emergency."

His mouth turned up crookedly. "Well, thank God for that."

Quickly then, he reached for the drawer and made short work of opening the sealed box. He used his teeth to open one of the wrappers inside and made even shorter work of unrolling the condom. But as he kissed her tenderly, pressed himself between her thighs, then filled her completely, she could tell he was going to take his time.

And thank God for that, she echoed silently, her head hitting the pillow as she completely succumbed to their mutual passion.

Brayden twirled a piece of Reggie's hair around his finger, then released it and watched as it bounced down to land on her bare shoulder. He was grinning like an idiot and he didn't care.

"Did I mention that I like dating you?" he asked.

She smiled up at him, her green eyes warm with amusement. "About fifty times."

"And did I tell you that you're beautiful fifty times, too?"

"Possibly. But it might only have been forty-nine."

"So I should tell you again?"

"Just to be sure I heard you."

"Reggie Frost, you're so damned beautiful that I think my mother will forgive the fact that I'm swearing about it."

"Thank you. And apologies to your mother."

He kissed her lips lightly, then leaned back. "I accept your apology on her behalf. And will now change the subject because it's a little weird to talk about her while I'm in bed with you."

She laughed. "*You* brought her up."

"Only because I couldn't stop the curse from coming out, and swearing makes her cringe. But seriously. Another topic?"

"What would you like to talk about?"

"You?"

"Suck-up."

"I mean it. Give me some random details."

"Like what?"

"Is *Reggie* short for something? *Regina?*"

She wiggled closer, tucking her head into the crook of his arm. "Nope. Just Reggie. But…my great-grandmother on my dad's side *was* a Regina. My parents wanted to name me after her, but my mother wasn't fully sold on the idea. She wanted something cuter and more modern."

He pressed his chin to the top of her head. "She got it."

"And now we're back to talking about mothers again."

"Hmm."

"What?"

"I think you should meet mine."

"Ha ha."

"I'm serious."

Reggie pushed up to her elbows and stared down at him, and the stunned look on her face made Brayden laugh.

"You'd like her," he said. "And she'd like you."

"We've been dating for five minutes."

"I'd like to think that was a *little* longer than five minutes," he joked as he tried to use his finger to smooth out the crease between her brows. "I told you that when I invest in something, I do it all the way. I wouldn't waste time on a relationship I didn't think would last."

"Oh. Now we're in a relationship?"

"Yes."

She made a face, but her cheeks were pink, and her eyes sparkled enough to tell him that she wasn't truly offended by his wild leap. "And what about your job in Freemont?"

He playfully dragged his finger down her nose. "I have it on good authority that someone on the police force here in Whispering Woods is probably going to get fired."

"So it's that easy for you? You'll just apply for a transfer? What if I turn out to be a crazy person who wants to live in a yurt?"

"I'm actually *hoping* for at least a touch of insanity."

"Oh, really?"

"Mmm-hmm. That's what it takes to settle down with a cop."

Her eyes grew impossibly wide. "You are *seriously* confident that this is going to work out, aren't you?"

He pushed his palm over her heart. "Of course I am, Reggie. I—"

Whatever over-the-top, emotional confession he was about to make was cut off as his phone came to life from somewhere inside the tangled mess of sheets.

"That's my brother's ringtone," he said without letting Reggie go.

"So you should get it, then."

"I don't have to."

"I don't think I want to start off our relationship with me asking you not to do your job. Especially not with this case."

Appreciation made Brayden's throat tighten. He dug

through the sheets until he found the phone, then met Reggie's eyes as he answered without excusing himself for privacy's sake.

"Harley. You've got something for me?"

"You don't check your texts anymore?" came the reply.

"Been busy."

"*Busy* good, or *busy* bad?"

Brayden fought a laugh. "Good."

His brother paused for a moment before replying, "Wanna tell me what's going on?"

"Didn't *you* call *me*?"

"Yeah. I sent you a picture about an hour ago. Tyler Strange."

Brayden sat up a little more. "Recent?"

"Took some digging. Guy's been a ghost. No employment record. No driver's license or passport. Nothing in facial recognition. When you see the picture, you'll know why the last bit is true."

"Looks different?"

"Hugely."

"But you're sure it's him."

"It's a mug shot. Proof is in the fingerprints."

"He came through the system recently?" Brayden asked, surprised. "How come that didn't show up in the first search?"

"It was out of state, for starters. Petty theft in a grocery store. But the report says it turned out to be a misunderstanding and the charges were dropped, and there was a request for the record to be removed."

"By Strange himself?"

"By a lawyer on his behalf," Harley replied. "We just got lucky. Another couple weeks and the request probably would've been met."

"I'll take any kind of luck we can get."

"Yep. Me, too. Any other news? Are those photos you sent yesterday connected to our case? Witness pan out?"

Brayden's eyes found Reggie. "Potentially. But nothing I'm going to report on yet."

A sigh carried through the phone. "All right. Have a look at what I forwarded you. Let me know if you need anything else."

"You got it."

He moved to end the call, but his brother's voice stopped him.

"Brayden?"

"Yeah?"

"Did you see him?"

His chest compressed. "I did."

There was a pause. "How was it?"

Brayden recalled the terrible combination of anger and helplessness. "About what you'd expect."

"Don't know how I'd handle it."

"Same as I did, I expect. Freeze for about ten seconds. Contemplate breaking a few laws. Then remember why we started the investigation in the first place, and carry on with the plan."

"Yeah, I suppose so."

"I'll talk to you soon."

"Yep."

Brayden clicked the phone off, then went immediately to his text messages. As promised, there was a digital image under his brother's name. And Harley was right. The man in the picture looked nothing like the previous shots he'd seen of Tyler Strange. Where the newspaper showed him to be a large, angry man, the mug shot showed him to be skinny and beaten down. His wild, thick hair was gone. In its place was a shaved scalp. His skin hung from his gaunt skull; his eyes were haunted and bloodshot. Brayden opened his mouth to wonder aloud what the man might have gone through over the last two years to reduce him to such a state, but Reggie spoke first, her voice quavering.

"That's him," she said.

"That's who?"

"The man that Chuck Delta shot in the alley behind the diner."

Brayden's gaze jerked from her to the photo, then back again. "You're sure?"

"A hundred percent."

"This is Tyler Strange's mug shot."

"What?" Her face came up, and it was clouded with confusion. "He looks nothing like the man in the other picture."

"I know. But I'm sure." Brayden recounted his brother's side of the conversation, then added, "So I guess we know for sure he was in town, too."

"I still don't understand," Reggie said. "Why come back?"

"There are always things worth risking your life for, sweetheart." He dropped the phone down and squeezed her hand. "Have you got a computer hidden in here somewhere?"

"My laptop. You want to use it?"

"Please."

"Okay. I'll be right back."

Wrapping a sheet around her body, Reggie stood and left the room. As he waited for her to return, Brayden considered his own words. There *were* things that made putting it all on the line worth it. But his experience taught him that they were few. Love. Family. Or the other end of the spectrum, for some. Hate. Revenge.

Something, though, has to have acted as a catalyst in this case, he thought.

He couldn't imagine that Tyler Strange had just decided to up and come back for no reason. He'd been well hidden for years. So what changed?

Reggie came back in then, the laptop in her hands. She set it on the bed and opened it up.

"My password is *SantaClaus*," she said.

"Santa Claus?" he repeated.

"All one word. Don't ask."

"I wouldn't dare."

"You want some coffee?"

"I'd love some," he admitted.

"I'll brew a pot. You sleuth."

He smiled. "Sleuth?"

"Detective," she amended.

"Better. But only slightly."

She rolled her eyes. "Just do whatever you do."

He grabbed her hand before she could step away from the bed and pulled her in for a kiss. He was tempted to toss aside the laptop completely. Might even have done it, if she hadn't broken their contact.

"You need to do this quickly," she said breathily. "Otherwise, Chuck won't be held accountable, won't get fired and sent to jail, and there won't be an opening for you on the Whispering Woods PD."

"All right," he grumbled good-naturedly. "You brew, I'll *sleuth*."

"Good man," she teased.

"I hope so."

She blew him a playful kiss on the way out of the bedroom, and Brayden had to force himself not to chase her down and tear off the sheet. He took a breath, cleared his mind of creamy skin and focused on the computer.

"Santa Claus," he muttered as he typed in the password. "Really?"

His amusement quickly took a back seat to his search for a clue to Tyler Strange's sudden return. The man's name in the search engine brought the typical results. The same things he and his team had found before he came to the small town. Newspaper articles around the time of his arrest, but nothing to indicate a preexisting tie to Whispering Woods or to Jesse Garibaldi. No social media, of course, and nothing more recent than the pipe bomb and resulting fire. Trying to look at it with new eyes didn't change what was already there.

Not discouraged, Brayden tried again, fiddling with the keywords until he pulled up what he could about Tyler from *before* the bombing.

He'd previously done his due diligence in researching the man's past as well, finding little. The man grew up in Freemont, graduated high school on time and worked as a grocery store clerk, then as a manager of the same store. His parents had been average citizens—a nurse and a limo driver—who divorced amicably when Tyler was in grade school with no hint of anything being amiss. Around the same time that he came to Whispering Woods, his father had passed away suddenly in a car accident.

Brayden paused in his scroll, thinking about the last bit. Had his father's death triggered the visit to Whispering Woods in some way? It had seemed unrelated the last time he considered it, the dates more coincidence than anything else. Now, though, something tickled at his brain.

Family.

That was one of the things he'd just told himself was worth risking a life for.

A hint of excitement gripped him as he highlighted Tyler Strange's father's name, then copied and pasted it into the search bar. A few dozen results popped up. An ad in the paper for the company where he worked. A commendation from a client that landed him a community service award. An obituary.

Actually...two obituaries.

At first glance, they looked the same. Identical man in the picture, no doubt about that. Matching birth dates and causes of death—a car accident, nine years earlier. As Brayden squinted at the obituaries, though, he realized they were different. Just marginally enough that it was easy not to notice.

In the second photograph, the senior Strange was older. He had a slightly more grizzled appearance. A deeper graying at the temples, a thickening of the creases in his forehead.

"Weird."

Puzzled, Brayden clicked on the first one. A quick scan told him the basics—survived by his son and former wife, a sister somewhere in Europe—and not much else. He closed it and moved on to the second one.

"'Predeceased by his loving wife, Cindy Stuart. Survived by his daughter, Nadine Stuart,'" he read aloud.

The scent of coffee alerted him to Reggie's presence before her voice did.

"Nadine Stuart?" she said, setting down two mugs on the nightstand.

Brayden lifted his head. "Does that name mean something to you?"

"She lived here in Whispering Woods until we were teenagers. In fact…she recently moved back."

"Well. If what I'm reading is correct…she's also Tyler Strange's half sister."

Chapter 12

It took a few seconds for Reggie to process Brayden's statement. And even when he repeated it, and she was sure she'd heard him right, she still couldn't really believe it.

"I don't understand. Nadine more or less grew up here," she said.

"Did you know her personally?"

"Not really. I mean, we weren't friends, and I can't say I've talked to her since she came back. But Whispering Woods only has the one elementary school—where I heard Nadine took a job, actually—and the one high school, so we crossed paths lots of times."

"Weird that she happened to turn up again now."

"It's been a month or so, I think."

"So maybe a coincidence."

"Maybe."

"What about this guy?" Brayden swiveled the laptop on the bed. "You recognize him."

"Yes. That's her dad. He came into the diner occasionally before he died."

"He's the shared parent. This man is definitely Tyler Strange's dad, as well."

"You're kidding."

"Nope."

"So…"

"The man had two families."

"At the same time?"

Brayden shrugged. "There's a six-year gap between Tyler and Nadine. I didn't see any divorce papers myself, but I do know the split came well after Tyler's sixth birthday."

Reggie studied the screen for another moment. "So this probably means that the whole reason for Tyler's visit to Whispering Woods was that he found out."

"Seems likely."

"So what now?"

"I question Nadine. Try to figure out if she's also the reason he came back, and see if she can connect her brother to Garibaldi."

Reggie sat on the edge of the bed, grabbed Brayden's coffee and held it out as she asked, "How?"

"Thanks." He took a small sip. "How do I question her, you mean?"

"Mmm-hmm. I mean, it's not like you can walk up to her in an official capacity, right?"

"No. But I did tell you once before that I have some experience with subtlety. I promise it wasn't a lie." He threw her a wink that was distracting in the sexiest way possible.

She pushed aside the immediate need to let her toes curl pleasantly and instead picked up her own coffee and replied, "I know it wasn't, *Detective*. But I'm just trying to think of an easy way to get her to talk to you without a need to fabricate another story about how we met."

"We could tell her we're thinking of having a baby and want to ask some questions about the school."

Heat crept up Reggie's cheeks. "Yeah, I'd prefer to take a route that doesn't make her think I'm crazy."

He slid sideways and wrapped his free arm around her waist. "Do I have to remind you so soon that I need crazy?"

Reggie rolled her eyes, but still pressed her face to his bare shoulder, a question popping out before she could stop it. "Was *she* not crazy enough for you?"

"Who?"

"Your worse-than-mine story. I assume it was a woman?"

"Oh. You actually want to hear it?"

"Of course. I showed you mine. You have to show me yours," she teased.

"Guess I should give you the background first. Through most of high school, I dated this girl named Chandra. Off-again, on-again kinda deal. At the end of our senior year, we were on. Or at least *I* was on. About two months after we graduated, she told me she was pregnant. Then she told me it wasn't mine."

"Okay, that's *far* more scandalous than my hippie wedding."

"See? I hate to use that phrase you don't like but...I told you so."

"Ha ha. Funny." She ran her hand along his forearm. "Sorry that happened to you."

"Not too sorry, I hope."

"Well. For selfish reasons...yes, I'm glad you're single. But I'm still sorry."

Brayden shrugged, then smiled. "Twelve years have given me enough time to acclimatize to being practically cuckolded."

"Practically cuckolded? Really?"

"If I'd married her like I thought I might, it'd be the right word."

"If you married her like you thought you might, it'd still be a *weird* word."

"Well. Now *they're* married. With five more kids. So practically cuckolded or not...things turn out the way they're supposed to sometimes."

"But you never regretted that it wasn't you? Never wanted to go that route yourself?"

"Nope. Never really made the time. Zero kids, zero hippie weddings. Of course, I also never met another woman crazy enough to take me on." She could feel him grinning even though she couldn't see his face. "Until we started planning *our* baby five minutes ago, of course."

"Shut up."

"It's not actually a bad idea, though."

"Are you drunk? Did I put whiskey in that mug instead of coffee?"

"I meant pretending to have one," Brayden amended. "Like, a preexisting kid."

"You want to create a fake kid?"

"I want to imply that I might be looking to place one in school here in Whispering Woods."

"Okay. But it's Saturday," Reggie pointed out. "The school's closed, and Monday seems awfully far away at the moment."

"Do you know where she lives?"

"Sort of."

"Anything nearby that would allow us to coincidentally run into her?"

Reggie thought about it, trying to remember if she'd heard what area the other woman had moved to. She was pretty sure it wasn't far from her own place. Maybe a block over. But there wasn't anything other than housing nearby. Not even a park or playground.

"I don't think so," she said after considering it.

Brayden didn't seem discouraged. "So we'll come up with something else."

"Like what? Getting her into the diner somehow while I'm at work?"

"Putting aside the fact that I'd rather you *didn't* go to work, that's not a bad idea."

"Yeah, out of our two jobs, mine is definitely the scarier one." Reggie made a face at him, then sighed. "Seriously, though. I'm scheduled for an opening shift tomorrow, and

I have to go in since I already got today's shift covered.
I'm the boss."

"I know. But I should warn you…I'm going to be sitting
in a corner booth…brooding."

"Oh, good. My own personal stalker."

"Bodyguard," he corrected. "And only because I care
about you."

Warmth blossomed in Reggie's chest. "I care about you,
too."

"Which is exactly why we need to sort out a plan."
Brayden strummed his fingers on her sheet-covered thigh.
"What would make *you* come to the diner to meet a strange
man?"

"Nothing."

"Literally nothing?"

She set her coffee back on the nightstand and slid back
on the bed to a more comfortable position. "I don't know.
I mean, I guess it's a public place. If I'd lost my wallet and
some guy found it or something, I *might* come in and meet
with him. But I'd probably ask Jaz to come with me."

"What if it was a woman? Would that change it?"

"Probably," Reggie admitted.

"So then it has to be you who finds her wallet. She has
more reason to trust you anyway. At the very least, she
knows who you are, where you work…"

"Sure. Except for the problem of neither of us actually
having her wallet."

"Yeah. We need a stand-in for the wallet. Something
she'd want to come and get."

An idea popped into Reggie's head. "A contest!"

"A contest?" Brayden echoed.

"We run a draw every now and then at the diner. Usually
for a gift card that's good for any of the businesses in the
Whispering Woods Downtown Association. I'll call and
tell her she won, and when she tells me she didn't enter,

I'll convince her that someone else must've entered her name, and get her to come down during my shift. No one says no to free stuff."

"True enough."

"Here, slide me the computer and let me borrow your phone again. I'll look up her number and call her now."

As Brayden handed her both the electronic devices, Reggie felt an undercurrent of relief buoy her mind. She wasn't fully ready to let go of the tension that'd been plaguing her since witnessing the shooting the day before—*how could it have just happened yesterday? It already seemed like so much had happened since then!*—but she was undeniably glad to see progress. They weren't in the clear from Chuck himself. But they'd figured out who was on the wrong end of the gun. And now they had a means of gathering even more information.

Thankfully, Nadine Stuart already had her phone number listed in the Whispering Woods online directory. Using the call-block feature to mask Brayden's number, Reggie dialed and waited, telling herself not to be nervous. The woman on the other end wouldn't have a reason to suspect anything was amiss. But four rings in, it was an answering machine that picked up rather than a person anyway. So in a quick and cheerful voice, Reggie left a message with the details, then hung up and turned back to Brayden.

"All right," she said. "That's done. What now? We've got a few hours until the Garibaldi Gala dinner. Assuming we're still going."

"We're still going," he confirmed.

"What should we do until then? More sleuthing?"

"Actually..." He set down his mug beside hers. "I've got a better idea."

"What?"

He raised an eyebrow, a slow smile lifting both sides of his mouth. And even before he leaned closer and tugged off her sheet; a delicious shiver of anticipation pushed thoughts of the case to the back of her mind.

Brayden held Reggie's hand tightly as they moved through the hall and down the stairs, and when they reached the lobby he pulled her close. Part of it was because he just plain wanted to. The dress she'd picked—above the knee, snug around the waist and with a temptingly scooped neckline—added more than a hint of sex appeal. Her makeup job was subtle, but elegant. Being close to a woman who looked like that was a privilege. But it was an instinctive need to protect her that made him tuck her under his arm and hold her tight. So once again, he made himself compartmentalize.

As they stepped into the cool night air, he scanned the area, then tugged Reggie along quickly. Though he saw no one, there was no doubt in his mind that someone could be watching the apartment. Maybe it was even likely. Either way, he didn't want to leave himself and Reggie exposed for any longer than he had to. Though he was convinced that public exposure wasn't on the agenda, he couldn't quite dismiss a nagging paranoia about long-range weapons and the surrounding buildings. He didn't breathe easy until they'd reached the car and Reggie was tucked safely into the passenger-side seat.

"You good?" he asked as he settled into his own spot and buckled up.

"Good as I can be." She gave a small, nervous smile. "You know where Garibaldi Hall is?"

"Yep. On the outskirts of town. Big building. Big sign."

"That's the one."

Brayden pulled the car out of the lot, and they rode in companionable silence through the streets of Whispering Woods until he finally spied the sign for Garibaldi Hall. He hadn't been kidding when he said it was big. The bright background was billboard-sized, and the red lettering emblazoned on it was an obnoxious set of slashes across the front. Seeing the company name, large and proud, made him grit his teeth, and he was sure there was something ironic to be said about the logo. It was a *G* turned into a paint palette, and there wasn't an artistic thing about the man.

Unless you count escaping from the law as art, Brayden thought, his hands tightening on the wheel.

"You okay?" Reggie's soft question brought his attention away from the sign and back to the moment.

He nodded, then flicked on his signal and turned into the lot, which seemed to be at overflow capacity already. People flowed in and out of the barn-shaped building. No one seemed bothered by the fact that their fancy clothes were oddly out of place with the otherwise-rustic feel of the place.

"Busy," he observed as he wove through the parked cars to the very end of the paved area and found an empty space.

"It *is* kind of a big deal," Reggie replied. "The food's good. Garibaldi gives out crazy prizes… No one who's invited wants to miss it."

"How many people are on the list?"

"Well. Garibaldi owns about seventy percent of the commercial real estate in Whispering Woods. That's gotta be fifty people. Plus the hotel. They have a decent-sized staff, and he includes them, so…a lot?"

Man's sure got ahold of this town. He didn't realize he'd muttered it aloud until Reggie responded.

"He does," she agreed.

Together, they stared silently out the front windshield. Worry hung heavy in the air, until a sharp rap on the window cut through it. Automatically, Brayden lifted his head, one hand nearing his weapon as he peered out the window. A smiling man—not much more than a kid—stood outside.

He wore a red-and-black uniform, and Garibaldi's logo was stitched into the pocket of his vest. He offered a cheerful wave and mouthed something incomprehensible.

"What does he want?" Brayden grumbled.

"I think he's a parking lot attendant or something," Reggie said.

He let out a breath. She was probably right. He dropped his hand from the general vicinity of his gun and opened the window instead. When he greeted the kid, though, his voice still came out a little on the defensive side.

He is Garibaldi's valet, after all.

"Can I help you?" he asked.

The attendant continued to smile. "Sir. Ma'am. It's starting to rain. Would you care for an umbrella to use while you walk from the car to the hall?"

"Thank you," Reggie replied, then swung open her door before Brayden could argue.

Moving so quickly that the kid had to jump back, he pushed out of the car and hurried to the other side so he could offer Reggie his arm as she stepped to the ground.

She lifted an eyebrow at his hand and said in a whisper, "I think you can hold off protecting me from the umbrella."

"Kid looks clumsy," he whispered back. "Might poke your eye out."

"Really? That's your excuse?"

"Yep."

She shook her head and tipped her head toward the valet, her face one part amused and one part doubtful. As if on cue, he slid open the umbrella in question, fumbled it, almost dropped it, managed to grab it before it hit the ground, then jabbed himself in the stomach before finally getting it opened. Brayden turned a knowing look Reggie's way, then held out his hand again. With a muffled laugh, she took it.

The kid turned out to be right, though. Before they made it more than a few steps, the sky opened and thick raindrops rat-a-tatted onto the umbrella. They huddled underneath it and hurried toward the hall, where the crowd was already pushing through the door in an attempt to escape getting soaked. A minute or two of organized jostling brought them inside, too.

A middle-aged woman with a carefully cultivated tan stopped them almost immediately, placing her hand on Reggie's arm with easy familiarity while her eyes kept flicking to Brayden.

"Hello, Ms. Frost," she greeted. "You coming in your father's place this year?"

"And every year from here on out, I hope," Reggie replied.

"You've finally talked him into retiring, then?"

"Working on it."

The woman eyed Brayden again, then released Reggie's arm. "Well. I wish you much success, dear. Don't forget to sign in at the table in the corner."

"You bet."

They got stopped a few more times on the way to the table in question, but no one asked Brayden who he was, even when they spoke to him directly. When they stepped into the small lineup of people waiting to sign in, he finally leaned down to query Reggie about their lack of curiosity.

She smiled. "Oh, they're curious. But half of them probably heard something about you today at the fair. The other half are keeping in mind that they're business owners in a tourist town. They're either too proud to admit that they don't know who you are already, or too polite to consider asking. Plus. You've got to factor *me* in."

"You?"

"They're probably more focused on whether or not I'm going to run off and get married again than who you are."

He couldn't help but chuckle. "You *really* think they're holding on to that?"

"I really do," she said solemnly.

"You want to keep them on their toes? Because I can think of a few ways to do that."

"Aren't we trying to keep a lowish profile?"

He let out an exaggerated sigh. "Fine. Should we sign in? Maybe give me an appropriate pseudonym to make them talk even more?"

"I do like to keep people guessing."

"So what should we call me?"

"Hmm. How do you feel about Elvis?"

"Costello or Presley?"

"I'm leaning toward Jones, actually."

"Elvis Jones it is."

He gestured to the small line around the table, and as they headed that way, he was glad for a moment to more thoroughly assess his surroundings. The room was big, with high ceilings and white decor. Numbered tables lined the walls, and a hardwood dance floor made up the middle. At the far end was a stage. Heavy purple curtains framed it, and a mirror ball hung above. It was the kind of setup that could be used as a catchall for every event people in the town wanted to host. For weddings. Or funerals. School functions and church pageants.

Pretty typical.

Except Brayden couldn't shake the feeling that something was off. He swept his gaze over all of it again, frowning. He tried to focus on some of the smaller details, searching for the source of the prick at his nerves. People milled around, laughing and talking, sipping wine and eating the delicate appetizers that were being served by the catering staff. Music—subtle and generic—carried from the small speakers overhead. Everything looked perfectly in place. Suits and dresses. Lively conversation.

He was about to give up and dismiss the feeling as a paranoid one when a flash on the stage caught his eye. For a single second, a stock-still hooded figure stood at the edge. Then one of the purple curtains flicked, and the person was gone. The same couldn't be said for Brayden's apprehension. His gut screamed a warning at him. And three seconds later, the worry came to fruition.

The empty space which had held the hooded figure was once again full. This time, it was occupied by Chuck Delta. The cop tossed a loose glance over the hall and its occupants, then slipped in behind the curtain, as well.

Brayden's instincts told him that things were about to go bad, and he knew he had two choices. Either chase down the hooded man or flee. And Reggie's hand in his ultimately made the decision for him anyway. The moment they *could* leave safely and unnoticed, they should.

Chapter 13

Though Brayden's expression remained neutral, Reggie felt the sudden shift in his attention. Automatically, she scanned the spot in the room that seemed to hold his focus, but she couldn't see anything out of the ordinary. So she lifted up to her toes and spoke quietly into his ear.

"What's wrong? Is it Garibaldi?"

Brayden tipped his face down, just enough that she could hear his murmured response. "No. Not him. Well. Always him, actually. But not him specifically right this second."

Something in his tone made Reggie's pulse skitter nervously. "What, then?"

"Nothing."

"I can tell the difference between nothing and something."

"Stubborn."

"And?" she challenged.

He nudged her. "And it's almost our turn."

She looked up. He was right. Only two people stood between them and the sign-in table. They inched forward again, and she tried to tell herself that everything was all right. Brayden was the cop, after all. The one with the gun and the know-how. It was his *job* to know if things were okay or not. But reminding herself of all those things didn't change the fact that she was worried about whatever it was that made him tense up. And she had to factor in that he seemed to feel compelled to keep her safe. So if something *was* wrong, he might err on the side of not telling her.

But he wouldn't actually put you in harm's way, she reminded herself.

With that in mind, Reggie forced her attention to the person behind the table. Thankfully, it was a woman she didn't know—someone from the outside catering company.

She let out a breath and issued a greeting. "Hi, there. Reggie Frost. The Frost Family Diner."

The woman's manicured nail slid down the guestbook, and when she looked up, she was frowning. "I see you here. But no mention of a plus-one?"

She made herself smile. "I wasn't expecting to have company. I was hoping we could sneak him in somehow. He's thinking about making Whispering Woods his permanent home, and I know Mr. Garibaldi would appreciate having a businessman like him in town."

The woman pursed her lips, made a few notes in her book, then looked up and smiled back. "Okay. I've got it taken care of. By the time you get to your seats at table eight, it'll be like we expected him all along."

"Thank you."

Slinging her hand through Brayden's crooked elbow, Reggie faced the room and searched for their seats. But her gaze didn't get past table two. Chuck Delta stood there, one hand resting on the back of a chair, the other clasped in a handshake with their host. Jesse Garibaldi. Neither of the men were looking their way, but when the latter bent to say something near the former's ear, Reggie's instinct told her she didn't want to attract their attention. At all.

Brayden seemed to concur. The moment they were out of earshot of the sign-in table, he dragged her close to a quiet space directly away from the two men and the rest of the crowd.

"I want to ask you something, but I don't want you to panic," he said.

"You saying that makes me *want* to panic," Reggie replied.

"Sorry, sweetheart. Not trying to scare you. I just want to know if there's an alternate way out of the building."

"Yes. Behind the stage, there's—"

"Not there, either."

Reggie's heart twisted unpleasantly. "Okay. Well. Do you see the brown door frame at the other end of the room? The one with the black curtain hanging over top?"

He nodded. "Yep."

"It's used as a storage space for all the tables and chairs, but it's actually a long hallway with an emergency exit at the end. I can't guarantee it's not alarmed, though."

"It'll have to do. Come on."

Pushing his hand to the small of her back, he guided her across the room quickly—but not so quickly that they would attract unwanted attention—to the door she'd pointed out. When they reached it, he paused, looked around, then dragged her inside. As he dropped the curtain and darkness engulfed them, Reggie turned to ask exactly what was going on. But she didn't even manage to say a single word.

Brayden's arms shot out. One hand landed on her mouth, the other clasped her stomach and he flattened himself against the wall, taking her with him. And before she could react, someone else came sliding into the dark space.

Reggie froze, afraid even to breathe. She could feel her pulse thudding through her veins. Throbbing in her neck. Pounding in her head. She thought it was a miracle that their shadow-cloaked guest couldn't hear it. But the sweatshirt-clad figure—whom she was 99.9 percent sure was the same person she'd seen leap from her balcony—seemed more concerned with something happening on the other side of the curtain. He stopped. He faced the way back into the main hall for a moment, head cocked to the side like he was listening for something. But silence reigned, and after just a few moments, he bolted toward the emergency exit.

As the door at the end of the hall flung open, Reggie braced herself for an alarm. Instead, the only thing that came blasting through the air was a gust of wind. Then the door shuddered to a close, and everything went still again. But the quiet only lasted for a second. It was interrupted first by the clatter of footsteps just outside—slow but heavy—and second by the abrupt call of a woman's voice.

"Whoa! Where's the fire, Officer?" Whoever she was let out a laugh. "Oh, wait. I guess that's not your department."

And there was no mistaking that it was Chuck who answered, his reply light, but laced with tension. "Nope. I'll leave the fires for the fire department and keep the mayhem and troublemakers for myself, thanks."

"We won't find either of those things here, I hope. Should I be keeping an eye out for trouble?"

"I'm here to make sure you don't have to," Chuck said. "Of course. If you *did* happen to see something—or someone—that looked out of place, I'd definitely be the man to call."

"I think everything is pretty copacetic, Officer. Well. Unless you count the fact that Reggie Frost has a new boyfriend as out of place."

"Reggie Frost?"

At Chuck's suddenly sharp tone, Reggie felt Brayden draw in the smallest of breaths. And she couldn't blame him. Her own heart rate—which had just barely settled—jumped yet again. Why, oh, why, did small-town gossip have to include her love life? Especially right that second.

But the unknown woman didn't seem to sense the tension in the way Chuck had repeated her name, and she just let out a second laugh. "You didn't hear? She brought some hotshot businessman as her date tonight. Spent the day with him at the fair, too."

"Oh, I heard. Met him, in fact." Now Chuck sounded too casual.

The woman, though, took his words another way. "Do I detect a hint of jealousy, Officer?"

The corrupt cop seemed to be content to go with it. "What can I say? She's a pretty girl. And now that you've brought it up, I actually couldn't help but notice that she's not around. She was supposed to be at table two, but I was just there a few minutes ago and saw that her name tag's been removed. You happen to have seen her?"

"You really gonna cut in? Tell the other guy it's illegal to date an out of towner now?"

"Wouldn't be too far from what people around here believe," Chuck replied drily. "An awful lot of Whispering Woods residents seem to have that opinion already."

"True enough," said the woman. "Oh. Sorry, Officer, but there's Mary from the deli. Mind if I go catch up with her? She's supposed to order me some cheese this week, and I think she'll forget—again—if I don't mention it now."

"By all means."

"Enjoy the party. And if you're really looking for Reggie, I'd say she and that cute date of hers probably sneaked away for some privacy. Might want to check all the nooks and crannies."

"Thanks for the tip." There was a long pause, then Chuck muttered, "Privacy."

And instinctively, Reggie knew his eyes were roaming the main hall in search of aforementioned nooks and crannies. She could picture him taking a little step back. Spying the curtain-covered doorway that was right in front of his eyes. Then moving toward it.

"We need to get out of here," she whispered.

"Too late," Brayden murmured back.

He was right. The sound of feet nearing the hallway carried in. And a thump, then a muffled curse confirmed that it was Chuck.

Reggie's heart seized, and her muscles tensed, preparing for a confrontation. But before the concern could come to fruition, Brayden took ahold of her shoulders. He pushed her back against the line of coats and pressed his body flush against hers. He stared down at her for just a single moment. Then he slammed his mouth to her mouth, and fear dropped away, desire blocking out all else.

In the back of his mind, Brayden knew it was an excuse. He could've come up with some other way to get them out of the situation. Create a distraction himself. Divert attention away from the fact that Reggie was there at all.

Maybe just start a conversation with Chuck?

Except he didn't want to do any of that.

What he *did* want was to explore her mouth with his own. He wanted to hold her sweet curves against him. He wanted to do exactly what he was doing right that second. So he embraced the opportunity with enthusiasm, sliding his hand down her arm, then slipping it to her hip. He tugged her impossibly closer, eliciting a pleasant little gasp from her lips. It spurred him on. He dropped a palm to her bare knee, and Reggie lifted her leg easily, curling it around his calf.

Vaguely, Brayden was aware that Chuck had actually entered the hall. He heard the awkward shuffle, then the throat clear and the muttered apology, followed by the man's somewhat-noisy exit. Really, though, most of his awareness was centered on the woman in his arms. On her soft, yielding kiss and the sweet cinnamon scent she still managed to exude, even though she'd been off shift for over a day. On the way she curved against him like she was meant to be there.

Because she is *meant to be here.*

The firm voice in his head made him forget that the kiss had had another motivation; Brayden brought up his free hand—the one that wasn't clasping her thigh like a lifeline—and dug his fingers into the thick tresses that hung down the back of her neck. He tugged, and her head dropped back, leaving his mouth momentarily bereft. The feeling didn't last long.

He dropped his lips to her bared throat and drew them over the tender skin, tasting every exposed inch. Her skin was firm and silken, and grew hotter under his attention. Had he really just met this woman twenty-four hours earlier? It seemed impossible. Already, he was sure what was between them was going to lead to so much more.

If you can keep her safe long enough for it to happen.

The thought forced him to pull away. "We should get out of here."

Reggie drew in a breath. "It won't look weird if we don't stick around?"

Brayden shook his head. "At this point, I think it's more important to figure out what's going on with our friend in the hood."

"Now he's our friend?"

"Sure doesn't seem to be fond of Chuck. Maybe it doesn't really make him our ally, but you know what they say about the enemy of your enemy…"

"So we're going to try to do what…work *with* him? He broke into my apartment. And hit you on the head."

"I know."

"But you still want to do it, don't you?"

"Yep." He gave her a light kiss. "C'mon, sweetheart. We can fight about it later. For now, let's slip out the front exit in case he's still out back. When I do talk to him, I want it to be on my terms."

Tucking her in under his arm and turning so that anyone

who looked their way would see only him, he eased out of the hall and into the main area. No one glanced their way, but before they got quite halfway across the room, he caught sight of Chuck Delta. He and Jesse Garibaldi stood close together, and they were all but clocking the main exit. As Brayden watched, Garibaldi gestured without looking toward the spot they'd just left. He had a sneaking suspicion that the crook was about to send his sidekick back their way.

Reggie seemed to reach the same conclusion. "What now?"

He quickly weighed their options. "Back to plan A."

"Out the emergency exit?"

"It's not ideal, but we already know that Mr. Hoodie doesn't want a fight. He wants to run. Can't say I'm as sure about Garibaldi and Chuck."

"Okay."

"Don't look up and don't stop. We don't want to give anyone an excuse to talk to us. We're not going to hurry, but we're going to walk with purpose. Once we're back in the hallway, we'll duck out and head straight for the car."

"Got it."

Holding Reggie close and heeding his own instructions, Brayden strode swiftly to their destination. They made it about three feet from their escape route before he felt the hairs on the back of his neck stand up. He didn't have to look to be sure that Chuck had spotted them. Moving even more purposefully now, he put his hand on the curtain and pushed. As they slid through, he was sure he heard the corrupt cop call out Reggie's name. He ignored it in favor of dragging the pretty waitress through the hallway, then straight to the emergency exit. He tugged her outside and pressed the door shut behind them. With his mind in overdrive, he debated just straight up tearing back to the car. First, though, he glanced around in search of the hooded stranger. The man was nowhere to be seen, but Brayden's hurried search did yield a means of buying a bit more time. He spotted a discarded umbrella a couple of feet away and decided to take advantage of the idea that sprang to mind.

Quickly, he released Reggie. The weather had worsened in the last few minutes, and as he darted out to grab the umbrella, he got pummeled by heavy drops.

Reggie gave him an incredulous look as he came hurrying back. "You're worried about getting wet? Now?"

He shook his head. "Not exactly."

Flipping the umbrella to a horizontal position, he slid it into the external side-by-side door handles. Just in time, too. The doors pushed out. Then stopped. A muffled curse carried through the one-inch crack. The trick bought them a minute or two, but they still needed to move.

Wordlessly, Brayden threaded his fingers through Reggie's and pulled her along the pavement at a run. Their feet smacked the ground hard, sending splashes of water up. Above them, the sky cracked once, illuminating the parking lot as they reached the gravel overflow area. Reggie jumped, then let out a cry and twisted out of his grip. A concerned glance her way told him why. One of her high-heeled shoes had snapped. She took two limping steps. Then a third. On the fourth, lightning sparked overhead again, clearly showing off the pained wince on her face as her foot hit the ground.

To make their situation even worse, a barely distinguishable shout came from near the front of the hall. Their pursuer had exited the building. He'd probably try to head them off first, and move toward the spot they'd just abandoned next. A little belatedly, Brayden realized his little trick might backfire. When Chuck found the rigged door, he'd have even more questions and even more of a reason to come after them.

Too late to reconsider now.

He'd have to come up with a valid excuse later; it

wouldn't take more than a minute or two for the cop to catch up.

Reggie lifted her eyes to meet his, fear translating even through the dark.

Brayden stepped closer, bent to position her arm over his shoulders and lifted her off the ground.

"The first thing we do when we get somewhere safe is find you a decent pair of running shoes," he said as he carried her over the ground. "No heels. No slip-on flats. Good, old-fashioned, lace-up sneakers."

The wind picked up suddenly, then, stopping him from saying anything more. In addition to cutting his breath away, it worked against him physically, sending the sheets of rain up like an angled wall. He pushed forward through the resistance and ducked behind the nearest row of vehicles. There, he inched along as fast as he dared, thankful that at least the storm covered the sound of his boots hitting the ground. His stealthy moves got them to the edge of the lot without detection. Then he had to stop. His car was a row over, and there was a wide space between where they huddled and where it was parked.

"What now?" Reggie asked.

"I run. You pray."

He waited until the sky lit up once more, then took advantage of the sudden darkness and rolling thunder that followed. Holding Reggie close, he crossed the exposed space in a few wide steps. He then crouched down even lower to hide behind the vehicle and set her on the ground. He dragged his key from his pocket. Then paused.

"What?" Reggie prodded urgently.

"Not sure how we're gonna get out of here with any kind of subtlety," he replied. "Even if Chuck didn't get a good enough look at me to know that he should be searching for my car specifically, the second he sees us pulling out of the lot, he'll make the connection."

"There's a back road. If you follow this gravel lot even farther back, there's a narrow path at the end. It's mostly used for people who want to bring dirt bikes or ATVs or whatever. But it's definitely wide enough for your car."

"And it'll take us out?"

She nodded. "It might not be the smoothest ride. Or the shortest. It'll probably add twenty minutes to the trip back to town. But it *does* lead to the main road."

Brayden tapped his key on his soaked thigh. "Now all we need to do is get into the car without getting caught."

"We can roll it back in Neutral," Reggie suggested. "As long as the rain keeps pounding down like this, he won't be able to hear us. And you can't see the car from here because it's sloped too much—which works in our favor too, actually—but once we get down there, we'll be able to push it all the way to the trees before we even start it."

It was a good plan. Except for one thing.

"The second we open the door, the interior light will come on," he said.

Reggie held out her hand. "Give me the keys."

"What?"

"Trust me."

"All right."

He held out the keys, and she took them. He watched as she held still and closed her eyes. She looked like she might be counting. He opened his mouth to ask her if she was, but lightning opened up the sky then, and Reggie came to life. She opened the driver's-side door. She leaped into the car. She lifted a hand and flicked off the light. Then she dropped down beside him with the keys on her index finger.

"Done," she gasped.

He stared at her for a second, then tugged her close and issued a swift kiss. "Genius."

She smiled. "My brain works better than my body, apparently."

Brayden couldn't help but shake his head and grin back. "I'd argue against that."

Even though he couldn't see in the dark, he imagined a blush as she deflected his statement. "Are we going to do this, or just stand around flirting until we get caught?"

"I'll assume the second part wasn't a real offer," he teased. "You want to guide me from the passenger side?"

"Sure."

She scurried around the car, and when the other door inched open, Brayden got to work. He put the car into Neutral and positioned his upper body against the steering wheel while keeping his feet on the ground. His visibility was terrible, but there was no way to make it any better without attracting attention, so he worked by feel. It didn't take much to get the vehicle moving. Reggie was right about the slope, and as soon as they hit it, the tires crunched along smoothly until they eased it to a stop near the trees she'd mentioned. It was pitch-black, though, and the roadway really was narrow.

It'll have to do, he thought, climbing into the car.

"Ready?" he said to Reggie, who was already waiting in the passenger seat.

"If I say no, will another option magically appear in front of us?"

"Doubtful."

"Then I guess I'm ready."

"Okay. Let's get this over with."

He turned the engine over, left the light off and plunged them into the dark woods.

Chapter 14

Even though Brayden was driving slowly and cautiously, Reggie held both her breath and the handle on the door. The blackness around them was broken only by the occasional flash of lightning. And rather than reassuring her, each brief moment of illumination just reminded her of how precariously close they were to the trees. And the subsequent darkness after each flash brought a terrifying near blindness. She was hyperaware that it would only take one strong bump—into a rock, a hole in the ground or just about anything else—and they'd find themselves slamming into a tree trunk.

Still better than facing Chuck, she thought.

But a moment later, they hit a particularly solid bump, and she wondered if it was true. At least Chuck could be deflected with words. Her fear…not so much.

"You okay over there?" Brayden's soft question almost made her jump.

She exhaled. "Just scared."

"Will it help if I turn on the lights?"

"Maybe. Are we far enough away from the hall?"

"Shouldn't you be telling me the answer to that?"

She made herself peer out the window, trying to assess the distance they'd traveled, then nodded. "I think we're good."

Brayden flicked the switch, and the path in front of them lit up. "Better?"

Reggie started to nod again, then sighed and shook her head instead. "It's not the drive that's scaring me the most. It's everything else."

"Break it down for me."

"What do you mean?"

"Tell me everything that you're scared of, one by one."

She frowned. "Well, for starters, I'm scared of Chuck."

Brayden tapped the steering wheel. "What scares you most about him?"

"Besides the fact that I saw him shoot someone?"

"Yep."

"I'm afraid that he's going to figure out for sure that I lied to him about not being at the diner when the shooting happened."

"So don't let him."

"It's not that easy."

"It is if you *make* it that easy," he argued. "Just keep everything as close to the truth as possible. You really only altered one little detail. The time you left the diner. A half hour earlier, and you really would've missed the whole thing."

Reggie fixed her eyes out the windshield for a second, watching the wipers swing back and forth. The truth of Brayden's statement hit her like a weight in the chest. *Thirty minutes.* It made the difference between her being an unwilling witness to a crime, and her being completely ignorant of it. Really, it could've been even less than thirty minutes. Maybe as few as ten. Or five.

What if she'd taken a few extra moments to look at her phone? What if she hadn't been so eager to be efficient, and so enthusiastic to get home to her bathtub and her wine?

"Hey," Brayden said. "I wasn't trying to make your face

get all scrunched up and even more worried. I was trying to make you feel better."

She fought to smooth out her expression and failed. "I know. But now I'm thinking about what being too efficient cost me."

"Would you rather be clueless?"

She considered it. Would she? On the one hand, she'd been perfectly content to *not* be chased around her own town in fear of her life. But was it really better to be unaware of the danger at all? She poured Chuck Delta's coffee in the morning. She served him pie. But underneath his polite expressions of gratitude and the badge on his chest... Now she knew there was something far more sinister. And that didn't even begin to take into account Jesse Garibaldi's involvement.

Reggie shivered again. She honestly wasn't sure if it was better to be blissfully ignorant or not.

"I don't know," she finally said with a sigh. "I guess it's probably different for you, because your job *requires* you to think about what's lurking around every corner."

"It's not always bad guys and imminent danger. Sometimes I meet a pretty woman," Brayden joked. "Every now and then I even get to kiss one and go all knight-in-shining-armor."

She opened her mouth to tell him she'd rather skip the damsel in distress role in favor of something else, then stopped as another worry hit her.

"The umbrella," she said.

"The umbrella?"

"When Chuck went around the building, he had to have seen it jammed into the door handles. I can't explain *that* away with an altered timeline."

"You don't have to. I'll take responsibility. I'll tell him I was trying to make sure no one followed us for *other* reasons."

"And if he wants to know why we weren't there when he came around?"

"I'll tell him my *other* reason was a fruitful endeavor."

Reggie couldn't quite suppress a laugh. "Okay, putting aside your lascivious-minded lies... You're going to accompany me if Chuck decides to interrogate me?"

"If I have to."

"Brayden..."

"Reggie."

"You can't do your job if you're just looking out for me all the time."

"I happen to be an expert multitasker." His mouth turned up for a second before he added, "And besides that, he can't really accuse us of lying about the umbrella without coming up with a good excuse for doing it."

"He's a cop. Isn't that good enough?"

"It might be good enough if he weren't corrupt. But since he is...he's got to tread lightly," Brayden stated.

"Unless he thinks he can come up with some other valid reason," she countered.

"Broken any laws lately?"

"No."

"Got a stack of unpaid parking violations?"

"No."

"So. No valid reason for questioning you."

"You make it sound so simple."

"What if he accused us of lying and we went to his boss? Or worse, what if we went public? I'm all about the logic, Reggie. Working things through, bit by bit. Makes it a lot easier to come at a problem if you're not overwhelmed by the scope."

"Is that what you do with work?" she wondered aloud.

He issued a nod. "Yep. Only kind of backward. I take all the pieces of a case, all the clues, then put them back together."

"Like a puzzle."

"Exactly."

"You must be pretty patient."

"One of my finer qualities. No hotheadedness for this cop." He smiled, then made a sour but rueful face. "Except where Garibaldi's concerned. Him, I wouldn't mind losing my temper over."

His admission tugged at her heart, and her mind went to the transparent fury she's spied on his face when he spotted Jesse Garibaldi. And the thick thread of sympathy and the accompanying need to ease his suffering hit her hard enough to startle her. Her throat tightened and tears threatened as Reggie realized that she wanted more than anything to see the case through so that Brayden could have some peace.

The need grew even stronger when, in a thick, emotion-roughened voice, he added, "I think that's the first time I've ever said anything like that aloud."

She reached across the center console to squeeze his arm. "I can't imagine holding it in."

"I don't even know if I could say I've been holding it in. That'd be giving me credit for doing it consciously. It's more like…being on autopilot, I guess. Working toward this end for as long as I can remember. I never paused to think about what would happen if I got close to success." His hands tightened on the wheel. "It sounds ridiculous, but I didn't realize how angry I am."

"You have every right to be angry," Reggie replied. "Garibaldi is responsible for your father's death."

A heavy exhale escaped Brayden's lips. "I know he is. And I know I can't put him away for that any more than I can haul off and punch him. But I'm utterly convinced that I'll catch him for something else here in Whispering Woods. Possibly something big."

"That's a good thing, isn't it? Catching him, I mean."

"It's the *only* thing."

"And *that's* bad?"

He seemed to hesitate before answering. "It's making me selfish."

The statement puzzled her. "What is?"

"I'm worried about what I'm going to do when it's over. I've dedicated so much time and put so much energy into finding Garibaldi. My only goal's been to bring him down…" He trailed off and shrugged helplessly. "What if shutting the case leaves a hole? What if it doesn't give me any closure?"

"I don't know about closure," Reggie admitted, "but I do know that there are *so* many other people in the world who've lost someone they love to other guys like Garibaldi. They need a good cop like you."

His shoulders straightened a bit, but he still sighed. "They do. But I'm not as sure as you are that I'll be able to shift gears so easily."

It was her turn to hesitate. Her heart was full of unnamed feeling. Probably far more than was reasonable for how short of a time she'd known him. But whether or not it was unreasonable didn't change the fact that it was there.

"Brayden." Her voice was so soft that it barely carried over the rain. "I know we just met, but I feel like I've known you for years. I don't think I've ever been more comfortable with someone. I've been unsure about a lot of things in my life, but I'm sure about who you are. You're a good man. You're kind and caring. And all of me is certain that those things aren't just going to disappear once you're done with Garibaldi. You'll repurpose your life, even if that just means becoming even more dedicated to the other parts of your work."

"You think so?"

"I know so."

At last, his hands loosened a little on the wheel, and he

turned her way just long enough to send her a heart-melting smile. "Where would I be if I hadn't met you?"

She couldn't help but smile back. "You'd probably have already solved the whole case because rescuing me wouldn't have eaten up all your time."

"Trust me. Even if that were true, it'd be worth the delay."

"Careful," she replied. "I'm going to get used to having you stroke my ego."

"That's not good?"

"I might start to expect a lifetime of it." The words were out before she could stop them—before her mind could catch up to her mouth and clue in to the implication of what she'd just said.

Brayden had to force his mouth from turning up into the over-the-top grin that wanted to surface, and instead made himself repeat the same sentence he'd uttered a few moments earlier. "That's not good?"

He caught the surprise on her face. "It's… I don't know. Presumptuous?"

"Did you think I was kidding when I said those things back at your place? That I didn't mean it when I suggested making Whispering Woods home?"

"I didn't think you were kidding, exactly. Just…"

"Just what?"

"It's crazy, isn't it? To talk about a lifetime after a day."

"Yep."

"That's it?"

"Yep."

She made an exasperated noise. "Brayden. If this is about you thinking that someone has to be insane to date a cop, I've got news for you. There are *plenty* of sane people in relationships with police officers."

"Have you got credible sources to back up that claim?"

"How about I'll research it and get back to you another day?"

"I'll hold you to it."

They both laughed, but after a few seconds, Reggie turned abruptly serious.

"What if it goes badly?" she asked.

"What makes you think it would?" Brayden replied.

From the corner of his eye, he saw her gaze drop to her hands, which fidgeted restlessly in her lap. "Because I've done the crazy thing once before, remember?"

"You mean yurt man?"

"Shut up. And yes, I mean him. That piece of my past doesn't worry you?"

"Why would it? You told me you ran away with him to prove something, and you also told me you're done with all of that."

"I know."

"But?"

"I'm scared of making a mistake."

"Do you think that's what I might turn out to be?"

Her response was immediate and rang true. "No."

Spontaneously, Brayden tapped the brakes hard, bringing the car to a complete stop. He shifted to Park, turned to Reggie and—ignoring her startled expression—cupped her cheek.

"Did you love him?" he wanted to know.

Her eyes were wide, and she shook her head as much as his light grip would allow. "I don't think so."

"Then you didn't."

"What?"

"If you loved him, you would know, Reggie. The fact that you said *don't* think *so* means more than if you denied it altogether."

"Did you love Chandra?" she asked.

He nodded once. "Yes. In a childish, knowing-it's-never-going-to-work-out kind of way. First love is like that."

"How do you know if you're in love?" Her throat worked as she swallowed nervously, but her eyes stayed on him. "Or if you're *falling* in love?"

He slid his hand up from her face to her temple, running his thumb over her brow. "It's partly in here." He dropped his hand to her chest and pressed his palm to her bare skin. "And it's partly in here."

"And you believe that someone just knows?" she wondered aloud.

"I believe it can take time to realize it's happening. And that love can grow slowly. But I also believe when you meet someone, you can already see the potential."

"And that's what you see now?"

He spread his fingers out so that each point touched her separately. "Don't you?"

Her eyes came up to his, their emerald hue darkening to forest green in the dim light. "Yes."

"See?" he said.

"See what?"

"There was no hesitation in that *yes*. When you know, sweetheart, you know." He leaned across the car and kissed her slowly and thoroughly. "Should we head into town?"

"Probably," she agreed breathlessly. "But I don't think we even decided what our destination is."

"Good point," he said as he realized she was right.

They hadn't discussed where to go next—getting away from the party had seemed like a good enough temporary goal. He started to ask Reggie what she wanted to do, but the abrupt ring of his phone cut him off before he could speak.

He pulled it from his pocket and answered without checking the screen. "Maxwell here."

The voice on the other end was worried. "You still with my daughter?"

"Mr. Frost?"

"Yes. Are you with her?"

"She's sitting right here with me in my car. Would you like to speak with her?"

"Please."

As puzzled as he was concerned, Brayden handed the phone to Reggie, who took it with a frown.

"Dad?" she said. "What's wrong?"

For several seconds, she listened silently, then she sighed. "Yes, Dad. We'll get there as quickly as we can."

A pause.

"I don't know. Ten minutes?"

Another pause.

"No, you don't have to come looking. I promise we'll head straight there." She hung up and held out the phone. "Sorry."

"Guess I don't have to ask where you want to go?" Brayden said drily.

"I'm pretty sure he'll *actually* come out looking if we don't show up."

He put the car back into Drive. "What happened?"

"The silent alarm was triggered at the diner about ten minutes ago. I'm the primary contact with the alarm company, and when they couldn't reach me, they dispatched an officer—not Chuck, thankfully—to the restaurant. Which they found unlocked. And my purse and cell phone were left behind, so then they showed up at my dad's door. He told them I was fine and at the Gala. But when he called a friend who was there, she told him I wasn't at the party anymore. He just asked me if you kidnapped me." She shook her head. "I'd laugh if the truth weren't so much worse."

Brayden asked for the address, then went silent again, his mind churning. She was right. The truth *was* worse. Or at least as bad. This development also added a whole list of other things to consider. Like whether or not the silent alarm was legitimate or fabricated. And what either scenario would mean.

As he navigated the car from the rough path onto the paved road, Reggie broke the silence, voicing the very things he was thinking about.

"Do you think Chuck staged the break-in?" she asked.

"To give himself an excuse to talk to you, you mean?"

"Yes."

"It'd be a gutsy move. And not in a good way. You're right that a break-in would give him a reason to talk to you, but it'd also give other people the same leeway. He'd have to be pretty desperate—or stupidly cocky—to let a whole other set of cops poke around near the crime scene he created."

"So if it's real…"

"It's not good, either. Chuck'll need to get in there fast to make sure he's on top of any damage control that needs to happen."

"What should we do?"

"Let's just start with talking to your dad. See what the police said to him and vice versa."

"Okay." She only went quiet for a moment, though, before asking, "Would the guy in the hood have broken into the diner?"

Brayden was surprised the idea hadn't occurred to him in the first place. "Could be. He does seem to be stalking us a bit."

"Me," Reggie corrected softly. "He was at *my* apartment with *my* shoe. He showed up at the diner where *I* was meant to be."

"Hey, now. He did clock *me* over the head," he replied lightly, trying to diffuse the fear that was evident in her voice.

"Who do you think he is?"

"I don't know. But figuring that out is pretty high on my to-do list."

His mind started working again, mentally prioritizing.

Making sure Reggie was safe was first, followed closely by seeking out their hooded friend's identity. He still needed more on Tyler Strange's presence—possibly through his sister—and to establish a connection between his shooting and Garibaldi, then find a way to bring down the man himself. It seemed funny to put Garibaldi near the bottom. Especially when justice was so close that Brayden could practically reach out and grab it.

So follow this case, he said to himself. *Connect the dots and it will work out.*

"Brayden?"

He jerked his eyes toward Reggie. "Uh-huh?"

"You've got a funny look on your face."

"Just thinking."

Without pressing for more, she nodded out the window. "We're almost there. It's left at the stop sign, then the third house on the right."

"Got it."

He followed her instructions, found a spot and guided the car to a smooth stop. He reached for the door handle, but Reggie's hand landed on his shoulder, stopping him.

"I need to say sorry in advance again."

He lifted an eyebrow. "For?"

"Look at the porch."

"At the porch? Or at the bearded man staring at us from the door?"

"That would be my dad."

"Hmm."

"What?"

"I can't tell from here whether or not he's packing a shotgun."

She groaned. "I guess we should get this over with."

Brayden fought a smile. "All right. But sit tight until I can run around and open your door. If I'm going to be accused of kidnapping, I at least want to do it in style."

She rolled her eyes, but waited as he let himself out, then made his way to her side, where he made a show of opening the door and offering her his hand. She even took it and let him pull her from the car, then threaded their arms together.

When they reached the doorstep, her dad was waiting, and Brayden suddenly felt self-conscious. A little nervous, even. He slowed a bit to process the unexpected feeling, and stared back at the man standing in the doorway. For a second, he felt like he ought to recognize him. Had he seen him around town? At the diner, maybe. Brayden squinted, trying unsuccessfully to place him. He had a grandfatherly appearance—white hair, matching beard and rimless glasses perched on the edge of his nose. His eyes, though, were sharp. Not quite calculating, but more than shrewd as they gave Brayden a solid once-over. As his gaze moved to Reggie, it changed. Her father's affection was clear in that single look. No matter what she'd said about his criticism of her past life choices, the man adored her.

The realization relaxed him. However overzealous Frost's protection was, it came from a place of love rather than suspicion. Brayden could appreciate that.

Giving Reggie a little squeeze, he disentangled his arm and reached out his hand toward her father. "Mr. Frost."

"Daughter's strangely mysterious and spontaneous date," the man replied, giving his hand a firm shake.

"Detective Brayden Maxwell."

A hint of surprise flashed across Reggie's father's face. "Is that right?"

"Yes, sir. Seems like a good idea to be upfront about that."

"Appreciate it. Helps make me feel a little more secure

about my only child running around with you, too." The older man lifted a craggy brow. "But I suspect you knew it would."

"Yes, sir."

Frost nodded. "Good to be honest with the future father-in-law."

Reggie drew in sharp breath. "Dad!"

Brayden's own mouth worked silently for a minute, unsure what to say. But then the older man let out a loud guffaw, and Brayden forgot his surprise as he suddenly realized why the man looked vaguely familiar.

"You're the parade Santa Claus," he blurted.

Frost scratched at his white beard and said, "Not sure what that has to do with anything. But yeah, for one day every year, I take on the role."

"Just something Reggie mentioned earlier."

"Already telling you our secrets, huh?" Her father's brows knit together for a second before he sighed and added, "Well, Detective Maxwell, it's more than a bit chilly out here. So why don't you go ahead and come in? I'll make tea, and while it brews, you can tell me a little bit about why the weekend you meet my daughter is the same weekend my restaurant gets broken into for the first time since it opened. Because my gut's screaming at me that it's somehow connected. And in my experience, gut feelings are rarely wrong."

"Mine, too," Brayden conceded.

"Good to know we're starting off on the same page. You can call me Cyrus."

Brayden grinned at Reggie's obvious embarrassment, but under that, he felt a tingle of anticipation, and he was doubly glad he'd been honest about his identity. Cyrus Frost was one of the men who'd objected to Garibaldi and his takeover of the town. He could potentially be an excellent source of information.

And Brayden was suddenly *really* looking forward to tea.

Chapter 15

When her dad disappeared to prepare the tea, Reggie shifted from foot to foot, feeling self-conscious as Brayden gave the sitting room a thorough once-over. His eyes seemed to take in every detail. The trinkets on the fireplace mantel. The drooping plant in the corner.

What did he think?

For some reason, she was more nervous now than she had been since the second she met him. Sure she'd been scared for her life. But this...

Much worse.

Being worried about what her father would think—and what the big cop would think of him in return—had been the furthest thing from her mind. But now it seemed all-important. This was her childhood home. Where everything good and bad happened for the first twenty years of her life. It was the space in which she was *built*. And the man she'd confessed to falling in love with was standing in the middle of it while the man who raised her brewed *tea*. It seemed more surreal than the fact that she'd somehow wound up in the middle of a police investigation.

She watched as Brayden's gaze came to rest on the only photo in the room. Automatically, Reggie tensed. In the framed shot, she sat at the front, young and fresh faced. Behind her, with one hand on her shoulder, was her father, just as white haired then as he was now. And beside him stood a frail-looking woman whose eyes were the exact same shade of green as her own.

"Your mom?" Brayden asked.

Reggie nodded and stepped closer. "Yes."

"You look a lot like her."

"Thanks." She exhaled a shaky breath. "They were both forty already when I was born. My dad always says his one regret was not having me earlier because it meant we got to have such little time as a family."

Reggie's hand sought his palm, her fingers weaving through his and offering a mutually reassuring squeeze. They stood like that for a long moment, both their gazes locked on the photo, united in an unspoken connection.

"Your dad still looked like Santa, even back then, hmm?" Brayden nudged her gently as he said it.

Reggie breathed out again, this time a little easier. "You do realize that I didn't think you'd be *meeting* him, when I told you that."

"You mean before he was offering up your hand in marriage?" he teased.

Heat crept up her face. "If he tries to give you a goat… just walk away."

He freed his fingers to slide them up her arm, then to her cheek. "Maybe I *want* a goat."

She leaned into his touch. "A goat *and* a crazy lady?"

"I'm a complicated man."

"Apparently."

His mouth came down to hers in a light, quick kiss. He pulled away just a heartbeat before her dad's voice carried from the hall.

"Can someone clear a spot?"

"Yes, sir," Brayden called back, then added in a low voice. "Or I could kidnap you for real and we could run away for good?"

"Don't make promises you can't keep," she murmured back.

"Trust me," he replied. "I don't."

With her heart fluttering pleasantly in her chest, Reggie perched on the edge of the couch and let her dad serve the tea. She was still nervous. She felt like a sixteen-year-old getting ready for prom. Hoping her date would meet her dad's exacting standards, and she was hyperconscious of every detail of the interaction between the two men.

Brayden didn't ask for coffee instead. That would earn a point with her father. He had a deep attachment to his British heritage, and resented those who rejected the homage he often paid to his roots.

Brayden complimented a small, carved box on the fireplace mantel, as well. Another big bonus. Most people thought it was just another knickknack. But it was actually a commissioned piece of work, made by a local artisan at her father's request as an anniversary gift for her mother. Truly one of a kind.

The real test would come, though, when her dad decided to cut through the niceties. Honesty and loyalty were the two things her dad valued most. It's what had made him so successful as a businessman.

She didn't have to wait long before her father set down his teacup and matter-of-factly stated, "Well, Detective Maxwell, I'd ask you what your intentions are with my daughter, but the truth is, she's more than capable of handling herself. And I'm a little more curious about what's brought you to Whispering Woods in the first place."

Brayden didn't hesitate. "I'm here on a scouting mission. Following a long-term lead."

"The details of which are confidential, I'm sure," her dad responded.

"Trying to keep it that way."

"Reggie's not making it easy?"

"You could say that."

"Pretty typical."

Reggie rolled her eyes. "You two do know that I'm sitting right here?"

Her dad gave her a too-innocent look, and Brayden seemed to be deliberately avoiding meeting her eyes. For a second, irritation reigned. But it faded quickly as a sudden vision of a future like this filled her mind. Comfortable bickering over Christmas dinner. Her father and Brayden teasing her mercifully, all in the name of affection.

"I could just poison your turkey, you know," she muttered.

"What?" The in-unison reply made her laugh out loud.

"Nothing," she said, fighting the need to giggle uncontrollably. "I am *not* intentionally ruining a police investigation."

"Not intentionally," her father repeated.

"Dad!"

Brayden finally came to her defense, a small smile crossing his face as he did. "She's actually been helping me quite a bit."

"By getting you access to an exclusive party?"

"Yes."

"What for?"

"To speak to Jesse Garibaldi."

Reggie saw her father's face sour immediately. And Brayden obviously picked up the disapproval, as well.

"Not a fan?" he asked.

Her dad turned her way for a long second, and she got the impression he was trying to decide what to say. For *her* benefit.

Why?

It wasn't exactly a secret that Cyrus Frost disliked the other man. He might not advertise it around town—it wouldn't have been good for business, after all—but he hadn't ever tried to hide the fact from Reggie. It seemed like a strange thing to start doing now.

"Dad?" she prodded.

"The man treats this town like his own personal bank account," he announced, pulling his gaze from her face to his hands, then grunting and lifted it again to look at Brayden. "Or maybe that's not the right label. He's more like a loan shark. Lending money to the desperate, then squeezing it back in blood when they can't afford to pay."

Reggie's stomach turned. She had a sinking feeling that she knew what he meant.

"You always told me that you sold the diner to him because you wanted to," she said. "That it was a better option than trying to mortgage it all over again."

Her dad sighed heavily. "What did you want me to tell you, kiddo? That I got scammed? You were sixteen. The bills for your mom's treatment were piling up. The travel expenses alone were enough to break us."

"I knew all that money stuff, Dad. But I didn't think you were forced to make the choice. How did Garibaldi do it?" Reggie asked.

"Came into the diner late one night with an offer. A loan. Said he'd heard about our problems and wanted to help. He put the loan in the form of a lease, which we were supposed to be able to work off. But when your mom died, he came after me with some fine print garbage about a time limit that we never discussed. Took the ownership of the business straight out from under me, and slapped down the real lease instead."

"So this whole time we've been paying him rent…you only agreed because you thought we'd continue to own the diner?"

"Yep."

"That's a whole decade of payments!"

"I know, kiddo."

Brayden's expression had grown dark, and when he interjected with a question, his voice was just as stormy. "I'm guessing you're not the only one he's done this to."

Her dad's mouth tightened. "Highly doubtful."

"Why didn't you go to the police, Dad?"

"All aboveboard," he said grimly. "Had a lawyer down in Freemont take a look. Even though I was damned sure that the fine print came *after* the contract was signed, it was my word against Garibaldi's. And he was—still is— the one with the money, isn't he? Plus, with everything we were going through at the time…I guess it seemed like I had more important things to focus on."

Reggie felt like her heart was breaking all over again. And she felt more than a little naive, too. For a decade, she'd truly believed her father had a choice in turning over the diner. Maybe not a choice he *liked*, but a choice nevertheless. And somehow she'd assumed they'd eventually get the restaurant back. Her father had talked about buying it again, but his dislike of Garibaldi had been holding him back. Or that's what she'd always thought. It was the reason Reggie had been seriously considering asking Garibaldi herself. That very night. She sat back against the couch and nursed the ache in her chest as her father and Brayden continued to talk.

"Who were the others?" the big detective asked. "Do you know?"

"I couldn't give you a list, even if I wanted to," her dad replied.

"Confidentiality agreement, or you don't know?"

"Both. I was never a hundred percent sure of who went in willingly and who was forced like I was. I tried to rally a few troops, so to speak. Went around and asked a bunch of business owners—or former business owners, I guess I should say—if they'd been through the same thing. Poked the wrong one somewhere along the line. Next thing I know,

Garibaldi's lawyer is on my doorstep with the threat of a lawsuit."

"And you backed off."

"I did. But a couple of the guys I'd talked to, they got loud instead. Decided they wanted to pursue getting their businesses back. Kinda hoped something would come of it."

"Nothing did?"

"Nope. They took off. Walked away from their businesses and Whispering Woods altogether."

Brayden's eyes sought Reggie. "These are the same guys you mentioned back at my cabin? The ones who questioned Garibaldi's motives?"

She tossed a regretful look at her father, then nodded. "But I didn't know about the rest."

Brayden's face remained grim as he directed another question toward her dad. "Cyrus, do you keep in contact with those former businessmen?"

Reggie's father shook his head. "More or less dropped off the grid."

"You mind if I grab their names? I can ask you in an official police capacity if you'd feel more comfortable."

"Not necessary. Francis Taulk and Vincent Overgaard." Her dad inclined his head. "Go ahead. I can tell that you're itching to call it in."

Brayden smiled gratefully, kissed Reggie's forehead, then pushed to his feet and slipped from the room, leaving Reggie to face her father alone. She braced herself for a hundred questions, cautions and accusations. Instead, her dad just lifted his tea and took a thoughtful sip.

"I like him," he stated.

"You—what?"

"I like him."

"You've known him for ten minutes."

"I'm a good judge of character."

"Ten min—"

"*You* like him," her dad pointed out.

"That's different," Reggie replied.

"How?"

"Because…"

"Because?"

"You think that I have terrible taste! You've told me that a hundred times."

"Only as far as Wave was concerned."

"His name was Ocean."

"Right." He took another small sip. "You know what?" She sighed. "What?"

"Just want to point something out."

"I'm not sure I want to know what it is."

"Just a small thing."

"Fine. Tell me."

"Well. It just so happens that *Brayden* is a name I can remember."

Selecting his brother's number from his phone's address book, Brayden slipped through the nearest door in the hallway to talk in peace. With his mind on the case, he was oblivious to the fact that it led to a bedroom until he was already standing inside. When he flipped up the light switch, though, he knew immediately that it had to have been Reggie's. It wasn't exactly a shrine, but the decor definitely paid tribute to her younger self. A large mirror hung over a desk, and it was decorated with concert tickets from all over Oregon and Washington. A faded poster—signed and dated—was mounted to the wall adjacent to the bed, and a stack of beaded necklaces hung from the footboard.

It all made Brayden smile. He had no problem imagining Reggie as a headstrong, rock-and-roll-obsessed teen. In fact, he didn't have to imagine it. There was photographic evidence tucked into one corner of a bookshelf. Reggie grinned at the camera, her fingers lifted in a peace sign.

Her fire-engine red hair was tied into a thick braid that hung down to her waist, and her torn jeans and black T-shirt said it all. Grinning, he leaned even closer, then ran his index finger over her image.

"Brayden?"

The disembodied voice startled him, and he jumped back guiltily before he clued in that it had come from the phone. He'd hit the autodial by mistake.

"Brayden?"

He lifted the phone to his ear. "Sorry, Harley."

"Still distracted?"

"You could say."

"Does this have something to do with the questionable witness you mentioned when you sent over the photos yesterday?"

"I didn't say she was questionable," Brayden protested.

"Also didn't say the witness was a *she*," Harley replied. "She pretty?"

"Are her looks relevant?"

"They are if *she* is the good distraction."

"She's not."

"She's not pretty or she's not a good distraction?" his brother teased.

Brayden ground his teeth together. "She's pretty."

"Not all that pretty if she's not a good distraction."

"Harley."

"Sorry, Bray. You're just leaving yourself wide-open." His brother chuckled, but his next question was spoken in a more serious tone. "You connect the shooting to Garibaldi? Or figure out what the hell he's doing there in the first place?"

"Not yet. But I'm working on it. In the meantime, I've got a favor to ask you."

"Anything that gets us a step closer."

"I want you to track two names for me. Francis Taulk and Vincent Overgaard. See if you can get current whereabouts."

His brother picked up on his doubtful tone right away. "You're thinking my search won't turn up anything good?"

Brayden cast a quick look toward the door to make sure he was still alone. "This entire town is full of people who owe Garibaldi something. But apparently, three men didn't like that much."

"And these guys you want me to look up…"

"Two of the three, yes."

"And the third?"

"Sitting in the other room with his daughter."

"His daughter," Harley said thoughtfully. "Ah. She's the pretty girl."

Brayden rolled his eyes to himself. "Yeah, just so happens that she is."

"Sounds like a potential conflict already, Bray."

"Not gonna argue that. But at least they're on our side. Rest of the town thinks that Garibaldi walks on water." He paused. "And speaking of the rest of the town… Turns out Tyler Strange has a sister."

Harley let out a whistle. "No kidding? How'd that slip by us?"

"Complicated."

"Damn."

"I know. I've got a potential meet-up set to go with her tomorrow. Hoping it'll be fruitful."

"All right. I'll look these names up as soon as I can get to the station."

"And I'll keep making connections on this end."

"Brayden?"

"Yeah?"

"Stay objective."

"None of this has ever been objective."

There was another long pause. This one heavy. Weighted

with fifteen years of searching and planning and searching some more.

"It's going to happen," Harley finally said. "We're going to make sure it does."

"I know."

"I'll call you when I have anything."

"Likewise."

Brayden clicked the phone off and closed his eyes. He wasn't anywhere near foolish enough to pretend that he'd be able to be objective where Reggie's safety was concerned.

It didn't mean that he couldn't do his job. Caring about her and taking down Garibaldi weren't mutually exclusive.

You hope.

The thought gave him pause. Mostly because he wasn't sure which side he would choose, if it came down to it. Would he pick Reggie over getting the justice he'd been seeking for the past decade and a half? Not her life—that would never be a question. Brayden valued life above giving the man what he deserved, no question.

But Reggie herself...

Could he walk away from her if it meant losing the momentum he'd finally gained in pursuing Garibaldi? His gut said no.

With a sigh, Brayden tucked his phone in his pocket and turned to leave the room. As he spun and stepped forward, though, he crashed straight into something soft and warm and already familiar.

"Reggie." His hands came up to steady her as she stumbled from the impact.

"Hey," she greeted breathlessly.

"Hey," he said back. "What's wrong?"

"Nothing. I just—" She glanced toward the door and lowered her voice. "My dad thinks I'm in the bathroom."

Brayden followed her look, then replied drily, "I somehow doubt that."

"Well I told him that's where I was going. He couldn't very well accuse me of lying outright."

"Why *were* you lying?"

"I wanted to warn you. I *may* have accidentally implied that you're spending the night at my house."

"What?"

Her wince was visible. "I complained about how late it was, and said I was looking forward to getting home. He tried to insist that I stay here. I love him, but as long as he's not a target, I *really* don't want to be here under lock and key. So…"

Brayden ran a hand over his head. "You don't think that might've been worse?"

"I don't know. I was desperate and he was going on about how much he liked you. It was the first thing that popped into my head."

"Is he readying his shotgun for real now?"

"My dad doesn't have a shotgun."

"Uh-huh."

"He doesn't. And besides that, he seemed relieved."

"Right."

"Really," she insisted. "He said having a cop on my couch seemed safe enough."

He stifled a groan. "Yeah. On your couch. He sounds thrilled."

"You don't have to actually do it. Just say you are."

"You want me to lie to him now, too? Nope. Not happening."

"If you don't, he's going to make me stay here."

"Maybe that wouldn't be a bad thing."

She shook her head right away. "If I do stay here, my dad won't be safe. So unless you're willing to sleep on *his* couch…"

This time, he *couldn't* stifle the groan. "Fine."

Her face brightened. "You'll do it?"

"I'm not going to lie. If I tell your father I'm sleeping on your couch, then that's exactly what I'm going to do."

"Seriously?"

"Yeah, seriously."

"But—"

Her dad's voice carried through the hall, cutting her off. "Brayden!"

Covering a smile, Brayden called back, "Sir?"

"Your tea's getting cold."

With a kiss on Reggie's wrinkled-up nose, he slipped back toward the living room, where he found the older man nowhere near the tea. Instead, he stood to one side of the wood fireplace, his fingers curled on the family photo.

"How long until she's done with her phony bathroom break?" he asked.

"Best guess? Two minutes."

"She probably thinks I called you back here to give you some kind of warning about staying on the couch."

"Did you?"

"No. I figure my thoughts as her father go without saying. But I want you to know that I trust you with her safety."

"Thank you."

"It's not flattery." The older man shook his head. "It's a responsibility. And a big deal. For me."

"I'm guessing you mean more than just the fact that she's your only daughter?"

"You guess right. Garibaldi is dangerous. And I'm going to tell you something I've never told my daughter, and which I'd prefer not to get back to her."

"All right."

"When all that stuff was going down nine years ago with him ripping me and my buddies off, Garibaldi came to the diner himself. Did you know there was a bombing on Main Street at about that time?" Cyrus studied him for a second. "I'm guessing you did."

"Yes, sir."

"Then I don't have to explain, and it probably won't surprise you that Garibaldi brought it up during our meeting."

"Not in the least."

"The man was smug. Pointed out that if the bomb had gone off just a few doors down, it would've taken out the diner. Said that things might be easier if we left town. And when I made it clear that we were staying in spite of his thinly veiled threats, he warned me that not keeping my opinions to myself could have some negative consequences for me, too. Not just *me*. Me, *too*. Heavy on that emphasis there."

"But you still chose to stay?"

Cyrus straightened up. "I don't like being bullied, and I'm far from a coward. I'd reached my breaking point. So I turned it around on him. I alluded to having some inside knowledge about Francis and Vincent and the bomb, too. Told him I had provisions in my will that could have negative consequences for *him* if anything happened to me."

"And it worked?" Brayden asked.

"Yep. The man wasn't too happy. Left in a big hurry that day. I sat on eggshells for about three months after. Was pretty damned relieved when Reggie went out of town for school. I waited it out. And nothing ever came of Garibaldi's threat. If anything, things became pleasant." He shrugged. "Thought it was worth mentioning, though. Figured you might want to know."

"Thanks, Cyrus."

Reggie's dad set down the photo, hesitated, then spoke again. "Did I do the wrong thing, son? Should I have left town like he said? Or informed the police?"

Brayden clapped a hand on his shoulder and squeezed. "It was a hard spot to be in. I think you did the best you could for you and Reggie. And for selfish reasons, I'm glad you did things the way you did."

"Because it helps you with your case, or because you're falling in love with my daughter?"

The boldness of the question startled him into answering honestly. "Both."

Cyrus opened his mouth again, but a floorboard creaked and a second later, Reggie cleared her throat from behind them.

"I hate to interrupt your bonding," she said, "but we left the party before dinner was served, and I'm starving."

Her father shot Brayden a look, his face a mask of bemused affection. "Did you notice yet how much she *eats*? Prepare yourself for a lifetime of empty cupboards."

Reggie groaned, her cheeks pink. "Are we back to this again? Dad, I don't eat that much. And you're going to scare Brayden away."

"I'm led to believe there's very little chance of that happening," the older man replied.

She threw up her hands. "Great. Now you're ganging up on me."

"Spaghetti?" said her dad.

"You can't placate me with pasta."

"Wanna bet?"

The banter continued for another few moments before Cyrus ushered them toward the kitchen, issuing instructions on who would do what. As they stepped from one room to the other, though, he grabbed Brayden's arm and spoke to him once more in a low voice.

"Do what needs to be done, son. And keep my daughter safe." Then he smiled and moved into the kitchen, asking affectionately if Reggie had any idea where the strainer had disappeared to.

Chapter 16

Reggie dropped the pile of blankets and the spare pillow onto the couch and shot Brayden her best disgusted look.

"I can't believe you're actually following through on this," she grumbled.

"My father-in-law wouldn't like being lied to."

"Ha. Ha."

Brayden reached around her to shake open one of the sheets. "Seriously. I think he liked me."

She made another face at him. "You think? He practically tried to write the wedding vows right then and there."

"Would you have preferred him *not* to like me?"

"No. But it would've been nice to have a little resistance."

"I thought you were over the rebellious phase."

"I am."

"So what's the issue?"

She sighed and flopped down onto the couch, dragging the pillow into her lap. "I guess I feel like he was passing me off to you or something."

Brayden sat beside her and pulled her hand into his. "He was."

"Gee. Thanks for reassuring me."

"Cut him some slack, sweetheart. You're all he's got. It makes him feel better to think someone's got your back.

Doesn't hurt that I'm a cop *and* share his distrust of all things Garibaldi."

"It surprised me that you told him who you really were, actually."

"Figured it would be better not to lie to the father of the bride."

"Seriously, Brayden. You've got to stop—"

He cut her off with a kiss, not pulling away until her head was spinning.

"No," he said against her mouth.

"No?" she repeated, already forgetting what it was that she'd said just a few moments earlier.

"I won't pretend that I'm not crazy about you. I won't pretend I'm not sure it's going to lead to more."

In spite of the way she willed it not to, her heart leaped. "You won't stop talking about marrying me?"

"Nope. And there's more."

She bit back a laugh at the serious look on his face. "What else?"

"I'll *probably* try to convince you to talk about it, too."

"Think you can persuade me?"

In a swift move, he put his hands on her hips, slid her down and pinned her to the couch. "By force if I have to."

She wriggled a little, but he didn't budge. "Oh, I see. If you can't ask a woman to marry you nicely, then you'll just *make* her do it."

"Only if the woman can't see what's good for her."

"What if you haven't even tried asking her?"

"Is that an option?"

"I don't know. Is it?"

As soon as the words were out of her mouth, she realized how they sounded. And Brayden realized it, too, apparently. With a devilish grin that made her heart flutter even more than it already was, he released her and rolled to the floor. She didn't have to look to see that he'd dropped to one knee.

"No," she whispered.

His smile didn't diminish in the slightest. "Don't say no yet. You haven't even heard what I'm going to ask."

"There's only one way a pose like that ends."

"I could be down here trying to retrieve an old, sticky lollipop from under the couch."

"Is that what you're doing?"

"No."

Her heart's *thump-thump, thump-thump* increased again. "Then I'm right."

His lips pressed together for a second like he was trying not to laugh. "Hold on now. Hear me out."

"Do I have to?"

"Yes. Relationships are all about compromise."

"I think *this* relationship is all about me climbing into some hole I can't get out of."

"Ouch. That hurts. Although…"

"What?"

"At least you acknowledged that we're in a relationship." He grabbed her hand and pressed it to his mouth, his lips searing her skin in a way that made her want his kiss everywhere else, too.

"Okay, Mr. King-Of-Cling," she breathed. "Tell me what you're proposing. So long as it's not actually a proposal, of course."

"I propose that you think about a proposal."

"Is this your attempt to trick me? Because I should warn you… I'm both smart *and* pretty."

"Smart and beautiful," he corrected, his voice serious as he reached out to cup her cheek with his palm. "I won't ever try to trick you, Reggie. I'm an honest man. Which is a big reason I want to lay it all out like this. As long as you don't mind hearing it."

"I don't mind. I think."

He laughed. "I'll take what I can get."

"Okay. Lay away."

"I think I've made it pretty clear that my life has been dominated by bringing down the man who killed my father. You're the first person—the first anything—that's reminded me how much more there is to life."

Reggie swallowed. "I don't want to become a source of resentment."

"Just the opposite, sweetheart. Right now, I actually kind of resent the fact that Garibaldi is getting in the way of me putting a hundred percent of my focus on you." He paused and ran a hand over his hair, his grin turning sheepish. "I'm seriously not sure when I became such a giant sap."

"Well. You've been like that since we met, so…" She trailed off teasingly.

"Yeah, it's definitely you," he agreed. "Which brings me back to my point. I'm not asking you to marry me. Not yet anyway. But I'm thoroughly declaring my intentions."

"Persistent, aren't you?"

"I'm a detective, and I'm after a sure thing. I'm not likely to give up."

Abruptly, Reggie's chest squeezed and her breathing tightened, and she looked down as she said, "Do you remember when we were in the car and you were asking me to list all the things that scared me?"

"Yes."

"I need to add this to the list."

"This?" he asked gently. "Or me?"

"This. The things you're saying. The way you're making me feel."

"Aren't those thing also *me*?"

"No," she said quickly. "You, I—"

"Me, what?"

She leaned over and kissed him solidly on the mouth. "That."

His lips turned up. "Yeah, I'm on board with that part, too."

"Come back up here."

Obediently, he climbed up and squished in beside her, then propped himself up on one elbow. "Better?"

"It's always better when you're close enough to touch," Reggie admitted.

"And that scares you?"

"Terrifies me. But maybe in a good way."

His hand found her face again, his thumb tracing a small, warm circle just to the edge of her mouth. "I didn't know that someone could be terrified in a good way."

Heat shot in from his touch, and her eyes wanted to close. "I knew."

His fingers slid from her lips down her throat, still circling. "How does it feel?"

"Wonderful."

His chuckle filled her ear. "Oh, really?"

"Mmm."

"You know that I'm asking about the fear and not *this*, right?" He dipped his mouth to her clavicle and traced his tongue along its line.

She couldn't contain a gasp. "Yes! I mean…*yes*, I know."

"So explain that one, then. How is something terrifying also wonderful?"

"Have you ever been skydiving?"

"No. You?"

"Yes. Once, when I was eighteen. It was exhilarating. That second right before I jumped was the scariest, most exciting moment of my life." She forced her heavy lids to open so she could look into his eyes. "Until now."

His returning look was warm, but he shook his head. "I'd still prefer not to scare you."

"Trust me," Reggie said. "It's a good thing."

"Does that mean you'll stop fighting the inevitable and consider my proposal to consider my proposal?"

She breathed out. "It means I've already accepted."

His face lit up. "Well, then. I've got two questions for you."

"All right."

"The first is, are you a diamond-ring kinda woman, or would you prefer something unique?"

A blush tickled her cheeks. "Um. Can I ask what the second question is before I answer the first one?"

"You sure?"

"Yes."

The warmth in Brayden's eyes turned molten. "How quickly can you get out of that dress?"

And Reggie decided that it was well worth putting off the first question in favor of showing him the answer to the second.

Brayden woke to the sound of running water and the smell of freshly brewed coffee. He rolled over, a crick in his neck making him groan as he blinked at the unfamiliar surroundings. For a moment, he was disoriented. Then he remembered, and his mouth tipped up automatically.

Reggie.

She'd made "sleeping" on the couch an experience and a half, and the evidence of their long night was clear in the disastrous state of the living room. The coffee table sat on its side, a sheet draped over top of it. Several books from a little shelf in the corner had been knocked loose and lay scattered in a mess on the floor. The remnants of their midnight snack sat on top of the TV stand.

Brayden's smile widened into a grin, and he allowed himself an indulgent moment of laying his head back on the couch and recalling a few of the spicier details. The curves of Reggie's body were permanently etched in his mind now; it required no effort to picture every inch of her. Zero to sixty in a heartbeat. That's how she made him feel. Like he'd been waiting his whole life for this one piece of the puzzle to make him right.

He closed his eyes, wondering how long it would take to wrap up the Garibaldi case. He was surprisingly impatient to get it over with. Yes, he still wanted to mete out justice. Still wanted to see the man behind bars. But he also wanted to move on. To start over here in Whispering Woods with Reggie Frost at his side. He wondered how long it would take to get a position in the small town. Or if he'd even want to continue in the same line of work. He loved being a cop. He'd never even considered another line of work.

But once Garibaldi's been put away, will you still feel the need?

He exhaled and folded his hands over his chest. Reggie had made a good point about other people needing a detective with his skills. Over the last decade, he'd helped put away a lot of unpleasant characters. He didn't want to just walk away, but he could picture himself taking a back seat. Maybe starting an online consulting business that he could operate from anywhere. Part-time, because if Reggie took over the diner the way she intended to, he'd want to be on hand to help her.

"You're lying there naming our unborn children, aren't you?" Reggie's wry question brought him back to the present.

He cracked one eye. "Thinking about how it'll feel to run a diner, actually."

"Guess you'll get a chance to find out. I'm just about ready to go to work." She straightened her uniform. "Good thing I keep extras around. I left my other one in the shed by Tyler Strange's hideout."

The reminder made Brayden swing his legs sideways and push to a sitting position. "Right. We should probably go retrieve that at some point. Preferably after food and coffee."

Reggie shook her head. "I've only got about fifteen minutes until my shift starts."

"So that pot of coffee I can smell is just a tease?"

"That pot of coffee has been there for an hour. As have the bacon and eggs I cooked, then gave up on and stuck in the fridge. You were dead to the world and missed out."

"I can't decide if I should say it was worth it, or beg you to be late."

"How about if you take coffee to go, and I feed you at work? At least eating at the diner will give you an excuse to lurk."

"I thought I was supposed to brood."

"You can brood *while* you lurk."

He sighed as his stomach grumbled a protest at having to wait, but pushed to his feet anyway. "Can I get pancakes?"

"Yes."

"Okay. Let's go then."

"Brayden?"

"Yeah, sweetheart?"

She cast an amused look his way. "You might want to consider putting on some clothes."

He looked down and realized the only thing he wore were his boxers "Whoops."

"Yeah."

"Speaking of naked..." He stepped toward her.

She backed up quickly. "Uh-uh. I *just* got clean and dry. And I don't want to be late."

"You said you have fifteen minutes."

"I know for a fact fifteen minutes is long enough."

"That's a compliment that feels like an insult."

"It's a fact."

He took another step her way and laughed as she tried to escape and instead banged into the upended coffee table, flailed a little, then tumbled forward and landed in his arms. "See? The universe wants us to stay here for a while longer."

"The universe, huh?"

"Clearly." He reached to tip her chin up for a kiss, but the noisy jangle of his phone made him pause.

"That's your brother's ringtone," Reggie pointed out.

"I know."

The phone rang again.

"So maybe the universe wants you to answer?" she asked.

"The universe hasn't even told me where my phone *is*," he countered.

"In your pants pocket. And before you ask, your pants are hanging on the lamp." She pushed to her tiptoes and gave him a light kiss. "I'll grab your coffee. You get dressed and answer your phone."

With a mutter, he moved to grab the phone, catching it just as the familiar jingle started up again. "This better be good, Harley."

"Distracted yet again, bro?"

"Could say."

His brother laughed. "Well. It's a good-news, bad-news situation."

"Give me the bad news first, then. I'm already annoyed."

"Your businessmen—Vincent and Francis—are still very much alive."

Brayden frowned and slipped on his pants as he said, "That's the bad news?"

"It is in that we can't track down Garibaldi for their murder."

"So what's the good news?"

"Vincent Overgaard is on his last legs. Terminal illness."

"Your idea of good and bad news is really starting to worry me, Harley."

"It means he was willing to talk to me a bit. Francis Taulk, on the other hand, hung up on me. Twice."

Brayden grunted as he buttoned his shirt. "Okay. I'll accept that as goodish news. What did Overgaard say?"

"That even though Garibaldi technically already owned his shop, he paid Overgaard double again what it was worth. Cash. He thinks Taulk got the same deal," his brother said.

Reggie stepped back into the room then, and held out a to-go mug. As Brayden took it with a nod, he couldn't help but wonder what offer Garibaldi had made her father. Had the crooked man given Cyrus Frost a comparable deal, even factoring in that he refused to leave town? Then he remembered another detail that Cyrus had revealed. His threat to Garibaldi. It had been effective.

But if the two other businessmen are alive...

It meant that the part of Cyrus's warning that worked was a hint that he knew more about the bombing. Not that Brayden really needed more to convince him that Garibaldi was behind it, but that fact sealed the deal in his mind.

"Bray, did you hear what I just said?"

Realizing he'd missed something completely, he turned his attention back the phone. "Sorry, no. Could you repeat it?"

"You really *are* distracted, aren't you?"

He eyed Reggie, who was mouthing at him that they needed to leave, and said, "Too mild of a word."

"I was just pointing out that the shops that were wrecked in the Main Street bombing were the very ones that used to be owned by Taulk and Overgaard. Only by the time they burned down, Garibaldi was on full title. Kind of begs the question of why he'd light up his own property. Insurance wouldn't have been worth it. Not with the kind of cash he'd handed out."

"So he was doing the same thing he did fifteen years ago."

"Torching some kind of evidence? I dunno."

"You disagree?"

Brayden grabbed his jacket and followed Reggie out the door, then overtook her so he could stay on the lookout as they moved through her building and headed downstairs.

"The bomb that killed Dad…" His brother trailed off, cleared his throat, then started again. "That bomb was the desperate act of a kid. Garibaldi's a little more sophisticated than that now, I think."

"So he wanted it to look like the act of a desperate kid, maybe."

"Maybe."

"Why the doubt?"

"Garibaldi basically runs Whispering Woods, right?"

"You could say."

He put up an arm to block Reggie in as he scanned the parking lot. Deciding it was clear, he led her to the car, offered her an apologetic look, then opened her door.

"It just doesn't make sense," Harley said. "He's probably got a hundred other ways to dispose of anything incriminating. The local law is at least partially in his pocket. And he had a scapegoat in Tyler Strange, but chose to pay a lawyer to get the guy off. There has to be some reason he decided to do things the way he did."

With a frustrated sigh, he climbed into the driver's seat. "Yeah. You're probably right. We're still missing too many pieces of the puzzle."

"But you're meeting with the sister today, right?"

"That's the plan."

"Hopefully that leads somewhere."

"Yep. Thanks for the info."

"You got it."

Brayden hung up and stared out the windshield for a long second before putting the key into the ignition. As he turned over the engine, Reggie's warm fingers landed on his forearm.

"Everything all right?" she asked.

"Depends on your definition of all right, I guess," he replied in a forcedly light tone.

"I meant relatively speaking."

"Everything's about the same."

"Are you sure?"

"Yeah, sweetheart. I'm sure."

But as he shifted into Drive, a sudden sense of foreboding hit him, and as hard as he tried, he couldn't shake it.

Reggie tugged the fresh pot of coffee out from under the machine, then carried it over to the table where Brayden had been stationed for the last forty minutes. He had a newspaper open in front of him now, and she could see that he'd made a fair amount of headway on the weekend crossword. She could also see the tension in his back, and the stiffness in the way he held the pen. In spite of the fact that he insisted otherwise, she was sure his worry had increased somehow. She wished she could ease it. But whatever his concern was, he was keeping it in.

With a silent exhale, she bent to refill his mug and spoke close to his ear. "Might want to slow down. You'll run out of excuses to keep sitting here."

"My girlfriend runs the place," he teased. "I think that's a good enough reason."

"Your girlfriend hopes you're a good tipper, because you're taking up prime space."

He cast a look around the near-empty restaurant, then brought his amber gaze back to hers and lifted an eyebrow.

"Okay," she grumbled. "It's a little slow. Especially for a Sunday."

The amused sparkle in his eyes faded as he gave the restaurant a second once-over, then dropped his voice. "No sign of Nadine yet?"

"No." She shrugged. "I mean, she might not have got the message. Or she might've got it, but then decided not to come."

"You think she'd say no to fifty bucks?"

"*I* wouldn't. But who knows?" Reggie paused as something else occurred to her for the first time. "Are we assuming that Nadine knows her brother is—was—here? Or are we assuming that she didn't know?"

"Either is plausible," Brayden replied. "What are you thinking?"

"Just that if Tyler was supposed to show up on Friday night and he didn't, wouldn't Nadine have done something about it?"

"Call the police, you mean?"

"Yes."

"Not if she was worried about him getting into more trouble."

"I guess." Reggie felt her shoulders sag.

Brayden reached up and squeezed her hand. "Why don't you sit down with me for a minute?"

She looked up at the clock overhead, then shook her head. "My coffee break isn't for another hour and fifteen minutes."

"Aren't you the boss?"

"Yep. And that's why I have to set an example." She sighed. "Speaking of which… I should go see if anyone else wants some more coffee."

He still held her wrist. "Hang on."

"What?"

"Is it a bad example to give a customer a kiss?"

"Definitely."

"You sure about that?"

"Yes. But I promise that the wait will only make it better."

He gave her a slow once-over that made her toes want to curl. "You have no idea."

A laugh bubbled up, and she flounced away, adding a deliberate bit of extra swish to her walk as she moved through the diner, filling partially empty cups and taking orders. She tossed Brayden a deliberately saucy look before delivering the fresh requests to the kitchen. He was watching her affectionately, the added tension she'd spied almost invisible now. She wished it was gone completely, but knew it wouldn't be until the case was closed.

Feeling a little pensive herself, Reggie slipped from the kitchen to the back room to sneak a sip of her own coffee and to take a ten-second breather. She suspected that Brayden was right about it being unlikely that Nadine would call the police to report her brother's absence.

But if she *was* aware that he was missing—or worse—and she was worried or afraid, that might be what was holding her back from coming to the diner. And who knew what other information the woman had? She could be familiar with Garibaldi's involvement. And if not, she might instead suspect that Brayden, as a newcomer, had something to do with what happened to Tyler. And there was the possibility that Nadine didn't even know her brother had come back to town. In fact, they had no proof that she'd ever found out about their shared parentage.

Too many possibilities, Reggie thought as she set her mug down.

She spun toward the dining area, determined to put it all aside until her shift was over or until Nadine came in, whichever happened first. But she only made it three-quarters of a turn before she froze. A hooded figure stepped from the shadows of the hall, hands outstretched and clasped around a gun.

Chapter 17

Brayden filled in the very last space on the crossword, then leaned back and looked toward the kitchen. Two minutes earlier, Reggie had waved her fresh order sheet at him, then disappeared through the swinging doors. He was sure she could've slid the order across the food service area, but he understood her need to be invisible for a second. Her smile—currently at the top of his list of favorite things—hadn't slipped once she started her shift. Not one of the customers would suspect anything was out of the ordinary. She gave no hint that her life had been upended on Friday night and hadn't yet been set right.

Soon, sweetheart, he promised silently.

His gaze drifted from the kitchen to the wide window across the diner, searching for any sign that Nadine Stuart was on her way in. On the drive from her apartment to the restaurant, Reggie had described the other woman as a petite blonde, but admitted that she hadn't seen her up close in several years.

Still, no one who came even close to the vague description appeared outside. The view hadn't changed in the near hour he'd been sitting there. Same tidy row of trees. Same group of mom-and-pop shops. Same three vehicles—one gray hatchback, one rusty truck, one red sedan.

Brayden glanced at the swinging door, waiting for Reggie to reappear. He wondered if there was an issue in the kitchen; she'd been gone longer than he thought she ought to have been. A tickle of worry nudged at him, and he pushed away the newspaper. Maybe he was being paranoid, but he'd far rather be safe than sorry.

As he moved to stand, though, the bell above the entrance jangled, drawing his attention. A young woman stood in the entryway, her eyes flicking through the diner. Her hair was blond, her frame petite.

Nadine.

Brayden eyed the swinging door that led to the kitchen for what felt like the hundredth time. It remained stubbornly still. Where was Reggie? If Tyler Strange's sister didn't see her, would the woman just leave?

With a frustrated grumble, Brayden decided he couldn't just wait and find out. He stood swiftly, slapped an easy smile onto his face and prepared to walk across the tiled floor, a greeting already half-formed in his mind. But before he could even leave the table, another woman—a redhead who'd been seated in the corner of the diner for almost as long as Brayden had been there himself—jumped up and squealed.

"Oh, my god! Ilsa! I was starting to think you weren't going to come! How did it go last night? Did he—"

Brayden tuned out the rest of the enthusiastic gush the moment he realized the blonde wasn't Nadine Stuart after all. He started to turn back to the kitchen, but paused again as movement outside caught his eye.

The red sedan was on the move, and from where he stood, he could see two people inside. One was a shapeless, hooded figure at the wheel. The other was hunched over in the passenger seat, a blur of brown waves tumbling over a teal-covered back.

Brayden's heart leaped to his throat and his stomach dropped to his knees. The diner uniform was teal, and Reggie's hair was that exact rich shade of chocolate.

"Oh, God," he breathed.

A snap from near his hand alerted him to the fact that he'd not only unconsciously picked up his pencil, but also snapped it in two. It was just the jolt he needed. Dropping the broken pieces, he darted across the diner with no regard for its patrons, slammed open the glass door and tore into the street. He was still too late. The red car was at the end of the street, its turn signal somehow managing to look menacing.

Fighting an urge to go futilely chasing after it, Brayden forced himself to stay calm. He told himself he had to work through what needed to be done. Panicking wouldn't serve any purpose.

First things first, he thought. *Verify that Reggie's missing from the diner.*

His gut clenched, and everything reasonable went out of his head. He was already sure it was her. He'd still do his due diligence and check inside, but only because that was the fastest route to his own car, which he'd parked near the alley on the other side of the building.

With a hard yank on the door, he flew back through the diner, ignoring the stares of the patrons inside. His feet hit the ground hard—probably harder than necessary—as he shoved back the swinging door, Reggie's name on his lips. The cook yelled something, then caught sight of Brayden's face and jumped out of his way instead.

Good, Brayden thought grimly, moving past the kitchen to the break room.

A quick scan told him it was empty. It also told him that the back door hung wide-open.

A string of curses left Brayden's mouth before he could even think to stop them. Dragging his keys from his pocket, he bolted straight out into the alley. He made it as far as his own vehicle before he stopped again. He had no clue where the red car was headed. Whether it was going somewhere local or out of town altogether.

Now his gut didn't clench. It *couldn't* clench. It was too busy being sliced by knifelike fear. He hadn't felt so helpless since the day he learned about his father's death, and for a second, it paralyzed him. If Reggie got hurt…

So do something.

He strode forward, his eyes on his car, his mind trying to come up with a plan. The only thing he could think of doing was to head in the same direction as the red car and hope for the best. It seemed like the only option.

"And it's not much of an option at all," he muttered, climbing in.

As Brayden shoved the key into the ignition, his phone— which he'd set to Vibrate while in the diner—buzzed to life in his pocket. On the wild chance that it might be Reggie, he freed the slim device. A glance at the screen told him it was his brother once again.

"Better be good," he snapped as he put the call onto speaker phone. "And quick."

Harley's voice crackled through the car. "Brayden?"

"Already taking too long."

"What's the—no, never mind. If you haven't already met up with Nadine Stuart, I'm going to advise you to proceed cautiously."

Brayden shifted into Reverse, threw on his turn signal, and eased out onto the road. "Why?"

"After I talked to you earlier, I was itching for something to do. So I looked her up."

"You found something?"

"A few things," his brother said. "After the Main Street bomb, she spent two weeks in the hospital down here in Freemont where she was treated for lacerations and burns."

"You think she got them in the bombing?"

"Official cause of her injuries was a car accident. But

her physician felt like her story didn't add up. He made a police report, which is how I managed to worm my way into the medical records."

"What happened?"

"That particular doctor was mysteriously replaced by another. And this is the clincher, Bray. That supposed car accident was the same one that killed her father, who, as you figured out, was also Tyler Strange's dad."

"I don't like where this going."

"You shouldn't. Nadine had no health insurance. Her mom was flat broke. But someone came in and paid her medical bills. The same someone who covered the funeral expenses for her dad, and who paid her way through college."

"Jesse Garibaldi," Brayden filled in.

He'd reached the stop sign now, and turned the same way as the red car. He was thankful that the road was straight up as far as he could see. No turnoffs that would lead out of town—just side streets and medium-density residential housing.

"So what was his excuse for throwing all that money their way?" he wanted to know.

"Dad was driving Garibaldi's car when it happened."

"Except there *was* no car."

"'S what I'm thinking."

Brayden slowed a little as he approached a cross street, and eyed the parked cars that lined it. Nothing in a shade of red, and no garages to keep a vehicle hidden, either. He moved on.

"So Nadine might be friendly with Garibaldi," he said.

"At the very least, she's probably grateful."

An idea struck Brayden then, and he almost sagged with relief at the thought of having a lead. "You in front of your computer, Harley?"

"Sure am."

"Do me a solid and look up Nadine Stuart's details."

"Okay. Hang on." The sound of a keyboard clacking carried through for a few seconds, then his brother said, "All right. There's an address here. Forty-two Pine Way, unit B."

"What color is her car?"

"What?"

"Her car," Brayden said impatiently. "Tell me the color."

"Uh...red."

"I've gotta go."

"But—"

"Later, Harley."

He turned off the road sharply, punched Nadine Stuart's address into his phone's GPS system, then pulled a U-turn as fast as he could.

From behind her blindfold, tears pricked at Reggie's eyes.

"Please," she said. "You don't have to do this."

It was the hundredth or so time she'd repeated a similar set of words, and even though her captor appeared just as unaffected as the first time, Reggie didn't seem to be able to stop herself from asking again.

"Really," she said. "The man I'm with isn't going to give up looking for me. But if you let me go, I won't say anything."

In response, her kidnapper gave her a little shove. She bit back a need to cry out as her foot smacked against something hard. She was utterly disoriented. She was sure only a few minutes had gone by since the hooded figure spoke his only words in a rough whisper—*make a sound, and I'll shoot*—but it was impossible to say where they were. The short car ride could've taken them anywhere in town. The subsequent push out of the car, then into somewhere warmer gave away the fact that they'd come inside. But whether it was a house or a shop or something else entirely… Reggie had no clue.

A hand landed on her shoulder, and at last he spoke again in that same whisper.

"Sit."

Stumbling a little, Reggie eased down until her rear end hit something hard.

A chair.

A ridiculous wave of relief hit her as she recognized the object for what it was. She pressed her hands to the seat, grateful for the solidity and familiarity. But her temporary break from distress was short-lived. Her captor had plans for keeping her in place, and she recognized the means as well as she recognized the chair.

A rope.

Light hands wound it around her body, cinching it tight as they worked. The tears came again, and this time they didn't just prick—they welled up and poured over, streaming down her face.

"Please," she begged.

But the rope kept coming. It had to have been wrapped around ten times before the guy using it jerked the ends—hard—and stepped back. Reggie braced herself for the worst. But all she felt was a set of fingers hit the blindfold, then yank it down. She blinked slowly, blinded by the sudden onslaught of yellow light.

Where am I? she wondered.

A throat clearing brought Reggie's attention to her left, where the shadowy figure stood, and she wondered if she should keep her eyes closed. Every movie she'd ever seen told her it meant bad things to be able to identify an assailant. But once her gaze had locked on her captor, she couldn't look away. And shock made her eyes not only stay open, but widen further.

The person who stood in front of her, staring out from

under the shroud of the hooded sweatshirt wasn't a man. Or even a stranger.

The petite blonde looked different than she remembered. There was less softness in her brown eyes. Something stiffer in her jaw. But she was the same person, no doubt about it.

"Nadine?" Reggie knew she sounded as incredulous as she felt.

The reply was soft, but still rough—like silk on sandpaper. "Sorry about all this."

"You're *sorry*?"

The blonde woman pushed back her hood, and Reggie was barely able to stifle a gasp. The left side of Nadine Stuart's face—the same side Reggie had glimpsed from her hiding spot in the closet the previous day—was dark, puckered, and uneven.

Not a beard, Reggie thought, realizing her mistake. *A scar.*

Nadine ducked her head as if she sensed the extra bit of attention, and a cascade of hair—chin length on the scarred side, and shaved short on the other, Reggie noted—immediately masked the damage. But the other woman flicked it back as quickly as it had fallen.

"I'm only doing things this way because I have to," she stated evenly.

"You had to follow us?" Reggie said, pushing off a stab of guilt for staring. "And you had to just about knock Brayden out, too?"

A hint of regret crossed Nadine's features, but she replied without hesitation. "Yes. And before you ask, I also had to kidnap you at gunpoint and tie you up, as well."

"Why?"

"Are you working for Jesse Garibaldi?"

"No."

Nadine eyed her dubiously. "But he owns your restaurant."

Reggie shook her head. "No. Well. Technically. We lease the property from him, but it was only out of necessity and—wait. Do *you* work for him?"

"I teach the third grade."

"I know. But…"

"Am I in his pocket?"

"Yes."

"No. Well. Technically." Nadine's scarred mouth tipped up as she echoed Reggie's words.

But Reggie herself had a hard time finding any amusement in it. "I don't understand."

"I need to be sure—really sure—that you aren't working for Garibaldi. I *want* to believe it. But I need some proof."

"Proof?" Reggie almost wanted to laugh. "You're standing there with a *gun* while I'm sitting here tied up. What proof do you think I can give you?"

"Tell me what you saw on Friday night," Nadine suggested.

Reggie opened her mouth, then closed it. Admitting to seeing Chuck shoot Tyler wasn't exactly proof of anything. And if the other woman was working for Garibaldi, it was a good way to trick Reggie into revealing more than she wanted to. So she pressed her lips tight.

The other woman flipped back her shock of hair, tucked it behind her ear and sighed. "I already know you were at the diner. I followed Tyler there. But if I can't figure out whether or not you set him up…"

In spite of the fact that she was literally tied down, the menacing trail off sent a shot of defiance through Reggie, and she glared as she replied, "I didn't set up your brother."

"Ah. But you knew he was my brother."

"Not then. After."

"How?"

"You've heard of the internet?" Reggie asked sarcastically.

Nadine snorted. "I somehow doubt my genealogy is laid out in black and white on the web."

"No. But your dad happened to have had two obituaries. Isn't that how Tyler figured it out himself?"

"He didn't figure out *anything*. I found a family picture in my dad's stuff, right before Garibaldi killed him. Only it wasn't my mom or me in the photo."

For a second, Reggie's head spun. "Garibaldi killed your father?"

The blonde woman blinked at her. "You didn't know?"

"How would I know?"

The other woman tapped her weapon on her thigh like she was considering it. "You saw the obituaries. Did you notice anything funny about them?"

"Aside from the double up? No."

"My dad went missing on a Monday. He didn't come home from one of his shifts."

"Driving a limo?"

"Driving Garibaldi's town car," Nadine corrected. "My mom refused to call the police, but I was too naive to take that as a hint that I should let it go. By Tuesday, I was more worried than she was. So I went looking for clues. Which is when I found the picture of Tyler and his mom and *our* dad, and things started to unravel."

Reggie frowned. "What does that have to do with the obituaries?"

"Like I said, my dad went missing on a Monday. By Wednesday night, I'd figured out that something was *beyond* not right, and by Thursday night I'd done my search, found the picture, confronted my mom and contacted Tyler. On Friday, my brother came to town. And you know what he had in his hands when he got here?"

"No."

"An obituary, fresh from the paper in Freemont that morning with the date of death listed as the *next day*."

Reggie's puzzlement only grew stronger. "Okay."

"Tyler thought the date was a mistake. A typo. He'd already convinced himself that our dad was dead, and thought that the real reason I contacted him was to share the bad news in person. But I hadn't placed the ad. He hadn't, either, of course. And his mom was on vacation in Mexico, so he knew *she* hadn't done it." Nadine paused and sucked her lower lips between her teeth, worrying at it for a second before she added, "Imagine meeting your brother like that for the first time. In seventy-two hours, I went from being an only child with normal parents, living a normal life to some weird world where I had an older half sibling whose first question was whether or not our father had been killed in a car accident."

Reggie started to say that she *couldn't* imagine it, then stopped. Because the last two days had shown her very clearly how quickly things could change. How easy it was to believe things were one way, when all along they were completely different. So she nodded instead.

"I get it," she said. "On Friday morning I woke up thinking my weekend would end normally. And instead…"

"It's Sunday, and you're tied up in a chair."

"Exactly." Reggie bit back an urge to ask again to be set free; she sensed the other woman was softening a little anyway, and she didn't want to jinx it. "So what happened with the obituary?"

"After an initial freak-out, we called the Freemont paper for some details. They were apologetic and told us that the ad was meant to run on Saturday. But they were insistent that the person who paid for the ad had listed his death as occurring the next day. They were apologetic about that, too, but refused to accept responsibility for the mistake.

They suggested that the whole thing might've been a prank. Tyler called it an omen. I called it a heads-up."

"You believed someone was planning on killing him?"

Nadine nodded. "It made perfect sense in my mind. I was sixteen. I'd seen enough crime movies to put together the clues. I mean, I didn't know *why* someone would want him dead. I couldn't imagine a reason. But I also never would've believed he had two families. So the latter seemed to make the former more plausible. And I thought I had an easy way to figure out who was behind it."

"You just had to figure out who placed the ad."

"Yep. But it didn't happen. Because Friday night, I woke up in the hospital in Freemont with this…" She pointed at her face. "And that wasn't the worst part."

In spite of everything, Reggie found herself interested. "What was?"

"That I didn't remember anything else."

"What?" Reggie thought maybe she'd misheard.

But apparently Nadine had meant it. "They told me I hit my head in the car accident. And it didn't seem that far-fetched. The last memory I had was of getting into a car with Tyler on Friday morning. I don't even know where we were going. After I woke up, I was in and out of it for a few days. When I finally managed to stay conscious for more than a few hours, they told me that my father had died in the accident. I thought they were mixed-up. That they meant my brother, not my dad. That's when they brought in the psychiatrist."

"But you had proof."

"I thought I did." Nadine shook her head. "But I was disoriented. Everyone around me—my mom, the doctors— were so concerned about me that I started to think maybe I *was* a bit crazy. And I was trapped in that hospital for a month, just for my physical injuries. By the end, the whole thing seemed like a faraway dream. My mom relocated us to Freemont because she thought it would be a fresh start."

Nausea built up in Reggie's stomach. "What about the obituary?"

"The paper copy was gone with Tyler, who—to me— had disappeared into thin air. By the time I'd recovered enough to start up my search again, Garibaldi came to me. Everything he said made me sure that he was the one who placed the ad. A perfect cover-up if it weren't for the date mix-up. And—" She cut herself off and eyed Reggie for a long moment. "You really aren't working for him, are you?"

"I said I wasn't."

"If I untie you, will you run?"

"No."

Nadine's entire body seemed to sag with relief. "I'm sorry for the kidnapping."

In spite of everything, a laugh escaped from Reggie's mouth. "Any other weekend, and I'd tell you to take that apology and shove it. Today...I'll accept it because it's not the worst thing to happen to me since Friday."

The blonde offered a tentative smile. "I think we can help each other. Or at least I hope we can."

Reggie held still as the other woman moved close and slipped one hand to the knots. She was eager to hear the rest of the story. To learn how the past and present fit together. And even more than *that*, she wanted Brayden to hear it. Somewhere in what the blonde woman had said was a key that would help put away Garibaldi. For good.

The rope came loose, then dropped to the ground, and Reggie let out a breath. But any release from the tension that had been hounding her was short-lived. Before she could even stretch out her arms to try to encourage some blood flow, a thunderous crash resounded through the space. As

Nadine dropped to a defensive crouch, Reggie's gaze flitted past her to focus on the source of the noise. A door across the room. Which was shaking with impact yet again.

Chapter 18

With a deep inhale, Brayden took four steps back. Then—with a forced exhale that came out as a grunt—he threw himself forward into the red-painted door for a third time. Under his exertion, it shuddered. It creaked. It bowed in, just a little. But it stayed closed. He drew back again, and this time, he lifted a booted foot and slammed it full force against a spot just below the handle. A satisfying, splintering crack heralded his success, and the frame fell apart as the door flung open.

Brayden slid sideways, pressed his back to the wall and readied his weapon.

"This is Detective Maxwell of the Freemont PD," he announced, his voice far calmer than his racing heart and mind. "I'm armed. Identify yourself."

His words were met with silence. He waited with as much patience as he could muster, straining to hear anything—a shuffle, a breath, a whisper—that would give away the occupant. He heard nothing.

Inching forward cautiously, he stuck the tip of the gun and the tip of his toe over the edge of the door frame and prepared to be jumped. Everything remained quiet.

"If you're in there," he called, "say something now, because I'm coming in hot."

Still nothing.

Easing off the wall, Brayden dropped down and raised

his gun at the same time. There was zero reaction, and as
his eyes scanned the exposed room, he realized it was not
only empty, but also completely dark. If Nadine Stuart had
taken Reggie by force, it wasn't to this location.

Fighting a maddening combination of frustration, helplessness and an anger that he knew stemmed from his
worry, Brayden stepped into Nadine's unit and flicked
his gaze around the living space. It was a crowded mess.
Knickknacks and photos dotted every surface. The air was
musty—almost rank—and everything was covered in a
layer of dust that appeared years old. A filth-crusted stack
of mail sat in the middle of a coffee table, open and waiting, as if someone were going to come back and go through
it at any second.

The place didn't look like it was lived-in at all, let alone
fit the bill for what Brayden imagined a single twenty-
something woman would feel comfortable with. He wasn't
coming at the assessment from a presumptuous point of
view. A decade of police work had given him a feel for how
people lived, and just the basic facts he had about Nadine
Stuart made him sure this wasn't her primary residence.
He doubted he'd find much of a clue in the apartment about
her actual whereabouts, so he tugged his phone from his
pocket and prepared to call his brother. He needed something else to go on. As he lifted his finger to dial, though,
he heard a muffled sound from somewhere up the hall.

Cursing his own stupidity, he dropped the phone back
into his pocket and readied his gun again as he moved to
the dark, open hallway. He flattened himself to the wall
and slunk along until he reached an open doorway. A quick
check told him it was an empty bathroom. A few feet farther, he reached two more doors. One was also open, and
was clearly as dark as the rest of the house. The other,
though, was shut tight, and a soft yellow glow was just
barely visible from beneath the bottom.

Jackpot.

Brayden snaked out his free hand and closed it on the doorknob. A quick, carefully silent turn told him that it was unlocked. He released it slowly and leaned back, working over what to do. Whoever was on the other side—*please, let it be Reggie, and, please, let her be safe*—had to know he was there. It wasn't as though he'd made a subtle entrance.

So why are they still hiding? They had an advantage, at least for the minute before I realized they were even here. Why not use it?

His only answer was a cough from the other side of the door.

"Seriously?" he muttered under his breath.

The cough became a thick, cringe-inducing hack. Then the hack cut off abruptly in a curse, which was followed by absolute silence.

Puzzled, Brayden grabbed the handle again, calling out as he turned it. "I'm coming in armed. If you've got a weapon, declare it now."

The reply came as a wet-sounding wheeze. "I don't have a damned weapon."

Brayden still proceeded with caution. He swung the door wide. Then waited. He lifted his gun and inched forward. Then waited some more. When there was no movement from inside, he pulled the same deal as he had at the front door—he dropped to one knee, weapon lifted.

"You can stop that," said the gruff voice inside the bedroom. "I can't even stand up."

Lowering his gun, marginally, Brayden brought his attention to the prone form on the bed. It was a man. So sickly looking that his face was all but gray, his hair a matted mess. And it only took Brayden a second to figure out why his appearance was so haggard. Though the T-shirt he wore was white, it was stained crimson and brown everywhere but the sleeves and collar. It was ripped open, too, and a six-by-six-inch piece of cellophane had been taped over a jagged, thumb-sized hole just below his rib cage on one side.

Brayden lifted his eyes to the man's face. "You're Tyler Strange."

He let out a coughing laugh. "You don't say."

"Where's Reggie?"

"Don't know." Strange closed his eyes.

"You don't know, or you won't tell me?" Brayden snapped.

The other man didn't answer. His breathing was shallow, the rise and fall of his chest inconsistent.

Brayden tried again, forcing himself to use a more conciliatory tone. "You clearly need medical help that's far beyond my training, so let's take care of that first. While we're waiting for the ambulance, you can tell me what you *do* know about Reggie."

"I'm dead already," Strange replied.

"You can't be sure of that."

"Thanks for the positive vibes, Detective, but I was beyond repair even before this whole gunshot-wound incident. Acute necrosis of the liver. Addiction's a son of a you-know-what. Booze, mostly, but I've always taken what I can get. And speaking of which..." The other man opened his eyes and swept a hand vaguely across the room. "I dropped some pain meds in here. You mind?"

Brayden spotted the little white pill bottle sticking out from under a chair. Shoving aside an urge to simply pick it up and hurl it at the man on the bed, he instead grabbed it gently, noted the oxycodone label addressed to someone else entirely and handed it over as politely as he could manage.

Tyler Strange lifted the cap, popped an indeterminate number of the painkillers, then closed his eyes again. "Thanks."

Brayden clenched his teeth. Every second in the dingy

apartment was a second away from Reggie. A second he didn't know whether or not she was okay.

"It was her, right?" Strange said.

"What was her?"

"She was the one who saw me and Chuck in the alley." Brayden saw no point in lying. "Yes."

"She startled Chuck just enough that he forgot to check if I was dead or just *nearly* dead. Gave me enough of a chance to hide. So I guess I can thank her for this slow, painful death."

"If you give me a hint about where she is, I'll happily pass along your message."

The other man choked out another laugh. "My sister."

"Nadine?"

"Yeah. You're a detective. Did I hear you say that?"

The man's seemingly random changes of subject was giving Brayden mental whiplash. "Yes."

"I don't usually like cops."

"Some people don't."

"I don't trust 'em."

"I guess your experience with us hasn't been too good."

"Corrupt cops, clean cops… You all hate guys like me." Strange's eyes drifted shut again. "It hurts."

"I can call someone."

"No. Don't. It'll just put her in more danger."

"Who? Your sister?"

"Can you help her? That's what cops are supposed to do, right?"

"I can't help anyone until I know where Reggie is, Tyler."

"One-track mind, huh?"

"As far as my girlfriend's safety is concerned, yeah."

The other man's lids lifted, and in spite of their glassiness, his gaze was sharp. "What's that like?"

"What?"

"Loving someone so much you can't think about anything else."

Brayden swallowed against the sudden roughness in his throat. "I'm new to it, actually. But I can tell you that right now, it hurts. It scares me, to think that she might not be safe, and even more than that, it scares me to think that I haven't had a chance to tell her exactly how I feel about her."

"She's safe," Strange mumbled. "Or I assume she is."

Hope buoyed under the surface, but Brayden forced himself to reply without betraying any hint of it. "Tell me what you mean."

"Nadine. She's been following you guys. Trying to figure out which side you're on."

"Which side?"

"If you were with Jesse Garibaldi, you would've shot me on sight. Like Chuck did."

"I'm not with Garibaldi." His placid tone was even more forced now. "And I'm nothing like Chuck."

"No." The other man breathed out a thick breath, then drew in another labored one. "I assume your girl is the same. That's all Nadine needs to know."

"All she needs to know for *what*?"

"Did she tell you what happened?"

"I didn't speak to her."

"Right. I keep forgetting."

"Forgetting?"

"Everything."

"What does Nadine need to know?" Brayden repeated, exasperated.

"There was a bomb here, did she tell you that?"

"She didn't—yes. I know about the bomb."

"Burned up her face something good. I liked her right away, you know? If I had to have a sister, I'm glad it was her."

"I'm not sure I'm following, Tyler." *Understatement of the year.* "And I'm not sure what this has to do with Reggie, either."

But the other man was on a roll, the words tumbling out. "She was mad when she found out about me, and even madder when she found out our dad wasn't the stand-up guy she always thought he was. Didn't like having him knocked down off that pedestal, and really didn't like that she couldn't tear a strip off him about it. Our dads were friends, did you know that?"

"I don't know if being the same man counts as being *friends*," Brayden replied drily.

Strange's greasy hair flopped over his eyebrows as he shook his head. "Not mine and Nadine's dad. I mean. Yeah. *Him*. But with Jesse Garibaldi's dad. Used to let Jesse babysit me. Scared the living hell out of me."

For the first time, the other man's rambling words truly piqued Brayden's interest. "Your dad was friends with Garibaldi's dad?"

"Back in Freemont City. Grew up together. Got involved in the drug trade together. Just about got killed together in some bust about fifteen years ago."

The last statement sent Brayden's mind buzzing. "What kind of bust?"

"Don't know the details. I was a kid when it happened. Dad got away. Not a scratch, not so much a dent in his reputation. He was too smart. Like my sister, I guess. My mom—and me—not so much. But I guess she knew what happened. Kicked him out. Heard the whole damned argument. Sent my dad to live with his *wife* for good. Learned my mom was the other woman."

Brayden tried to muster up some sympathy. "Must've been hard."

"I don't know if that's the right word. I grew up in a house with a criminal father, who was only around about forty percent of the time. Who used me and my mom as his cover. Such a joke. Strong possibility that his leaving was the best damned thing that happened to me."

"What about Garibaldi's dad?"

"Jesse's dad wasn't so lucky. It was his mistake that got them caught, and he stayed behind to try to clean up his mess. But he was killed in the bust, and the cops took everything. They tossed Jesse into foster care and launched some big investigation."

The revelations sent a dozen questions spinning through Brayden's head. Fifteen years earlier... No chance that was a coincidence. He had more than a sneaking suspicion he knew which cops had begun the investigation in question.

"What happened after the bust?" he asked carefully.

The man's shoulders moved up and down in a horizontal shrug. "Dunno. I didn't see my dad again until Nadine called me and told me he was missing. Never looked him up and steered clear of all things related. Kept my life on the straight and narrow until all hell broke loose nine years ago. Then I found out I really am my father's son."

"But you *did* see him?"

"Yes. Once. Me and Nadine both. The bomb..." He trailed off, then added something incomprehensible, shuddered a little and went silent.

"Tyler?"

The addict said nothing in response to his name, and Brayden had to fight a need to shake the other man into coherence. He might've even done it if he hadn't been worried it would result in immediate death. Strange's chest was already barely moving up and down.

So Brayden mustered up the last bit of patience in his very limited reserve and said, "Listen to me, Tyler. I don't know what happened all those years ago when the bomb went off on Main Street. I don't know how you were involved, or if you were at all. Right this second, I don't even care. Just give me a hint that'll lead me to Reggie."

"The Main Street bomb," Strange mumbled.

"It doesn't matter."

"No."

"No, what?"

Strange's eyes opened halfway, a stoned, almost smile gracing his face. "That's your hint. In fact, it's more than a hint. It's the answer."

"The answer to what?"

He couldn't tell if the other man was being deliberately mysterious, or if he was just so out of it that he had no clue what he was saying at all. Then Strange coughed, and a bubble of blood formed on his lower lip and Brayden decided it was more likely the latter. He also thought the man couldn't have much time left.

"Give me a bit more," he urged. "Something else to go on."

"All I wanted to do was one thing—keep Nadine safe. I stayed away because I said I would. That was the deal."

"You're not making much sense." Brayden scrubbed a frustrated hand over his chin.

"I'm passing the torch."

"Nadine. Where *is* she, Tyler?"

"I did it."

More mental whiplash. "Did what?"

"When my sister called me up here, I came. I thought my dad was already dead, and I thought Nadine was wrong about him just being missing. But then Jesse called me…" His breathing grew labored for a moment.

"Jesse called you and said what?" Brayden prompted as gently as he could manage.

"I swear I didn't know." Tears leaked from the other man's eyes and trailed down his dirt-streaked face as he babbled on. "He said to bring my sister with me, and I did.

He said my dad was working on some secret project for him, and he'd take us there. I don't remember anymore what I thought would happen. A reunion? Something good? I was too stupid to realize it was a setup. Too eager. We got down to that cellar and we found our dad. Unconscious, tied up. We tried to free him. Then we smelled the smoke and heard the explosion. He wanted to kill us all, I think. And I had to make a choice. So I saved my sister. I've been saving her ever since. She needs to keep not remembering."

Brayden's mind worked to connect the disjointed information into a proper narrative.

Nadine and Tyler's father—a long-time associate of Garibaldi—had gone missing. Nadine had initiated a search which ended in an attempt on her life and on Tyler's, too. Their father was probably the original target. Why? And why had Garibaldi wanted to destroy those properties in the first place?

"And why did he let you live after all that, Tyler?" Brayden muttered, more to himself than to the wheezing man on the bed.

Tyler answered anyway, "The blackmail."

"You couldn't blackmail him if you were dead."

"Not me."

"Not following again, Tyler."

"She doesn't remember."

It still didn't make sense in Brayden's mind, but the repeated phrase about Nadine *not remembering* finally clicked. "She doesn't recall the accident at all?"

"I promised I'd keep her away from Whispering Woods." The crimson bubble on Strange's lips blew out again, then dribbled down. "But you should go."

"I don't know where I'm going, Tyler," he pointed out. "You still need to tell me."

"She could, if she remembered."

The final sentence seemed to push him over the edge. He

shuddered again, this time almost violently. Then his eyes rolled back in his head, and his jaw went slack and the pill bottle—empty—slid from his hand and fell to the ground and Brayden knew he wouldn't speak again. A quick check of his pulse confirmed it, and there was no sense in trying to perform CPR. A stab of regret hit him. Loss of life, no matter whose, was never welcome. Right that second, though, he didn't have time to dwell. Renewed futility was threatening to settle in.

"The Main Street bomb is my hint," he muttered to himself.

The only thing he could think to do was to head straight to the scene of the crime. Before dragging his keys from his pocket, though, he paused long enough to give the dead man a moment of silence. He mentally promised to personally see that Tyler Strange was given a proper burial. With a final, respectful nod, he turned to go. Before he even reached the door, though, his phone rang from inside his pocket.

Hoping yet again that it would be Reggie, he pulled the slim device free. A local number scrolled across the screen, buoying that hope.

He swiped the phone on. "Maxwell."

The voice at the other end was as unpleasantly familiar as the reply itself. "Mr. Maxwell. I believe I have something that belongs to you."

Brayden's throat went dry, and he had to clear his throat before answering. "Officer Delta. How can I help you?"

"Me? I'm not the one who needs assistance." There was a pause. "Say something to your boyfriend, sweetheart."

For a second, no sound carried through the phone. Then there was a shuffle and a squeal, and Reggie's plea filled his ear.

"Brayden! Please. I don't want you to—"

Chuck cut her off. "That's more than enough."

Brayden gritted his teeth. "What do you want?"

"I want to know what the hell's going on. I want to know who you really are, and I want to know what this has to do with my employer. And I don't mean the Whispering Woods PD."

"Tell me where to find you."

"I have a few conditions first."

"I'm listening."

"I'm assuming you have a weapon. Leave it in your car. I'll be checking. I'm assuming you have some kind of fail-safe network. Don't contact them. I can't check, but I'll know. And finally, I'm assuming you'll spend the whole drive here trying to figure out a way to sneak in without me knowing. Stop before you start. I've got guys watching."

"Done, done and done."

Chuck let out a dark laugh. "Damn. That was easy."

"Should've asked for something complicated," Brayden said back, his tone matching the other man's laugh. "Give me an address."

"I'll give you some instructions instead. You know where the movie theater is?"

"I can find it."

"Good. Drive there. The parking lot should be completely empty at the moment. Put your car right in the middle. When you get out, lift your jacket, pant legs and shirt. Spin in a slow circle. If any of my guys see something suspicious, they'll shoot first and ask questions later. Once you're done with the little dance, go to the back of the theater. There's an unlocked emergency exit. Go through it. It'll be dark inside, but you'll find a low ledge on the right. On the ledge will be a bandanna. Tie it over your eyes and wait. Could be a few minutes until I've sorted out who's going to bring you down. Got it?"

"Is all of that really necessary?"

"I don't know. Why you don't you ask your girlfriend when you get here?"

Then the line went dead.

Chapter 19

Reggie swallowed nervously as Chuck hung up the phone and turned his attention back her way. The fact that Brayden was on his way did little to alleviate the fear she felt under the corrupt cop's scrutiny. He'd wound the rope around her again, securing it far more tightly than Nadine had done.

And Nadine herself...

Reggie swallowed again. The other woman lay in a crumpled heap on the floor, her already-scarred face now also marked with a bloody wound just at the edge of her hairline.

At least she's breathing. If he'd fired at her instead of hitting her, things would be much worse.

But the self-directed reassurance did little to ease Reggie's mind. All Nadine had done was take a step toward Chuck, and he'd lashed out, slamming the butt end of his weapon into her head. She'd collapsed instantly.

"Just be glad I didn't shoot her," Chuck said.

His words—which were far too close to what was going through her mind for comfort—made Reggie cringe back. She didn't know why he'd left Nadine alive. She didn't know why he hadn't shot her, too. He sure hadn't hesitated when it came to Tyler Strange on Friday night.

Chuck paced the room for a second, then paused, his words once again echoing her thoughts in a way that made her shiver. "It was easier to take down her brother. I knew

what I was up against. Or thought I did. Th[...]
hand…"

Reggie drew in a breath and made herself answer[...]
ing that if he kept talking, he'd slip up in some way—giv[...]
her a clue as to where they were and how she could regain
her freedom. "This what?"

He lifted his gun and used it to scratch his head. "It'd be
a lot easier if you just told me what you know."

"I don't know anything."

"You know that I shot Tyler."

Reggie swallowed a third time, her throat aching with
the continued effort to keep in her tears. It was bad that
he'd said it aloud. Very bad. It meant he didn't *care* that she
knew. Probably because even though he was keeping her
alive for the moment, as soon as he'd extracted whatever
information he needed, she'd become dispensable.

"I don't know what you're talking about," she whispered.

"I want to know where he is."

The statement startled her. "What?"

Chuck's eyes flicked from her to Nadine's unconscious
form, then back again. "One of you knows."

Reggie pressed her lips together to keep from expressing
her surprised aloud. Tyler had survived the gunshot. But she
didn't need the policeman to know that it was news to her.

"I have no reason to tell you anything," she said, infus-
ing her comment with an extra bit of defiance. "And since
Nadine *can't* tell you anything now, I'd say you've screwed
yourself over."

Chuck narrowed his eyes. "Who *is* Brayden Maxwell,
Ms. Frost?"

She feigned innocence. "My boyfriend."

"I don't feel like playing games. The last number that
called Nadine's phone belonged to the same man you've
been hanging off all weekend. Who didn't exist in Whis-

...day. And he just happened to
...ay night?"

...well. Didn't I already introduce

—which he'd dragged unceremoni-
...cket—from hand to hand and sighed
loud... ...ss owner. Real estate developer. Land
buyer. Excep... ...all bull. There isn't a single person with
his name listed in all of Freemont City. Not in business, and
not anywhere else. Bit strange, don't you think?"

"Maybe he's a private man."

"And maybe he's a fake."

"What reason could he have for being a fake?"

"Two words. *My boss.*"

"Who *is* your boss? I thought you were a cop. Maybe
you're the fake."

He blinked. "Do you have any idea how little your average civil servant makes?"

"I've always heard the job itself is supposed to be re-
warding enough," she shot back.

"You're awfully mouthy for a waitress."

"And you're awfully scummy for an officer of the law."

"This isn't going to end well for you if you don't co-
operate. I *am* a cop. And you're just the daughter of some
disgruntled man who's mad that Jesse Garibaldi got the better of him." He shook his head and gestured toward Nadine.
"She's got a history of mental illness. Did she tell you? And
her brother is an alcoholic drug addict. I'm sure Maxwell
will turn out to be more or less the same. Once I've figured
out what the hell the four of you are up to, whose story do
you think will come out on top?"

"Except what *I* have to say isn't just a story," Reggie
countered. "It's the truth."

"In the end, the truth won't matter. Only what's printed
...he police report and in the news."

He smiled. And she suddenly knew why he sounded so convinced that he was right. No matter what she told him, no matter what he found out about Brayden…he had no intention of letting them live. *He* would write the story. He'd bend whatever truth he needed to so that it would fit his narrative. For a second, Reggie was paralyzed with fear. Then a thought occurred to her.

Brayden won't fit any narrative.

He was a real cop. A good cop. And killing him wouldn't be easy to trivialize. Sure, his childhood intertwined with Garibaldi's, and that might come out. At first, Chuck might even think it worked to help him. But it wouldn't. It would just expose his boss for who—for what—he really was. It would get Brayden exactly what he wanted—Garibaldi behind bars.

Chuck would make him a martyr.

The dark thought brought something else with it. A bargaining chip. Hope flooded through Reggie. She exhaled a breath she didn't know she'd been holding and lifted her head. She suddenly felt very, very calm.

"Before you start making stuff up, you might want to ask *your boss* what he's willing to lose," she said slowly. "Ask *him* if the truth matters."

A shadow passed across Chuck's face, and the expression puzzled Reggie for a moment. Then something else clicked in her mind.

"He doesn't know about any of this," she stated.

"Nothing for him to know."

"You screwed up. You let Tyler live."

"Won't matter once everything's taken care of."

He put a menacing emphasis on the last three words, but Reggie just shook her head. She knew he wouldn't kill her right then. He had to put the pieces together first. He'd made one mistake, and he wouldn't take a chance on making another.

"Even when you think you've got it figured out, you still won't have it all," she said to him. "Garibaldi will kill you, too."

Genuine fear filled Chuck's eyes for a second before he managed to cover it with a sneer. "You have no idea what you're talking about."

"Don't I?"

The corrupt cop's lips dropped, doubt threatening to take over his features. He opened his mouth, then snapped it shut again as an electronic-sounding alarm blared from inside his pocket. He pulled out a phone, slammed his thumb into the screen a few times, then flashed a dark smile.

"Our mutual company's arrived," he told her, his smile widening to show his teeth. "Don't go anywhere. I promise I'll be right back."

He spun on his heel and marched out the door. The lock clicked loudly, echoing through the room. But Reggie refused to give in to the finality of the sound. There was a solution. A way out. There had to be.

She counted to one hundred, then tilted her head to the side and listened. When she was sure—about 80 percent anyway—that Chuck wasn't coming back right that second, she did a slow inventory of the room. Between being tied up twice, under close watch by the sleazy cop and being afraid for her life, it was the first time she'd really taken a thorough look around.

The room wasn't big, maybe ten feet by ten feet, and the ceiling was low. Of the three walls she could see, one was bare, and it was made of concrete. An oversize table had been haphazardly shoved against it, and was littered with what looked like reams of tissue paper. Except the sheets were huge.

A second wall held floor-to-ceiling shelves, which were too narrow to store anything she could think of off the top of her head.

The third wall held the door, a keypad and what could only be some kind of blueprint. For all intents and purposes, the space screamed of being a basement, albeit a weird one.

Reggie inhaled and worried at her lower lip, trying to puzzle it through. She knew she should be thinking of an escape plan, but for some reason, their location seemed to matter. Her gaze drifted up for a second, and she saw that the ceiling was lined with an odd assortment of vents. As she frowned at them, a buzz filled the room and the vents came to life, pushing a stream of air downward. It ruffled Reggie's hair, and as she breathed it in, she couldn't help but note that while it was cool enough to make her skin prickle a little, it was also strangely humid.

"Where are we?" she muttered, her eyes dropping to Nadine's still form again.

As if in reply, the other woman groaned. Hope pricked at Reggie once more.

"Nadine," she said, her voice urgent but soft. "You need to wake up. Please."

The plea got no immediate response, so Reggie turned her attention to trying to loosen her bonds. The rope was so tight that she could barely get a wiggle in, let alone find a way to work herself free. Just pushing at the tight fibers made her skin burn.

You're not giving up, she told herself sternly.

She drew in a deep breath, then exhaled hard and strained again. Her eyes watered. Her hands went white. But she swore that when she ran out of breath, she felt a little bit of give.

"C'mon, c'mon," she muttered.

She pulled the same set of moves a second time, and this time, the rope stretched enough that it actually sagged a bit. She did a mental fist pump and moved on to round three.

Inhale. Exhale. Push-push-push, and—

"It's going to take you an entire day to get free like that."

At the unexpected observation, Reggie's breath came out in a splutter, and her attention jerked back to Nadine. The blonde was sitting up now, one hand covering the fresh wound on her hairline.

Reggie couldn't even muster up a snappy reply. "Either help me, or go back to being unconscious."

Nadine pushed up to her feet, swaying a little as she stood and moved closer. "Where's our friend Chuck?"

"He went to let Brayden in."

The other woman paused, her hands poised over the rope. "To let Brayden in *here*?"

"I don't know. I don't know where *here* is."

"We're underneath Main Street."

"What?"

"Underneath—"

"No, I heard you. I just don't understand. Any of it. Chuck was talking about having Brayden meet him in the theater parking lot. But that's across town from Main Street."

Nadine dug her fingers into the closest knot. "Remember when I was telling you that Garibaldi came to me?"

Reggie nodded, unsure how the question connected back to their current location. "Yes."

"He was there for two reasons. The first was to see for himself if my memory loss was real, or if I was just faking it. The second was to make me an offer which was really a carefully worded threat." The first knot came free and she moved to the next. "The offer was basically hush money, I guess. He'd already paid my medical bills, and was willing to cover the cost of our move from Whispering Woods to Freemont. He wanted to put a college scholarship in a trust for me. He said it was all because he felt responsible for the car accident that injured me and killed my dad."

"But you knew there wasn't an accident."

"I really thought there might not have been. And I had

this one weird memory. It was of Tyler—who the doctors said was a figment of my imagination—carrying me *up* from under a pile of burning rubble."

"Did you tell Garibaldi that?"

"Yes. And he said it was because of all the stuff on the news about the explosion in Whispering Woods. That the TV had been on in my room and the info had seeped in somehow."

"You believed it?"

"No. But do you remember being sixteen? You're caught in this spot where you think of yourself as an adult while all the *real* adults around you think you're a kid."

"Someone should have listened."

"Should've, yeah. Didn't…also, yeah."

The second knot came free, and Reggie was able to lift her elbows. "Thank you."

"Don't get ahead of yourself," Nadine cautioned. "There are a few more to go."

"So what about when you actually got out of the hospital?"

"Well, like I said, my stay wasn't exactly short. When I did get released, my mom kept me housebound and watched me like a hawk. And honestly, as self-centered as it sounds, I kind of wanted to get on with my life. My dad was dead. I was starting over at a new school. I didn't know for sure that everything wasn't just in my head. And the more time passed, the fuzzier things got."

"I get it. But it sounded like you were so determined to find out the truth before you went into the hospital… Why didn't you try to track Tyler down?"

"I did. Once. Almost a year later. I sneaked away from school, caught a bus to the low-income area where he lived with his mom and I confronted him. At first, he pretended not to know me at all. When I finally gave up and left, he followed me. He dragged me into an alley and told me that we were both dead if I kept pursuing the situation."

Reggie's heart squeezed with sympathetic fear. "That must've been scary."

"Terrifying. And to be honest, I was just as frightened of Tyler as I was of what he said. He was a mess. High on something, barely holding it together. Totally different than he had been a year earlier. He warned me that we were probably being watched, then said I should forget him that same way I forgot the car accident, and never come back up the mountain. And I didn't hear from him again."

"Until now."

A third knot sprung open, and Nadine dropped down to work at the one behind Reggie's knees. "Actually, it happened almost by accident. My mom passed away about a year ago, but just this month some paperwork finally caught up to me, and I found out she still owned her apartment here in Whispering Woods. The accident happened a long time ago. So did Tyler's warning. And it seemed like kismet. The job opening up at the school after my contract in Freemont had just expired. Suddenly owning an apartment, free and clear—even if it's one that needs a huge overhaul—right after my ex forced me out of my place in the city. I couldn't get here fast enough. I set myself up in the temporary place, got settled at the school, then got ready to clear out Mom's place. But when I went over there, my brother was waiting for me. He'd been holed up there for almost as long as I'd been in town, just waiting to tell me to leave. That Garibaldi would find me, and that would be the end." She paused to tug off the remainder of the rope, then stood up again. "Okay. You're good."

Reggie stretched out her legs and sighed. It felt good to be free. But she knew it was only the first step in escaping. She stood up and strode across the room to the door and gave the handle a yank. Not because she expected it to open, but because she had to at least try. It didn't budge. But when she turned back to Nadine, she just about crashed into the other woman, who stood to the side, her hand on the blueprint that was affixed to the wall.

"This," she said, "is our way out."

"What do you mean?"

In reply, Nadine strode to the oversize table. As Reggie watched, the petite blonde lifted one knee, then pulled herself up on it completely. Finally, she stood and pushed on one of the vents.

"You can't be seriously considering going out that way," Reggie said.

"That blueprint says that this vent system leads straight out."

"But…"

"But what? You see an alternative?"

"No. But will we even fit through there?"

"The last three weeks of stress have lost me ten pounds. And you're about as thick as a piece of straw. We can squeeze."

Reggie stepped closer and peered up at the dark, narrow opening. "It doesn't look very promising."

"We won't know until we try. Climb up and give me a boost."

Lifting a cautious knee, Reggie pushed onto the table, knocking some of the thin paper sideways as she did. She paused to straighten it, still not sure exactly what it was for.

"You never did say what this place is," she pointed out as Nadine grabbed her hand and helped her the rest of the way up.

"I was kind of hoping you could tell me, actually."

"Why would I know?"

"Because it's almost directly under your diner."

"What?"

"That's why I brought you here. I figured if you were

with Garibaldi, you'd know for sure. And if you weren't, you might have an idea, since you work upstairs."

"I guess that plan didn't pan out."

"Nope. C'mon. Bend down and put your hands down like this." Nadine cupped her own fingers together to demonstrate.

Frowning so hard it hurt, Reggie complied. The other woman wedged a foot onto her clasped palms, then bounced up and grabbed ahold of the opening in the ceiling.

"It's actually pretty big," she announced. "I'm going in. Then I'll help pull you up, too."

Reggie watched as the blonde grunted her way into the smallish opening, impressed at how easily she performed the feat. She was even more impressed when the woman's head and arms popped out a few seconds later.

She grinned. "Guess those Pilates classes are really paying off. Let's get you up here."

"What about Brayden?"

"You think he can't handle himself?"

"No. I know he can."

"Then what are you worried about?"

"I don't know? Abandoning him?"

"We're going to cut them off."

"What?"

"Think about how easy it would be to get from Main Street to the theater if there weren't all those pesky roads in the way."

Reggie pictured it in her head; it was a straight shot, theater to diner. "Sure, it'd be quick. But—oh. You think Garibaldi built some kind of connector underneath the town?"

Nadine's smile became a little triumphant. "Exactly."

"For what?"

"My guess is transporting something illegally. What,

though, I don't know. But that doesn't mean I'm not willing to take advantage of it."

"Am I crazy for following you?"

"Possibly."

"Thanks for the reassurance," Reggie said with a sigh.

But in just a few moments, she was grunting her way into the space with the other woman, and was surprised to see that it actually was a reasonable size. The most uncomfortable thing about the whole setup was the air that was being forced through the metal ducting. The combination— cool but moist—made a sticky sweat break out on Reggie's forehead and sent a shiver through her at the same time.

"This is…" She trailed off, unable to think of a word that accurately described the unsettled feeling the whole setup left in her stomach.

"Weird?" Nadine filled in.

"To say the least." Reggie cast a final, puzzled look into the room below. "I feel like I should know what the room is for, but I just can't put my finger on it."

"Me, neither. But I can tell you what the space used to be. A cellar." Nadine grabbed the grate and placed it back over the opening. "Let's go."

Reggie followed the other woman at a crawl. "A cellar? What do you mean?"

"Under those two shops that were destroyed in the pipe bomb fire."

"So…when Garibaldi rebuilt the store, he added this?"

"Exactly. And I don't know about you, but I'd really like a concrete explanation."

They shimmied along the interior of the silver piping, Reggie trusting—or maybe just hoping—that the other woman would lead her to Brayden.

They made their way across the ceiling, presumably far enough that they'd come out to the other side of the odd room. They hit a narrow part of ducting and had to lie flat and inch along slowly for a full minute. Then they reached a fork. On one side, the pipe narrowed; on the other, it led to a wide panel, held in place by four screws.

"What do you think?" Nadine whispered. "Take our chance with getting stuck, or try to force our way through?"

Reggie looked from the flap to the skinny pipe, then gestured to the first. "I think this is one of those times when size *does* matter."

Nadine let out a raspy laugh. "All right."

A few seconds of twisting at the screws, which turned out to be a little rusty, and they were able to lift the panel off completely. And on the other side, they found a much bigger opening. There, they had enough room to sit up and pause for a breath. As Reggie drew in a few gulps of the still-thick air, her gaze drifted forward, automatically searching for a way out, and she spied a gap in the ceiling of the room below just ahead. She opened her mouth to mention it to Nadine, but the blonde woman abruptly covered her own mouth with her hand and shook her head vehemently, then pointed toward the split. And after a second, Reggie knew why. A bobbing light flashed through the space below. Then a voice carried up to them, the words indistinguishable, but the tone derisive. And finally, she caught sight of a familiar head of sandy brown hair.

Brayden.

Reggie's heart beat so hard that she was surprised that both men didn't tilt their heads up in search of the source of the sound.

Chapter 20

Although the walls around him were wide enough and tall enough, Brayden couldn't help but feel claustrophobic. Just knowing he was underground was enough to do it. It made his feet move heavily.

So far he hadn't seen a single reassuring thing. No hint of Nadine Stuart's red sedan. No sign of the woman herself, or of Reggie. He also had a sneaking suspicion that Chuck's supposed lookout team may have been a ruse. If they *were* real, why would the corrupt cop have shown up at the parking lot alone? The answer was easy. He wouldn't.

Brayden breathed out and tried to keep his jaw from clenching. It was hard. Each step made him more uneasy. Having a gun jammed into his back and his hands zip-tied together didn't help the tension coursing through him, either.

Just until you get to Reggie, he reminded himself. *Then you can do something about it. And do something about Chuck, too.*

As if the other man sensed his ill will, he spoke up then, his voice an overconfident growl. "I told you a second ago not to slow down, Mr. Maxwell. You're only delaying the inevitable."

Brayden's irritation momentarily got the better of him. "Maybe if you stop jabbing at me with a deadly weapon, I'll feel more inclined to be cooperative."

"And maybe if you seemed a little more concerned about the fact that I *have* a deadly weapon, I'd step back a bit. I may not know exactly who you are, but I do know when a man isn't afraid of a gun. And I also know that isn't going to work in my favor. So keep moving."

Brayden took a step forward. Then paused. He could swear he'd just caught a whiff of a familiar cinnamon scent in the air. His eyes traveled the length of the hallway, automatically searching for a door which might hide Reggie. There was nothing to be seen. When he inhaled again, though, the scent filled his nose once more.

"Get going, Maxwell," Chuck snapped.

Brayden took another step, stumbling deliberately as he moved. He hit the ground with one knee, feigned a wobble, then collapsed to his side. By the time the other man reacted— hollering and waving the gun around—Brayden was on his back, staring up at the ceiling. And what he saw there just about made him forget all else. A set of flashing green eyes blinked down at him from a narrow slit in the ceiling. Then the eyes pulled back and he could see most of her face. She flashed a finger to her lips in a be-quiet gesture and disappeared.

Reggie. Dear God.

What was she doing up there? He didn't know, but it only took a second to figure out what she was *going* to do. As he watched, one of the ceiling panels lifted and made him realize he was staring hard enough that he might attract unwanted attention from Chuck. Brayden averted his eyes and blinked slowly at the corrupt cop.

"Get *up*," the man snarled.

"I am," he replied.

"If by getting up, you mean you're lying there like an idiot, staring straight at the ceiling." Chuck gestured with his gun, then started to lift his eyes, too.

Thinking quickly, Brayden lifted a foot, then twisted to slam it into the other man's foot.

Chuck jumped back, his face filling with surprise as he growled, "What the *hell* are you doing?"

"I slipped."

The crook's expression went from surprised to confused to angry. "Do you *want* me to shoot you?"

Brayden didn't bother to answer. Mostly because he didn't need to. A blond-haired woman—presumably Nadine Stuart—came flying out of the open space in the ceiling. She landed full force on Chuck's back and sent the other man to the ground. The gun went flying. It skidded down the long hallway, struck the wall a dozen feet away, spun for a second, then stilled.

For a moment, the silence was overpowering.

Chuck appeared stunned.

Nadine seemed triumphant.

And Brayden's focus was on Reggie's face, which hovered across the space in the ceiling, her eyes wide with surprise.

Then everything started up again at double speed.

Chuck let out a curse and shoved the petite blonde aside so hard that her arms spun and her back smacked the ground with a resounding crack that made Brayden cringe. Except he didn't have time to help her. There were more important things to worry about.

Like the gun.

He knew it was what Chuck was after, and he had to be after it, too. With his own wordless growl, he tried to push to his feet so he could jump toward the weapon. He almost made it. The other man was quick, though. Motivated, too. They reached the gun together, both of their hands closing over top of it. The result was a dangerous tug-of-war. Back and forth went the shiny object. The only saving grace was the fact that neither of them could get a grip that allowed him to get ahold of the trigger. As badly as Brayden wanted control, he was far happier that Chuck *didn't* have it.

And help came quickly.

A thud carried over the sounds of their struggle, and suddenly Reggie was there. She was a blur of messy hair and flying fists. One of her hands hit Chuck's shoulder, then the side of his head, then arm, and at last his grip weakened.

Brayden seized the opportunity. He jerked backward, pulling the gun with him. For a second, he was triumphant. He secured a proper hold of the weapon, pressed a finger to the trigger and aimed up, an order on his lips.

But Chuck was in fight-or-flight mode. He issued a wild kick forward—aimed just close enough that Brayden had to pull out of the way—and pushed Reggie sideways at the same time. Then he spun on his heel and ran at full speed up the hall, his footsteps echoing noisily off the walls.

Jumping up, Brayden steadied Reggie with a touch, then tore off after the other man. The blonde woman was quicker. She'd recovered from the fall, and was on the move. She dived forward, her arms closing in on Chuck's knees, making him stumble then fall. He went wild once more, kicking and flailing. Brayden fought through it until he finally got ahold of the other man's hair.

"Stop," he ordered, his voice low.

"What does it matter?" the other man spit. "I'm a dead man whether you put me in jail or whether Garibaldi finds out what happened."

"I can help you," Brayden replied.

"If I do what? Turn on him? Not a chance in hell."

Then, with a surprising amount of ferocity and complete disregard for the fact that Brayden was both armed and held him tightly, Chuck threw himself forward hard enough that a clump of hair stayed in Brayden's hand, and his forehead cracked into Brayden's with a force that made him see stars. They stumbled apart. Then Chuck bolted again.

Reggie came to Brayden's side, her warm fingers touching his face gently. As she asked if he was okay, her voice echoed a little. Like it was underwater.

"Fine," Brayden managed to say.

"You don't sound fine," Reggie replied.

"We need to go after Chuck." When he tried to move, though, the world swam.

"Don't chase him," Nadine said.

"Can't let him get away," Brayden muttered.

"We aren't going to. He's headed back out the theater exit. It's a longer trip that way than it is to the spot where I came in. So we can head him off." The petite blonde flashed her teeth, then held out a finger and jangled a set of keys. "He's not going to get far without *these*."

Reggie's hand tightened on his arm. "You can trust her."

"Pretty sure she kidnapped you, sweetheart."

"I know. But she has as much reason to hate Garibaldi as you do. And she wants to help."

"I did tell her I was sorry," Nadine added.

"Right," Brayden replied. "I forgot that we'd done away with jail time for felonies and instead replaced it with apologies."

Reggie gave him a squeeze. "I already forgave her."

"Time's running out," the blonde pointed out.

Brayden weighed his options, decided he didn't really have any and met Reggie's eyes. "I can't say I trust *her*, but I do trust you. So if you think she'll help us…"

"She will."

"All right." He gestured up the hall. "Lead the way."

The blonde woman offered him a tight nod, then turned in the other direction. Brayden gripped Reggie even closer to his side, and together, they followed her up the hall.

Reggie was afraid to let Brayden go. She had an unreasonable fear that if she did, he'd slip away. And having just had an hour of forced separation, she knew it was something she didn't want to experience again anytime soon. Just the thought was enough to make her throat scratchy. But thankfully, Brayden didn't seem interested in letting her go, either.

"Doing all right down there?" he said, dipping his mouth to her ear as he spoke.

"Much better now."

"My fault for not seeing this coming."

"I shouldn't have taken off into the back room like that."

"No." His tone had more than a hint of irritation. "You should be able to walk around your own restaurant without worrying about getting taken against your will."

Reggie cast a glance toward Nadine's back to see if she'd heard the comment, but the other woman was a few feet ahead of them, her pace brisk and her attention focused forward.

"Cut her some slack," Reggie said softly. "She's been looking for answers for close to a decade, too."

Brayden let out a sigh, and his response was a little less brusque. "I know. Her brother told me she doesn't remember the accident."

"You talked to him? He's alive?"

He shook his head. "He was, but not anymore."

A stab of sadness and sympathy for Nadine pricked at Reggie as she listened to Brayden recount his conversation with Tyler Strange. As much as it sounded like the man had led a troubled life, she knew it was going to hit the other woman hard when she found out her brother was gone. He'd died trying to protect her, too. Trying to make up for the past. That made it even sadder.

She exhaled, realizing she'd been lost in thought and missed the last part of what Brayden had just said. All she'd heard was one word. *Blackmail.*

She frowned. "Sorry. Can you repeat that?"

"I was saying that I'm not sure if Tyler was all that with it at the end, but he told me that Garibaldi couldn't kill him or Nadine because of a blackmail threat." He paused. "Except if it were true, I don't really understand why Garibaldi would just let Chuck shoot Tyler now."

"He doesn't know," Reggie replied.

"What do you mean?"

"Chuck was acting on his own. Maybe Garibaldi just sent him to talk to Tyler, I'm not sure. But I do know that Garibaldi doesn't know anything about *us*. Chuck was trying to figure it out without making his boss aware of what he was up to. Everything else you said matched up with what Nadine told me."

Brayden's eyes sought the blonde's back. "So the blackmail bit might be true."

Reggie followed his gaze. "Are you going to ask her?"

"No."

"No?" She couldn't keep the surprise from her voice.

He shook his head. "Once we have Chuck, I'm taking a step back, sweetheart. Who knows? He may change his mind and turn on Garibaldi in exchange for a plea, and that could just be the end of it. If not…my partners are ready—eager, even—to step up."

"You're not curious?"

"I am. But I did what I came to do. I found the man responsible for my dad's death. And I found something even more important in the process."

"Something more important?"

He paused in their walk to look down and lift an eyebrow. "Yep."

Heat crept over Reggie's cheeks as she clued in to what he meant. "Oh."

"Yeah. *Oh.*" One corner of his mouth tipped up. "Listen. I'd rather this not be the place I tell you this for the first time, but—"

Nadine cleared her throat, cutting him off, and Reggie fought a need to shush the woman. Whatever Brayden was going to tell her seemed imminently more interesting than the fact that they'd reached their destination. But it was too late. Brayden shot her a wink, brushed his lips over hers, murmured, "Later," then brought his attention to Nadine.

"That's it?" he asked, nodding toward the end of the hall. "Looks like a cargo bay."

"You know what they say about books and cover and all that," the blonde responded. "It's an elevator. There isn't one like this at this end?"

"No. Just a set of stairs."

"Hmm."

She reached down then, took ahold of the handle near the floor and rolled up the door. Sure enough, just on the other side was an industrial-sized elevator.

It could almost fit a car, Reggie thought.

Momentarily forgetting that Brayden had been about to make a big confession, she stepped into the wide space.

"Whatever it is that Garibaldi's moving illegally, there's either a lot of it, or it's very big," she stated.

"What he's moving?" Brayden repeated as he joined her inside.

"I don't know yet," Nadine said. "But my theory is that he built this space to store and move some kind of goods."

"It's a good theory," Brayden replied, his eyes moving over the interior of the elevator.

She hit the up button. "I like to think so."

The mechanism jerked to a start, then slid smoothly up for several seconds. When it came to a stop, they were in front of a second cargo door, and this time when Nadine slid it open, Reggie saw why it had been set up to look the way it did. It *was* a cargo bay, and it was definitely designed to hold something as big as a vehicle. Or maybe an *actual* vehicle. Because they were in the Main Street Garage, complete with all of the usual tools of the mechanical trade. Reggie's dad regularly got his own car maintained there.

"I'd never have suspected this was here," she murmured.

"That's the whole point, I guess," Nadine replied, stepping out of the elevator. "Come on. My car's over there in a real service bay."

They moved through the darkened shop together, then climbed into the car—Reggie and Nadine in the front, Brayden in the back. A scant few minutes later, they were on the road, the air in the car thick with tension. And it was the blonde woman who finally broke the silence.

"I really am sorry," she said, her voice softer than Reggie had heard it yet. "The last few days have been... I don't even know if there's a good enough word. I've been hiding half the time, but trying to live my regular life the other half."

"I get it," Brayden said from the back seat, his eyes finding Reggie's in the rearview mirror. "It's hard to compartmentalize."

Nadine rolled her shoulders. "When I came back here, I didn't think I'd be running for my life. I didn't think that my brother would be—" She cut herself off and swallowed. "I know that if he isn't dead already, he will be any second now."

Reggie continued to hold Brayden's gaze as he answered, "I'm sorry, Nadine."

"You spoke to him?"

"He just wanted you to be safe."

"That's what he said to me, too, before he took off to try to confront Jesse Garibaldi." Nadine's reply was a rough whisper. "I thought it was just part of his addiction."

"Trust me when I say it wasn't."

"Thank you."

Reggie reached a spontaneous hand across the console to squeeze the other woman's forearm. "We're here."

"I know." Nadine breathed out, then nodded toward the windshield. "And *we* are *here*, too."

Reggie moved her gaze out front. Sure enough, the old theater loomed ahead, looking far more threatening than she'd ever thought of it before. Brayden's car sat in the middle of the parking lot, somehow adding even more gloom.

"You think Chuck's made it this far?" she asked.

"It was just under ten minutes from the theater to where you found me," said Brayden from the back seat. "But we were moving a lot slower."

"So he could be here," Nadine mused as she pulled in. "But where's *his* car?"

The reply came in the way of an engine's rumble. And about ten seconds later, a set of headlights flashed from a bend in the road.

"Crap," muttered Brayden.

"I thought you had his keys," Reggie said.

"He must've had a spare set. Or hot-wired it," Nadine replied.

"What do we do?" Reggie couldn't keep the edge of fear from her voice.

"You get out," the other woman replied.

"What?" she and Brayden said together.

"He doesn't know yet that we're here," Nadine said.

"So?" Brayden said back.

"So I'm going to run him down."

Reggie inhaled. "You could—"

The other woman cut her off. "I know. And we've only got about two minutes before he gets close enough to see us. The car's the only weapon we've got."

"I'll do it," Brayden said.

"No," Reggie replied immediately.

The big man reached over the seat to put a hand on her

shoulder. "I've got tactical experience. Neither of you has ever been involved in a high-speed chase, I'm assuming."

Nadine nodded her head slowly. "It makes sense."

Reggie's heart wanted to seize. "No."

"Reggie…" His hand tightened.

"You want me to just let you deliberately risk your life? I can't lose you like that, Brayden." The last sentence was a desperate sob and she didn't care.

He lifted his fingers from her shoulder to her cheek. "I'll be fine. I promise."

"We need to hurry," Nadine said, pushing the driver's-side door wide.

Tears blurred Reggie's vision as she pulled away from Brayden and flung open her own door. She knew he wouldn't make her a promise he wasn't sure he could keep, but that didn't mean she was any less scared. And as he climbed out after her, she wanted to cling to him and beg him to stay. But she settled for his quick embrace instead, then stepped back as he moved toward the other side of the car. He didn't even make it as far as the trunk before Nadine slammed her door shut again. The tires squealed and dirt flew up and then the car fishtailed and went screaming across the gravel toward the road.

"You've got to be kidding me," Brayden growled.

Reggie opened her mouth to say something, but before she could even manage a word, Chuck's police cruiser became visible again. It was traveling at breakneck speed up the hill, straight toward Nadine's sedan. And the blonde woman showed no sign of backing down. If anything, the car seemed to speed up.

A scream built in the back of Reggie's throat, and even the sudden, reassuring warmth of Brayden's chest pressed to her from behind wasn't enough to calm her. She wished she could close her eyes, but her lids refused to drop. Her gaze stayed wide. Fixed on the scene in front of her. The blur of red, the streak of white, each headed toward the other at an unstoppable pace, tires spinning and rocks flying out from under the rubber.

Reggie stiffened, bracing for the impact she knew she was about to witness. But just as it should have happened, Chuck's car veered wildly to one side. Nadine's car skidded past it and clipped the rear bumper. And for a second, everything seemed to move in slow motion. The cruiser spun. Then it flipped. It somehow *bounced* across the pavement. It spun some more as it slid across the road to a grassy embankment where it at last came to a shattering halt against a concrete barrier. The entire roof of the car collapsed in, and Reggie knew—even before the first lick of flames crackled to life—that there was no way Chuck had survived the crash.

And a hundred yards away, Nadine's car had its own impact—head-on into a tree. From where she stood, Reggie could see the woman's head slumped against the steering wheel.

And that's when everything sped up again.

Slamming her feet against the ground, Reggie pushed to reach the red sedan. There, she ripped the door open and called the other woman's name. For a moment, there was silence, and she feared the worst. But when she reached out to place her fingers on Nadine's arm, the blonde woman jerked back.

"Did I do it?" she asked weakly. "Did I stop him?"

Brayden's voice answered grimly from behind. "You did."

"It's over?"

"Yes."

Nadine's head sagged again. "Good."

But as Reggie pushed to her feet and collapsed in Brayden's arms, she knew there was a silent "for now" at the end of

Brayden's affirmative reply. Chuck might be dead, and Tyler Strange's murder no longer a mystery, but Jesse Garibaldi was still free.

Epilogue

Five days later

Reggie frowned down at the envelope in her hands. It was an obnoxiously bright shade of yellow and embossed with an equally bright blue sun.

"What is it?" she asked.

Brayden shot her an eager, little-boy grin. "Open it."

"I'm kind of afraid to."

"Why?"

"It looks like it might shoot out glitter or something."

Brayden's mouth tipped up a little more on one side. "One can only hope."

Reggie rolled her eyes. "*You* open it, then, if you're that enthusiastic about it."

"I can't. It's a gift from me to you."

"Fine."

"Hurry."

She snorted a laugh. "I don't want to get a paper cut."

But she slid her thumb under the sealed flap anyway, then flipped it open and dragged out the contents. And she frowned.

"It's…plane tickets?" she said. "To Mexico?"

"Yep."

"But…"

"But what?"

She looked around the diner in case anyone was listening, then dropped her voice a little lower. "The case."

He leaned over the table and pressed his finger over top of hers. "I meant it when I said I was bowing out for the rest. I did my part. I completed my scouting mission, and I've set the guys up for the next part of the investigation. Or I should say that *we've* set them up. Anderson's already in town."

Reggie couldn't hide her surprise. "He is?"

Brayden nodded. "I want some time with my girlfriend. I want to see her relaxing and not looking over her shoulder. And I'm hoping that after a few weeks of margaritas and snorkels and lazy afternoons, she'll think about accepting a big fat diamond ring on her finger."

Heat crept up her cheeks. "She could do that here."

"Not a lot of snorkeling to be done in Whispering Woods."

"You know what I mean."

"Do I?" he teased.

She rubbed subconsciously at her ring finger with her thumb. "Yes."

"Do you hate the idea of seeing me in my swim trunks?"

"No. Of course not."

"So what do you say?"

"What about work? The diner?"

"I've got a ton of banked time. And your dad's agreed to come out of semiretirement to run things. But only until we get back. Then he's said he's washing his hands of the diner business completely."

"For real?"

"He's ready to put your name on the lease. As soon as things are all clear, that is."

Excitement bubbled up at the idea of being officially in charge. And she had no doubt that Brayden's partners would see to it that Garibaldi was put where he belonged.

"When do we go?" she asked.

He scratched at his chin. "Pretty quick, actually."

"This week?"

"No. In two hours."

"What?"

"Jaz packed you a bag."

"You're kidding."

"You're the one holding the tickets."

She looked down. The departure time was listed as nine o'clock that night.

"At this time tomorrow," Brayden said, "you'll be sipping coffee in your bikini."

"I don't have a bikini."

"Hmm. Guess you better check your bag, then. I swear Jaz said she packed one."

Reggie groaned. "Oh, God. Where *is* the bag?"

"In the back room," he replied.

"I'll be back."

She jumped to her feet, but before she could get even a step away, Brayden snagged her by the wrist.

"Hey," he said. "You forgot something."

"I did?"

"A kiss."

She bent down and brushed her lips to his. "Good enough?"

"For now," he joked.

She lifted an eyebrow. "Anything else?"

"Just one thing."

"What?"

"I don't think I've said this officially yet. Which seems kind of crazy. But, Reggie…I love you."

The words sounded so natural coming from his mouth. Like he'd said them a million times before.

"You *are* crazy," she replied. "But I love you, too."

She was a little surprised to hear that they seemed just as natural coming from her.

He smiled. "Good. Glad that's settled."

"I really should check the bag."

"All right."

She dusted another kiss over his mouth, then slipped away, her mind reeling with excited anticipation.

Brayden waited until he was sure Reggie was out of earshot before grabbing his phone from inside his pocket and hitting the second number in his speed dial.

On the third ring, his friend's familiar voice filled his ear. "Hey. You on a plane yet?"

"Not quite. Just wanted to check in and see how things are going over there."

"You mean with Princess Prickle?"

Brayden had to bite back a laugh. "You can't call her that, Anderson. You need her to trust you."

"Sure I can. Ever since she opened those big brown eyes of hers, she's been cranky as all hell."

"Big brown eyes, huh?"

"Not my point."

"Look. I know following her around wasn't your first choice, but you're supposed to be Mr. Nice Guy, remember? Patient and understanding."

"Yeah. So the fact that I can't manage it should really tell you something."

"It's not going to be all bad."

"So you say."

"She's a schoolteacher."

"With a temper. I think I just saw her take a swipe at a doctor."

"You did not."

Anderson sighed heavily. "Okay. I didn't. But seriously. Isn't there some other way to do this? She might *actually* kill me before I figure out what it is that Garibaldi's transporting. Did you say she was a schoolteacher, or some kind of Special Forces trainee?"

This time, the laugh couldn't be held in. "She's a schoolteacher."

"With a vendetta."

"She wants what we want. To see the scumbag behind bars. And she's been through a lot, so cut her some slack."

Another sigh carried through the phone. "Fine."

"I'll keep in touch while I'm in Mexico."

"For the love of all that's holy…please don't. Just enjoy your vacation and your girl."

"Likewise. About the girl, that is."

"Riiiiight."

"Well. At least keep her out of trouble."

"Can we settle for *alive* rather than *out of trouble*?"

"Anderson."

"Brayden."

"Stay safe. And figure out what Garibaldi's long game is. We all want this to be over."

"You know I'm on it."

"Yeah, I do."

"I'll talk to you soon."

"'Bye, Anderson."

Brayden hit the hang-up button, brooding for just a second over everything that had happened over the last few days. Chuck's death had been officially ruled an accident by the authorities, and Brayden's own boss had seen to it that he and Reggie were labeled discreetly as witnesses. The accident should've been big news locally, but a freak snowstorm had trumped the story, and quickly distracted the town's focus. Unsurprisingly, Tyler's body had mysteriously and miraculously disappeared from Nadine's mom's place. Brayden knew Garibaldi was on cleanup duty.

Sipping his coffee, he turned his mind to what was to

come. Anderson would keep an eye on Nadine, and if her memories started to resurface, his friend would ensure her safety. He trusted that the other man would work to figure out the exact purpose of Garibaldi's underground storage system, too. He did wish that—at least a little—he could stick around to see it through. But his face was already too well-known in Whispering Woods. So even if he didn't want to take Reggie away for selfish reasons, he wouldn't have been much use if he stayed behind.

"You look awfully serious for a guy who's about to head to Mexico."

At the sound of Reggie's voice, a smile immediately overtook his frown. "Planning the proper proposal is serious business."

Her cheeks went a bit pink. "Now you're just trying to distract me. I know your thinking-about-the-case face."

"Hmm. Is the distraction working?"

"A bit."

He slid out from the booth and stood so he could wrap his arms around her. "How about now?"

"A lot," she admitted.

"Good. Because I've got a lifetime of distraction planned, and I'm kind of eager to get started."

"You sure this is what you want to do?"

"A hundred percent."

It was definitely the truth. With Reggie under his arm, he was far more interested in the future than he was in the past. And the future looked good.

* * * * *

And don't miss Anderson and Nadine's story,
coming in spring 2018
from Harlequin Romantic Suspense!

And check out other suspenseful tales by
Melinda Di Lorenzo:

SILENT RESCUE
LAST CHANCE HERO
WORTH THE RISK

Available now wherever
Harlequin books and ebooks are sold!

Get 2 Free Books,
Plus 2 Free Gifts—
just for trying the Reader Service!

After giving up her son as a surrogate,
PI Adeline Winters must work with Jeremy Kincaid, her
baby's father, to save their son from a vengeful kidnapper—
who might be Livia Colton herself!

Read on for a sneak preview of
MISSION: COLTON JUSTICE
by Jennifer Morey, the next book in
THE COLTONS OF SHADOW CREEK continuity.

"So, why you? Why Jamie?"

"Not everyone is rich like me," he said. "That would narrow down her options."

"You suspect Livia because she had a reason to despise Tess, but other than her nefarious character, I don't see enough to suspect her."

"If Livia survived that accident, she's desperate. Desperate people do desperate things."

Adeline nodded, folding her arms. "Desperation is valid." All this depended on Livia having survived the accident.

She went to the bookshelf along a side wall of the family room, where an electronic frame switched through several photos. Most included Jamie. His adorable, smiling face and bright blue eyes spoke of a happy boy. The pictures of Tess haunted her. She felt at odds falling for Tess's husband, especially knowing how much Tess had loved him. Although now Adeline questioned that love. If Tess had approached

Oscar with a proposal to start up their affair again, could she have loved Jeremy as much as she'd claimed?

Jeremy reached to the photo frame and pressed a button to stop its cycling. Adeline didn't realize he'd followed her across the room until then. He'd moved closer and she felt his warmth. She also sensed his absorption with one photo, in which Jamie must have been about two. He sat at a picnic table with a cake before him, and what looked like half his piece covering his face around his mouth. He smiled big.

"That was the first time he was really happy."

After Tess died.

"He had all his friends over. I set up an inflatable bounce house in the backyard and gave him his first tricycle for his present."

Adeline stared at Jamie's playful face and felt a surge of love. She'd helped to create such an angel. Now that angel was in the hands of someone evil, and they might not ever get him back. He could be killed. He could be dead already.

Unable to suppress the sting of tears, she turned to Jeremy for comfort. "Oh, Jeremy."

Jeremy took her into his arms. His hands rubbed her back, slow, sensual and firm. Then he pressed a kiss on her head. She felt his warm breath on her hair and scalp. With her arms under his and hands on his back, she snuggled closer, resting the side of her head on his chest.

"We'll find him," he said.